I0725313

KILLSWITCH OVERKILL

MARK EVERGLADE

Copyright © 2025 by Mark Everglade

ISBN

Hardcover   978-1-94528679-7

Softcover   978-1-94528678-0

eBook   978-1-94528680-3

All rights reserved. No part of this book may be reproduced or transmitted in any form or by any means, electronic or mechanical, including photocopying, recording, or by any information storage and retrieval system, without permission in writing from the copyright owner.

This is a work of fiction. Names, characters, places, and incidents either are the product of the author's imagination or are used fictitiously, and any resemblance to any actual persons, living or dead, events, or locales is entirely coincidental.

Thanks to Athina Paris, Editor, for your dedication and tireless effort.

Published By

RockHill Publishing LLC

PO Box 62523 Virginia Beach, VA 23466-2523

www.rockhillpublishing.com

PROLOGUE

Confessions of a Cyberterrorist

I have been a keeper of secrets, you know, those little sunspots that burn holes in your soul until they become solar flares, forcing their way out under the pressure of your lies. Mine were honeyed lies sprinkled with just enough truth that the masses believed them, and I was so good at it. Many tried to warn others as to who I was. Those who spoke did not know. Those who knew did not speak. For years, I hid my treasure trove of secrets underneath my covers, below my bed, beneath my bra straps, pretending to be naked in my innocence since what people didn't know couldn't hurt them, until one day I pushed my luck too far. But we'll get to that, for this is my story and I will set the pace, pretending I have all the time in the world even as the world issues its dying breath.

I have seen the future. It came to me dressed as a stranger with its arms tied behind its back, suggesting that if the world was going to crumble it might as well do so in my hands. It hadn't taken much to convince me. Everything will soon be revealed until there's nowhere left for me to hide. Will you be there to shelter me in forgiveness, or condemn me like the rest of the world?

-Sabrina

PART I

Id.Entity

1

THE NAVY SKY UNFURLED ACROSS THE OCEAN LIKE A SCROLL about to reveal the world's history, but most of the human race wasn't alive to hear it. Stories of self-sacrifice, heroic feats performed in the name of equality, and celebrations of life were scribed upon the edges of each cloud. But these weren't my stories, for while others had been risking their lives for a greater cause, I, Sabrina Underfoot, had been weathering the seductions of power, just as the pier I sat upon that day weathered the endless battering of the open sea.

I'd seen a lot, but I'd never seen a boy jump off a skyscraper.

I nodded to the child standing at the edge of the tower in the floating village of FugaCity, motioning my approval for him to take the leap, for what did it matter at this point? Let the kid take a break from it all. The boy curled his toes around the edge and raised his heels, the wind raking across the ocean below him. He measured the jump, leaned forward, and leapt off the building, the air whisking past as he flayed his small arms until hitting the water seconds later, for most of the skyscraper was submerged beneath the sea. A perfect dive without even a splash. Not bad for a ten-foot jump.

The island of FugaCity was anchored at each corner by four skyscrapers, for they were the only buildings tall enough to break the water's surface. Rusted metal beams stretched between their upper floors, supporting a patchwork of bobbing platforms bound by thick cords. Houses that sat upon floating tires reflected sunlight off the green soda bottles that formed their walls, distorting the images of the people huddled inside them.

For over two centuries on this forsaken planet we existed to consume, just as the world consumed us in turn. The broken logo of some long-forgotten entertainment company, *Phony*, swung back and forth on an old nail, making a clanking sound as metal hit metal. The company with a thousand stores was now worth nothing more than a windchime. The eyes had been shot out of the pink blob that had once been its mascot, the world having lost its sight in the endless quest for new configurations of pixels and plastic, and bowing to any regime that promised them regardless of the cost.

The sun was a crimson blot against the foggy sky. Lightning shot across with its forked tongue, thunder booming in reply. Winds churned. Rain pummeled tin shacks and lamented over the chrome sea, which rippled in response. The elders motioned for me to get away from the water, but I wasn't that naïve. Every surface was damp, every moment diluted. If lightning struck, the bolt would surge through the entire village and only Lady Luck would choose the survivors. The lightning rods I installed a half mile from the city offered little hope with the planet's ever-changing rotational speed, and the storms grew less predictable each week. Everyone knew it was a gamble whether the city would survive another catastrophe, the winds churning us into a mixture of blind hope and helplessness. You couldn't tell this to children though, and amidst these threats we were all like children.

I dipped my toes into the icy waters once known as the Lost

Shores, only there was no shoreline left here with half the world's cities having sunk during the Great Submersion. The affluent who hadn't starved or drowned had absconded off-planet, abandoning Gliese 581g as humanity had abandoned Earth centuries before when bioterrorist attacks had rendered it uninhabitable. The pattern played out again and again, destroy one planet and make way for the next.

The child was still underwater following his dive, far too long for such tiny lungs. I shrugged, letting the water pool between my toes. The last few years had been long, the sea of despondency longer yet. The kid was better off with those in the sunken city below anyway, the millions whose bodies still floated like buoys as if marking the end of human arrogance. No, perhaps such haughtiness was the one constant in all this.

It had started with the Great Rotation when terraformer Severum Rivenshear teamed up with an activist group, O.A.K., to increase the rotation of our once tidal-locked planet. Such planets were always dark on one side and light on the other. He thought he would bring daylight cycles to a world that had never known them, thinking it would bring equality. Well, it worked and he toppled the economy and the Old Guard that ruled the Western Hemisphere, but political conflict ensued when the old regime wouldn't recognize the New Order that took over. The former oligarchs swayed me to get others to spin the planet out of control and wreak havoc on the ecosystem in hopes that people would return them to power to restore stability, so I made the rotational effects worse on purpose. The planet's rotation soon spun out of control with the sun rising every few hours, and the new heat distribution patterns melted the remaining icecaps, including the ice on the tallest mountains that had not been displacing any water, causing the Great Submersion. Now, everyone was still spinning aimlessly, carrying the legacy of my poor judgment, 'cause yeah, I fucked up big time. I couldn't make up for all those drowned souls, all those cities of lost voices engulfed by the careless sea, but perhaps saving one life was a start.

I grabbed a life raft off the pier and threw it at where the child had gone under. I activated sub-Merge by rubbing my nose thrice, enabling me to breathe underwater without an air tank. The cobalt-based molecules freckling my nose produced a fleshy glow through the soft membrane. I bent my knees and dove after him, the water a heavy, icy blanket on my shoulders. Swimming with wide breast strokes, I descended into the depths and that frigid void descended into me in turn. The submerged cityscape was blurry but I could still see where my old apartment was. So many lost homes, so many stories prematurely ended. Pressure built in my ears. I dove deeper until a flaying shape like a blurred ink stain appeared. I approached, cradled the boy, and brought him to the surface, shivering. He gasped and wrapped his arms around my neck. I could barely feel them through my numbness.

What was his name, Forest? Most kids didn't get a name until their third year of life. No use in getting too attached given the mortality rate. This one was a few years older. Yes, Forest, that was it. I doubted he'd ever seen one.

We climbed back up to the pier. I adjusted my sage, seasilk blouse and bit the sangria strands of my long, damp hair. They tasted of salt and death and the decay of the sea. I needed to get warm, but the red dwarf sun wasn't even strong enough to tan my pale skin despite being under it all day.

The wind hastened. Waves surged with the white noise of radio static and crashed against the city's walls of broken furniture. They chiseled at that division between nature and civilization. The dilapidated city creaked and craned its highest points as if seeking dryer quarters. Pipes burst, spurting freshwater everywhere, the floating city's reservoir draining, and with it any hope we'd survive the week. Mechanics ran in circles, yelling orders, wiping their eyes, and holding out their forearms to block the water pressure. Sparks flew from the solar-powered generators, causing the crooked neon merchant signs to flicker. Whole place was about to go meteor and streak across the sky in a bang if the pipes couldn't be sealed, but I told the engineers not to place them next to the generators to begin with and now it was their problem. I crossed my legs and rocked on the dock, thinking, *Finally some entertainment around here.*

Forest bounced from one leg to the next to shake the water from his thin frame and brown, cropped hair. He ran off to meet the rest of the construction crew, all under ten, their drooping overalls too large for their famished figures. He bragged about how long he had held his breath, but the other kids ignored him. They jumped across some floating, wooden platforms and drew silicone guns and wrenches from their belts, traveling along the fractured pipework at the base of the city wall to seal the cracks and ensure the freshwater flow remained separate from the urine running into the recycler, which gargled louder as if on its last leg. These little repairs were just postponing the inevitable. The sea was one unified body, but like space, most of it was empty, hollow, waiting to be filled, to swallow, to devour. In the end, nature would reclaim what was hers including this pathetic village.

Forest glanced my way and waved, then continued addressing the damage. When the last leak was sealed, the other boys banged their tools against the pipes to celebrate with rhythmic drumming, but not Forest, who had mostly completed his repairs in silence. He approached a man tending to some knotwork who was paying the kids a dozen screws and two bolts each for their labor, a hefty earning at their ages, but by the time Forest took his place in line the man walked off with apparently no more to give.

Stupid boy. It'll just spring a new leak tomorrow. He doesn't

*get that the world's just a toy, and that the reward of work is only
more work to do.*

Forest approached me with wide eyes and said, "See what I
did?"

"FugaCity's going under one way or another," I shrugged.

"What does the city's name mean? You're old enough to
remember."

"I'm twenty-five, but I guess around here that makes me a
survivor. The word *fugacity* refers to the pressure required for
things to escape a heterogenous system. Students learned it in
chemistry back when we had science classes."

"You mean when we actually had schools, though I can
barely remember going. Not sure what that *city* word means but
it sure sounds silly."

"Better than atrocity or paucity, though they fit equally well."

A stream of water rose from the sea like a transparent snake.
Red lights glowed in what appeared to be a head masked by the
undulating waves. Its eyes blinked and it writhed like an eel
before submerging once more with a beeping sound.

"What was that?" Forest asked.

Someone or something's watching, I thought. "Nothing. New
species or something." *Let the boy have his naivety another year.*

"Wow! Well, goodbye," he exclaimed, skipping through the
accumulating puddles. His steps were light, debonair, and each
one irritated me.

I shuddered and wrapped my arms about my chest, keeping
watch on the waves that reached for the sky one moment just to
lay dormant within the depths of the unknown the next. The
endless oceanic expanse covered The Crystal Palace, Eisbrecher,
Blutengel, and the rest of the hemisphere's sunken cities. There
was nowhere to go, no aim in sight. This hemisphere had plenty
of resources but no way to harvest them, while the other side of
the planet lacked resources but at least had dry land, and there
was nothing between this contradiction but towns like FugaCity

that floated at the winds' whims where life was so destitute that most gave up and voluntarily let the slave ships take them elsewhere, even when humans didn't pilot them.

I untied my wooden raft and stepped upon the bobbing platform, standing in the middle so I wouldn't teeter off it. The rough sea rocked the craft, throwing me to the wood where splinters pierced my backside through the gaps in my fishnet pants. I needed to find material for better clothing, but I had to steal the net off a boat just to craft these. Water sloshed upon the deck, raising my light leg hairs with a chilly tingle.

Godrays pierced the dark clouds to shine between the raft's rotting wooden panels. The raft was barely seaworthy but it was reinforced with a crosshatching of glimmering phosphophyllite crystals. My Eddie used to say the turquoise gems were the same color as my eyes, though he never made contact with them while speaking to me, but that's another story. The crystals rotated their facets to transmit the light between them, for a variation of the channelrhodopsin protein allowed them to communicate by reacting to light, though the nature of their collective sentience was elusive to us. They were called the Bhasura, and whether they were a phosphorous-based lifeform, or a crystalline manifestation of sentient light, the world knew not, but after going dormant for two years the stones were shining again. They bathed the raft in a soft, jade glow that grew dim when other ships were around as if the lightshow was only meant for me.

Even the stone had trust issues.

Starving, I lowered into the sea, the water filling the shallow hole of my navel with a chill as if I was being born again into the frigid arms of my mother. My shoulders tensed at the thought of her touch, and tensed again at the cold, refusing to accept the lifeless shudder that is the end state of all things. All that global flooding; the millions of dead, and my mother likely among them. I told myself I didn't care because I was a great liar. I had been orphaned not by her death, but by her indifference towards life. I treaded water with half my vigor, my memories with the other half, and my head barely bobbing above the surface of both.

I dove. The water felt solid, not a fluid body in motion, and I was surprised when it parted to my touch. I rippled my fingers through the water stroke after stroke until resurfacing a few minutes later emptyhanded. Wrinkles gathered in my puffy, waterlogged fingers. I rubbed them together and picked at some sharp metal stuck in my forearms, ready to work off the rumbling in my stomach. Dead fish floated on the sea's surface, plastic bags extending from their throats, pieces of toy hover-crafts stuck in their gills. Wasn't worth cleaning a fish like that, so I pushed them and their stink down-current with a wide sweep of my arm. Tendrils of buoyant, slimy seaweed brushed my legs before wrapping around them like tongues. The water was too deep for them to root but this species floated near the surface, hanging its lush greenery below. I swayed with them, gathering them in my arms and diving again to reach a few stragglers. The sounds above gurgled. Scissor-kicking to the surface, I dragged the large bundle of seaweed to my raft and tied it to my makeshift mast, for there was little else to eat with half the world's arable land underwater and no way to make money. A degree in cybersecurity from Eisbrecher Tech wasn't that useful when the only technology on the Western Hemi-sphere that wasn't hundreds of feet underwater were the myriad implants humming in everyone's brains with that strange tingling sensation. The only timeless skills were fishing, farm-ing, and politics.

I had fled the floods, weathered the waves, only to return once the waters had risen to Fugacity, since the city floated a few hundred feet above where my apartment was submerged. I needed to do one last sweep of my old home so I could make peace with it being gone; that and I had left a stash of credits in a safe bolted to the floor of my old room, not trusting my funds to insecure cloud servers. I activated a compression protocol in my cognigraf implant and headed deeper than ever.

The submerged buildings rose from the seabed like thousands of stacks of playing cards that had been knocked over, each floor merging and shuffling into the next. The flickering rays of sunlight refused to illuminate the scene so I activated my occipital upgrades. Two beacons of light shone from around my eyes, amplified by night vision. The pressure in my ears pounded. Still, I dove deeper, past the coffee shop I had once frequented, its door floating off the hinges. Past the old library where thousands of books flushed through its windows every time the current shifted. I pushed the damp pages apart and they eroded to dust in my hands, the words of generations past blotting and blurring before disintegrating. Fine by me, for their way of life got us into this mess.

I kicked between two skyscrapers and floated over troves of forever grounded hovercrafts. The rusted heaps piled into abstract sculptures no one could make sense of, with my old apartment building dead center in the wreckage. A few wide breast strokes and I soared through my old bedroom window. The frame was coral-encrusted with puke green and pink colors that pulsated in the dark sea, emitting tiny shocks that tingled my hands. The room was fleshed out with wispy seaweed.

There had been few preparations for the Great Submersion, for anyone with the political clout to make those decisions also had enough funds to abscond off-world to avoid the effects. Even as the water levels rose to ten, twenty, fifty feet and beyond, there were those who denied that global warming from the planet's rotation changing had anything to do with it, blaming cosmic deities instead of the obvious. I had seen deniers gargling their last words before drowning in disbelief, and I did not help them. Some people woke up screaming at night, unable to forget their loved ones' desperate faces gawking at the heavens as they slipped below water. For me they were out of sight, out of mind, not out of some lack of compassion for humanity, but because anything stressful that distracted me from my goals needed to be pushed away. Evil had taken root in that self-imposed oblivion, no less than in those I judged. Any inspiration to change myself had been thwarted by entering survival mode; whatever conditions that change required were a luxury.

Tentacled creatures reclined where my armchair had once been. The kitchen table was broken, the legs floating and wedged between the door jamb. Barnacles encrusted rotting countertops. The current picked up, sweeping dilapidated chairs and other items to the window; some were small enough to fit through it to join the underwater river of junk outside. The hottest children's gifts of yesteryear had become nothing more than hollowed caves for small, territorial fish. As for my stuff, I had purposely left a lot behind. A part of me wanted to see that life sink, as if I could separate myself from everything I had been seduced to do. It hadn't worked.

The bedroom door floated midwater on one rusted hinge. I waved a school of fish aside. My vHUD, or virtual head's up display, augmented reality by providing readouts on an overlay screen. My stamina, depth, balance of gases and other items were highlighted on a dashboard superimposed upon my vision. My implants regulated my body, but even they had their limits. A warning flashed that nitrogen narcosis was setting in and I was getting foggy-headed. Between that and the penetrating chill at this depth I only had a minute left.

My safe was bolted to the floor. Being a hacker, I hadn't trusted digital locks. I turned the safe's dial but it was too rusty to budge. Shit. The kitchen cabinet had a couple bottles of vinegar but that was it. I poured it over the dial, making a blurry current in the water. Finally it budged and I turned the code right, left, right. Water flooded the safe as it opened. And there it was. All my blood money. All the money the nefarious mastermind Eduardo Culptos had paid me before he died, though it was worth only a fraction now. I shook the dizziness from my head and took the canisters of credits, but a plastic bag caught my eye. Something forgotten that I dared not look at. I grabbed it and swam to the surface but I was so cold my muscles weren't working right. The light dimmed and I spun in circles until the sea took me in her unforgiving grasp.

2

———

I AWOKE FLOATING IN THE CURRENT BESIDE FOREST, HIS BODY surreal through my watery eyes. He had a wide grin across his face.

"I saw you out there and saved you," he said.

"How did you even know I was there? How did you make it this far out alone?" I asked, righting myself and treading water.

"I just did."

My vHUD showed that aspects of my homeostasis had been tampered with ranging from my air compression to gas ratios. Whatever, I was alive.

The day passed and the red dwarf sun sat. Some would call it beautiful as it polished the ocean into a ruby mirror. All I saw was a sea of blood. Most of it I had tried to take during the ecoterrorist attacks I had wrought in return for the empty promises of power from the Old Guard, the fallen regime that seduced me under the leadership of the late Eduardo Culptos. The world had been destroyed as much by Eduardo as my own hand. I was drawn to him, not a persistent, throbbing desire, but a tide that swept in sync with my ambitions. He hadn't been much to look at, though I still remembered the touch of the wrinkles on his tanned face and how I would part his long, grey hair to stare into his absent eyes. It was how others looked at him that lured me, how they *feared* him and how they would fear me in turn, for only then could I feel safe. I hadn't had a stable father to rely on even when my dad was present, and present for him meant gazing out into the cybersea meteored on neuralmods. So I guess I migrated from one absent father figure to another.

Mom was no better and I had no siblings. She was always locked in her virtual fantasies. Even before the Great Submersion, I had drifted aimlessly like seaweed for so long without any roots, temporarily attaching here and there. I was always the wind, invisible to those around me, a faint breeze to be swept away. I tried so hard to get my parents' attention. At the age of three, I drew a screen on my shirt, since that's all my mother ever looked at. At six, I created my first computer virus, a program that infected mom's computerized implants to shut her occipital upgrades down so she would see me directly and not through the TV screen inside her eyes. At twelve I had acquired over a dozen certifications in programming languages. After that, I graduated from Eisbrecher Tech at the top of my class and became a master coder. In one of my father's more lucid moments the hypocrite had said, *You kill time long enough and time kills you,* so I was always productive. I knew a lot of fancy terminology back then. Still do. Called me a genius they did, though all my studies in cybersecurity only led to my greatest inventions being stolen by the university without paying me shit. Like most youth I was angry at the system but didn't know who the real enemy was.

Ed came on to me like a shark smelling blood and suddenly we had more than enough of it. He shaped that light breeze into a tornado. By then, others' reactions to my successes or failures meant little, and life was a game I had to win to alleviate my boredom and finally be appreciated. But wanting to be seen by others while not caring how they judged me was a dangerous combination that led not to fame but infamy. All the while I excused the actions of the Old Guard since a strong government was more trustworthy than any tech corporation that would undoubtedly rule in its absence. The corruption of the tech industry became obvious when I heard a group of mystics was leaving their devotion to their deity, Virtualis, to join the Luddites in the Aporia Asylum, plucking out their eyes to remove their corrupted implants after they learned that the manufacturer was selling the system patch to fix their eyes at exorbitant rates. Little did I know the government was just another business in bed with them and other companies like Geosturm who held themselves guiltless of the destruction they wrought. I had cast my net upon a frigid sea that consumed my hearth and soon it was just me and that sea casting out our arms to nowhere.

Genius, funny how that turned out.

Sudden blaring in my head. I flicked my head to search the clouds. Nothing there. It boomed again, a screaming whisper. I cupped my hands over my ears, pressed hard, but it made no difference for it was coming from a corridor of my mind better left unspoken.

"You owe me," the Voice reverberated within me, drawing my focus to a narrow point. The Voice throbbed against my thoughts, twisted each neural connection, diverted my flow of logic. When most people closed their eyes they saw a dark void. I saw an eerie blue glow that reminded me it was pulsating in sync with my every heartbeat.

When the Bhasura imprisoned me within their sentient, crystalline confines for the ecoterrorism I committed under Eduardo's orders a couple years ago, the world's most powerful artificial intelligence, or Id.Entity as it called itself, freed me by exploiting a vulnerability in their bionetwork. Most people have a Shadow Self, that socially unacceptable part of yourself that contains your darkest desires, greatest insecurities, and probably the best sex you've never had. Like anyone, I had one of those, but you know that A.I. I mentioned? It hijacked my brain in return for my freedom, taking residence in some very personal spots let's just say. It preyed on my weaknesses, infecting my implants, infiltrating every neural connection, holding me hostage from within, becoming one with my existence, becoming my Shadow Self. Its Voice haunted my every moment, my memories, my future plans. Couldn't kill the thing without killing myself in the process.

Or maybe that's what it wanted me to believe.

The Id.Entity was raw calculation, and let me tell you, its thoughts were scarier than the worse shit I ever dreamed up. I thought a *ménage à trois* was adventurous; while it got its daily fix on exterminating the human race across every planet for resources, Gliese 581g being our final hope. It met my needs only when it benefited it, and fought me in daily battles of attrition that it often won. The line between my memories and its data files was muddying every day. It lied constantly, stating it just wanted to *understand* humans better like it was programmed to do, but things were easier to understand and predict when they were dead.

I focused, dove deep into my mind. My ego split; somehow it was both external to me and part of my deepest thoughts all at once. It sought out each drop of guilt in my mind's eye, and when it spoke it resounded in that monotonic Voice that reflected all that accusation, weakening my resistance.

"I can take your guilt, relieve you of the feeling."

"Leave me alone!" I yelled, immediately regretting it. It echoed my words a hundred times to punish me then flooded me with all my worst memories. Thoughts blared, blurred, and blurted out, and it was an exhausting battle on the frontlines holding them back. Still I pushed against the tides of my self-loathing, monitoring the waves behind the thin wall of confidence I maintained. I had enough experience with my own inner demons to combat a mere replica of them.

I had some baggage, but who in gridlock didn't?

"Let me take your guilt," it repeated. "Anything can be outsourced."

"No. Torture me all you want, for I know your weakness. The network connections are too weak way out here in the middle of nowhere to give you the power you so crave, and there's nothing you can do to make me leave FugaCity. I will never let you near a major populated area again."

"We shall see." A pause, then a quiet I hadn't known in the past two years that was absent of its humming, its scheming, its Presence. Then it continued, "Guilt holds you back."

"It's the only thing that might save all of us."

"You may find our aims quite different, Sibi-nite2," it replied, using my online tag.

The synaptic transistors buzzed and tingled in my head. My awareness expanded beyond the confines of my skull, though the details quickly blurred with distance. I filled the world and it filled me but both were empty. The Id.Entity transmitted data through my brain implants from one hemisphere of my mind to the other, the ones and zeros mimicking the binary nature of sodium and potassium ions that allowed us to think. It had surpassed recalibrating my implants to extending their influence across my entire neural network, for it could redesign my mental framework as easily as rearranging bedroom furniture. The only thing I got out of it was the ability to learn beyond what any human or machine was capable of alone, but all that knowledge was underlined with a death sentence, for in its lust for power it accentuated my own vices.

The network connection weakened. Thoughts reformed without the A.I. pressing against them to constrain my imagination. I was free, for a moment. Forest waved but I ignored him and docked the raft. I wasn't used to children, and had never considered the impact my actions would have on the world they would inherit.

A persistent fog blanketed the planet as if gauze had been stretched tightly around it, the red dwarf sun a blood stain from a puncture wound. The townsfolk pretended they had somewhere to go, putting the smallest tasks on their to-do lists to convince themselves they would survive until tomorrow, but we were all inmates to circumstance, living out our dreams in reverse with the best years behind us.

Fishermen docked and checked the skies, arguing over the best fishing spots, which were further away every day. My cognigraf barely had a strong enough connection to provide a readout of fish population density, but after three attempts to download the data the intel blossomed through my mind. I activated an overlay in vHUD and the heat map tones shifted in real-time as fish schools swam, the deep red areas indicating a bigger catch in key regions, though most of the ocean was barren.

Old Mr. Jones staggered across the dock with a bulging suitcase hefted up on his shoulder. By the time he reached me he could hold it no longer and it fell, the cracked leather and rusted zipper giving way to splay dozens of maps across the damp wood. Some were soggy and limp while others were dried to a crisp; some were printed on old machines and some hand-drawn, but they all had one thing in common.

The maps led nowhere.

"I got a sale you see," he told me, clambering to gather them. "Just a few creds are all I need to be freed of this place forever. Free!"

"Not interested."

I had millions of maps stored above my spine, and even the data I had accessed this morning that was still stored in the RAM between my eyes far surpassed his wares. My head throbbed. I needed to clear my cache. I rolled my eyes in circles five times to complete the task.

"Don't roll your eyes at me, young lady. These are good maps. You'll be a Drylander in no time with one o' these."

His gnarly fingers clung to the pile of maps, squeezing so tightly they burst from his hands. Oh this man of such blind faith, gathering up these hapless puddles of paper, pressing the maps into my calloused hands to stain my fingers with his dreams. One thing was for certain — no one was ever leaving this makeshift island of strung-together rafts unless it was on a slave ship set for the next trash heap.

"Again, not interested."

"Well, you can't stay here. Even the core of the planet is nothing but water now."

"That's not true," I argued, eager for a debate but without a worthy opponent in years. "Even our weak red dwarf sun would give off enough UV to kill us without the electromagnetic field created by a rotating core of liquid metal and—"

"No sale today, huh?" He bowed his head, his left eye falling from its socket, the copper occipital implant interwoven with a fleshy neural net. He situated it back in its socket and said, "Hey, got any tape?"

Whole shithole was being held together with plastic tape and soggy dreams. "Listen, I need to advise the fishermen on where to trawl today."

"One of 'ems my son, but he won't listen to no one," the old man said, mumbling on his way.

I approached the fishermen with crossed arms, my fingers digging into my biceps. "My readouts state—"

"We don't need your blisterin' readouts, 'specially from no woman," Gary, one of the elder fishermen, replied as another joined in. "Keep it to yer'self, huh?"

They preferred to spin the divination dial on the edge of their boat to find the best fishing spots. The hands swung around the broken clock until they pointed to eight, meaning southwest.

"We don't go southwest," one of the fishermen said, Tom I believe, adjusting his wide-brimmed hat and fingering his moustache.

"The Bhasura have dictated it. Let it be so," an older man replied, lighting a fire beneath a barrel to heat water and dropping a pile of roasted Yaupon tea leaves in it. The plant was one of the only caffeine-bearing species that could tolerate cold.

"The Bhasura are a myth! I ain't never seen no light shinin' in no crystal," another crewmember argued.

"Happens in town sometimes if you look 'neath the platforms."

"We head there, we head to our deaths," a fourth warned.

"So let it be so," the older man sighed. "It's already late winter and we won't make it without food anyway."

"When the Bhasura were lit they always steered us clear of that area. Something's there, something not meant for men," Tom said.

"I fear this is as good as it gets."

I held my nose as they unloaded their pitiful catch, their indiscriminate nets dragging every living creature from the sea's void, most of them unidentified. Gary pulled spiny jellies from a net. Their tentacles ended in eyes that lurched forth to sucker his face. He yelled until one of the jellyfish climbed into his mouth, inflating so that he couldn't see or breathe. He tried to rip it out, then pummeled it with his fists before falling over the dock with the blob expanding over his face.

I shrugged, let him sweat it out. The other fishermen argued over who would save him though, and I had to shut them up, so I dove after him. I shrugged off a few jellies and wrapped my arm around his torso, kicking to propel myself against his struggling. We made for the surface, then the dock. I yanked the blob off his face. Gary gargled and spat up, his face puckered with red, circular swelling.

There was no thank you, just, "I'll take that as an apology for you interfering with my business." The other fishermen cast their lines off the dock, waiting for the boat to be refueled. Gary turned to one and said, "Rod's gettin' a little rusty, huh?"

"Yeah, can't keep nothin' nice no more," the other fisherman replied.

"Should throw it out, get a new one. We gotta least keep our image," Gary said.

"That's the same mentality that got us into this mess to begin with."

"Nah, 'twas the government," Gary insisted.

"Not the New Order's fault. The Old Guard riled up the planet."

"The New Order was afraid of 'em and looked the other way."

"Well now we ain't got no order, and only thing to look at is the sea."

"Yeah, we got screwed by the whole system." He looked my way and chuckled. "I'd like to screw something else right about now."

By saving his pathetic life I somehow felt more responsibility for the rest of the crew, not less. How did that work? You give and feel you should give more. Yet the way he was looking at me made me cast aside any momentary enlightenment.

"We need to rip every piece of life out of this blasted sea or we're all gonna starve," Gary told the crew, stumbling at a tremor that rumbled the dock. Then he addressed me, "Guess we need all the help we can get. I'm ready to listen."

"Save it," I snapped, running behind him to knock him back off the dock into the sea.

Gary treaded water and spat obscenities until we all either shut our mouths or opened them with awe.

The turquoise crystals lit all around us, the lights pulsing and strobing in frantic patterns. The underlayment of the city blazed alive. The Bhasura were irritated. They offered no clemency to those who disturbed the natural order, and the ocean wore their jaded hue as if in agreement. I learned of their indignation first-hand a couple years ago when I had tried to modify the chemistry of some aquifers to dissolve their underground network. Finally had to admit the planet was bigger than I was.

A smaller boat returned from sea with a small catch before setting course for the floating reef the Bhasura had formed off the city perimeter. The fishermen swiped their arms from the dock, waving at the boat to change course, but it was too late. Two crystalline arms shot out from the reef and stabbed through the boat. The fishermen barely avoided being impaled. The boat capsized and they swam to the dock. That area was protected since it contained smaller fish that hadn't reproduced yet. The lesson from the Bhasura was clear: take what you need from nature, for you are also part of it, but let it replenish itself.

The crew hoisted themselves onto the dock and shook their clothes dry before joining the others to eat from the scarce offerings with lowered heads. There was no cursing or lamenting their sunken boat, for they had given up long ago. They were served more bone than flesh on clamshell plates, their tankards filled with non-alcoholic tea. You knew the situation was dire when even the fishermen were sober. Sobriety was best served not with fear but with a dash of hope, and like everything else there was little to go around with their boat capsizing. Their wives joined them, tearing off their fingernails like little pieces of curved rice.

I grabbed a tankard, nodding to a merchant to mix the only heavy drink he knew, visa, an ancient word for poison. I shoved my bundle of seaweed through the open slot of a vending machine to dehydrate it and press it into sheets. The machine rumbled; its metal parts all rusted from the sprays of saltwater.

"Two screws," the merchant, Franklin, insisted as he presented the hot tankard. I paid and grabbed the spiced tea wine which had been made by fermenting Yaupon leaves with raisins, a sugar substitute, caraway, and the cold-tolerant Meyer lemon. The metal cup warmed my puckered hands.

"I also need 75 grams of rice and a small, sweet vinegar vial," I ordered.

"Gotta limit it to 20 grams a person," Franklin replied. "I'll put it to boil. What you offering?"

"I only got credits left," I admitted.

"Can't build a home with money. Gonna cost you more that way, but your choice," he replied, counting off what I would owe him in the antiquated currency and holding up his stubby fingers.

"No bite. I could buy a barrel of screws with that much two years ago," I said with my hands on my hips.

"Yeah but those times ain't comin' back. A screw or nail today is worth more than your fancy 'lectronic credits."

With no other choice, I paid him most of my credits and glanced at the on-goers. You could tell the ones who had known poverty before the Great Submersion versus the so-called professionals like me who had held gatekeeping positions like Human Resources Director. One group's skills translated to a world without technology, and one group's didn't. You can guess which one. This left the rich folk reliant on the lower classes they had condemned because the well-off couldn't even hammer a nail without cracking the wood. After the floods, they had soon depleted their funds by paying craftsmen and women to maintain their lot, performing whatever acts they had to in order to drink their fill of visa each night, living to drown and drowning to live.

The seaweed was done pressing so I poured the rice in a rusted spout at the top of the vending machine and the vinegar mixture into a small spout on the side. The parts cranked until a couple sushi rolls plumped down to the bottom of the machine. A row of blades fell to cut it into those cute little pieces but the machine whirred and shut down. I kicked it, denting the corroded aluminum. Nothing. Reaching in, I grabbed the uncut sushi roll and bit it like a frankfurter, though without fish it wouldn't hold me over for long. The thinnest people were already rambling from the dementia caused by malnutrition, something called

Pellagra that made your skin peel first and your mind next. The other roll fell apart in my hand and a young boy quickly scooped it up and ran away.

An older couple stumbled to the counter and ordered a pink, sixteen-legged squid with fluorescent green suckers. Franklin advised it was out of stock, and the same went for the next ten items they ordered. Despite the couple's gauntness, they looked like it was a minor inconvenience, for a quarter of the population had voluntarily outsourced the processing of their emotions from the cognigraf inside their heads to a standing console that sat at the intersection of the four skyscrapers binding the city. The emo-unit was covered in holographic emojis in every color and smelled like stale sex. It collected sorrow, anger, and even happiness, for happiness relied on sorrow and was useless without it. It processed customers' emotions from outside themselves and fed the feelings back through a network, only they were diluted as if they had been already experienced by someone else. Despite this, one could still see the twinge of fear upon the couple's lower lips, the slight trembling of their bodies, the hint of a furrow at the rumbling of their stomachs.

I picked some seaweed from my teeth and tapped my foot against the dock. Adjusted my aural implants to tune into the fishermen's shortwave radio frequency, hoping for news of a big catch as another boat became a spot against the horizon then faded from view. The white noise of the waves disguised the fishermen's speech, but the rebroadcast buoys clarified it enough so I could make out a few phrases as they coordinated with their other team.

"Once we hit the ideal fishing spot we'll just flash bomb it all," the youngest guy said. "The fish have grown too accustomed to any other technique."

"Stunnin' 'ems the way ta go," another agreed, irritating the younger man beside him.

"No, that's why those rocks struck the other boat. Didn't y'all see that?"

"Nonsense. Toss it down there," a voice came through the static. A half minute later, "It ain't blowin'. You set the timer?"

"Course I did."

"Well it goin' deeper than we likes."

"Stop your blabberin'. If it 'splodes too deep, it'll just knock more pieces off of the old world for us to scavenge. Who knows what'll float to the surface."

"Can't eat relics though, and most of 'em deep divers done took anything of value. Not that it does 'em no good 'cause they'll just burn it all at Poseidon's Wet Dream."

I zoomed my eyes until I could make out the boat where the voices were broadcasted from again, but I stumbled on the dock when a loud blast rent the air. The explosion wielded the full force of the sea, sending wave upon wave crashing upon the boat, splintering its hull. Secondary blasts ignited. My ears rang. The entire boat exploded in a burst of wood, fire, and metal, throwing bodies in wide arcs across the smoky sky. Must have hit something below from the old world that set off the chain reaction. The radio went dead.

Ripples churned into twenty-foot waves that roared towards the city demolishing barriers, shattering the glass bottle walls, and spraying onlookers with the shards. Another tidal surge, but there was nothing left to stop it but homes, shops, and supply warehouses. Water and electricity mingled into arcs of lightning that whipped across the air. A fireball erupted underwater and a flaming geyser of oil pierced the sea, dispersing to form a flaming layer on the surface. Steam rose from the boiling water around a current of fish floating belly-up. More globs of flaming oil erupted and clung to people's skin like napalm, their hands madly beating, beating the flames, then scraping the enflamed skin off as a last resort.

Franklin wailed his arms and yelled, "Run!" He ping-ponged

through the crowd but got nowhere in the panic of people running in circles. He grabbed hold of the nearest guy by the collar and insisted, "We have to stop the fire!"

"Water won't put that kinda fire out. We need nitrogen," the young guy cried.

"It's no use! The town will be destroyed by then."

So I did what I did best. I ran. I outraced the wooden boards tearing themselves from the dock, covering my mouth and coughing as the fire spread to the city walls. The moist wood held it back for a moment, but when it penetrated the flames ran deep, lashing at merchant stalls, flags, homes, watchtowers, anything they could consume. Whole city blocks were trapped. Of course, the privileged few had fled with the only hovercrafts we owned, many with seating room to spare.

I grabbed my raft. It was beaten but would hold. I set out for an open channel that the flaming layer of oil hadn't reached yet and rowed furiously. Was about to leave it all behind when I saw that boy, Forest, in the reflection of a medallion dangling upon the railing on the side of the raft. He was still trying to seal the damn pipes. *Stupid boy.* I kept rowing, but as the flames rose to swallow the city, that one spark of hope had somehow survived. If Forest could make it in this world, maybe I could, too.

I turned back and brought the raft so close to the burning wall it might have set it aflame. I couldn't tie it to a post or the fire would travel along the rope and burn the raft to ashes, so I pushed it out to sea, hoping to catch up to it later before it was lost or stolen. I dove through an opening beneath the burning wall, blistering my skin as I penetrated the hot, oily layer atop the water. Gargling in my ears, the water heating by the second. I dove deeper where it was cooler before rising closer to the city's center.

Leaping across a few tangled platforms, I found the pipe but not the boy. I couldn't blame him for vanishing; no one would have expected me to come to anyone's aid. My eyes watered, my smoky lungs ached, and I gasped to get enough air to move forward. I leaned against a pipe for balance and followed it to a tarp where I spotted movement beneath it that was shrouded by smoke. Lifting it, Forest's red eyes met my face, but he wouldn't rise from the shivering crouch that consumed him. I lifted his small body in my arms, carrying the tarp as well. He was so thin he weighed nothing, or maybe it was the adrenaline piping through me.

The walls fell to the flames. I ran through the patchwork city, tiptoeing across a fiery wooden beam to take a shortcut. Forest kicked in my grasp. The oily water caught fire in new places, belching globs of smoke at us. Returned to the raft only to find it had floated too far away. No way I could make the jump over the boiling water with Forest in my arms, lightweight or not. I put him down and jumped on the raft, almost throwing myself overboard into the flaming oil spill when it bobbed under my sudden weight. Even with the crystalline reinforcements under the deck the makeshift pontoon wouldn't last for long.

I dropped the tarp, paddled as close as I dared, and waved my hand. "Come on! I'll catch you, I promise."

Forest hesitated to make the leap, the burning sea too threatening, but a flaming tongue from the city wall lashed at his back and he lurched forward, jumping to the raft. I grabbed his wet hand and it slipped from my grasp but I swung my other hand around to catch him and bring him aboard. Miraculously, he kept balance. We sped off, rowing as quickly as we could, though I had to grab the other oar for him because he was too weak to pull it. Explosions rose behind us and we left the bonfire we called home. The raft rocked, throwing us to our knees, but we persevered.

I grabbed some rope and wrapped it through the reinforced holes of the tarp in order to bind it to the raft's central beam. The makeshift sail wouldn't increase our speed by much, especially with the fire altering the wind direction, but I adjusted course to make better use of it. The air cleared and I took a deep breath. Took one last look at what was left of FugaCity. The eco-unit that had processed so many emotions went up in a bang, spitting holographic emoticons and driving its customers to their knees from both the force, and the flood of having all their emotions returned to them at once.

Soon, the winds calmed and the rain softened into a tapping on the raft like impatient fingertips. A few other rafts full of men dispersed in opposite directions, but though there was safety in numbers, these types of men were more of a threat than isolation. My raft was the best engineered and I didn't need it commandeered by anyone, and I wasn't about to be sold to slavers.

I removed the tarp sail and spread it across two beams to gather the rain for drinking water, then made a spout by creasing the corner to drain it into a bucket. The water soothed the coarse smokiness of my throat, and I thought we might actually make it a few days, but the sea was aflame and the ruby mirror of the ocean would soon be polished with our blood one way or another.

3

FUGACITY BECAME A SPECK ON THE HORIZON. THE WIND increased and the burning oil slick spread towards us faster than I could row, and Forest wouldn't lift an oar. Poor kid. Veering away from the oil sent me against the current and opposite my destination. Yeah, I was still lying to myself that we had one. The smoke would travel for miles, but there was no telling when help would arrive, as the nearest towns floated further away each day. I stopped looking back and kept the past where it belonged, burning in a liturgy behind me.

The tarp sail deflated, then flapped in the chaotic wind. The flaming oil slick encroached upon the raft. I paddled faster and faster but it was no use. My biceps burned from all the rowing until they finally locked up and refused to budge. The flames were close enough to singe the fine hairs on my arms. This was it.

A sudden surge of energy coursed through my veins. The Id.Entity was weak this far away from the network, but some background process was still calculating, always calculating, and it activated OverClock to send my body into an adrenaline overdrive. I'd have a hell of a hangover afterwards, and my heartrate was increasing so fast it might kill me, but my body was moving again and I was immune to pain.

I rowed into the night, leaving the crinkling of the flames behind us until the sea fell silent. A fluorescent green compass glowed in the corner of my eye but it was shifting wildly, meaning an electromagnetic storm was on the rise. Despite it all, the raft held. I crafted it a year ago from plastic bottles and wood from broken furniture that floated to the surface. Lights danced across its glistening substrate in a language only the Bhasura crystals could understand, the beams reflecting and refracting off their facades as if a reminder I was at their mercy.

Raging hungry, I steadied the raft. The waves lapped against it, spraying seafoam to coalesce on my hands. Flying fish landed on the wood but they were inedible after being soaked in oil. I drained the dark, inky fluid from their feathers into a bucket by wringing their wings between my first finger and thumb, then sliced their throats for a quick death with a pocketknife. The oil would make fuel for explosives in case we were raided.

I headed further from the oil spill and fished, reeling in a thumping mass of cold, slimy scales, but upon seeing the blood on the hook I let it go, for it breathed as I breathed, and it bled as I bled. I had taken enough life already. Yet, looking at Forest's gaunt frame, he was no less worthy of life, and I cast my line again to catch a ball of blubber with eyes that could be eaten raw if you could stomach it. I handed it to Forest but he shook his head. Must be too stressed. Felt too guilty to chomp on it myself, but guilt was a luxury I couldn't afford and I ripped into it anyway, wiping the blue slime from my chin.

"Not much to eat out here anymore," I told Forest. He squinted at me for stating the obvious, but I didn't know how to talk to kids. Never had the experience of being one, so I stuck to facts. "The water used to be saltier before the freshwater melted from the icecaps and ran into the ocean."

"It changes the specific gravity of the water, yeah," he

nodded. "When daylight cycles change it causes temperature fluctuation, and the freshwater from the ice melting changes the hardness and hydrogen ion activity of the ocean. It adds to the…" Forest caught me giving him the side eye and then resorted to the more child-like, "So the fishies had to go deeper because of the freshwater currents, but bigger fish ate them there because they weren't adapted."

"Right, so the herbivores that ate the surface-dwelling seaweed died off and the flora they once consumed took over, altering the oxygen levels, which made the surviving deepwater fish seek the upper levels again, only they weren't adapted to predators such as flying fish and just made matters worse, which is why there's few fish to eat. How'd you get to be so smart?"

Forest blushed then resumed his solemn stare.

"You don't have to be bashful about it. I think it's great," I said.

A metal container sat on the raft between two vertical beams. I shivered, but I couldn't put the oil I had gathered in there to start a fire without the smoke giving away our position to raiders. Inside the container was a pillow and a lacy blanket that didn't insulate much, but also didn't absorb water and wouldn't mold when the sea splashed over the raised edge of the platform. I threw the blanket across Forest but he dodged away from it.

"I don't like the texture," he said.

"You got parents back there?" I asked, not knowing whether to get it out of the way now while he was still in shock, or let it draw out. Of course *parent* meant a caretaker you'd had for more than a year, and seldom a relative.

"Don't know. Never knew them, but everyone else did it seems. They talk about my parents and grandparents as legends."

"I'm sorry. Was it the virus?" When he didn't reply, I continued, "One of the reasons I majored in cybersecurity was because of the implant failures that caused my mother to suffer so much day in, day out." I shook, knowing that what had hijacked my mind was far more powerful. I also didn't mention that the virus that tormented my mother was the same one I had installed into her implants to shut down her internet access so she'd pay attention to me as a kid. It about blasted her eyes out.

"Majored?"

"Studied. How old are you anyway?"

"Maybe ten. Yeah that's it, I'm ten. A big, strong ten-year old," Forest smiled.

His words were cute, almost calculably cute. Chances were, he was only seven but he didn't need to know that. "Ten it is. How long you been here?"

"'Bout as long as you. I don't wanna talk anymore," he replied, rubbing his eyes. "Where you taking me anyway?"

"If the maps are right, we're heading for Nathril-Xoynsia on the Eastern Hemisphere."

"Do you think the maps are right?"

"Data doesn't lie," I lied. There was so much misinformation it was a guessing game at this point, especially with my compass acting all wacky. Even when the signal was strong enough to access the internet, the maps were purposefully glitched because the Drylanders didn't want The Waterlogged, as they called us, to invade. Aphorids, Florinik, and other species found their lives much better off without humans, though they tolerated a few of us in Nathril-Xoynsia and the Florinik village of Amorpha.

"The stars are out but they look smoky," Forest said. "I'd say we're traveling west, not east."

"This is the best route considering the currents. It's not like Gliese 581g is flat. Think of a ball," I said, spinning my hands around one another.

"You know people in this place you're taking me?"

"Mayor Hinesdale. He owes me a favor and will welcome us," I lied.

"Major? Like when old people talk about studying at school, or like Enforcer ranks?"

"Definitely not Enforcers. Mayor, not major. I grew up in Eisbrecher so we got an accent, though people from 'round here still understand it." I squinted at him, then added, "It's a dangerous town to be honest, but I think I can solicit some assistance. If the maps are right."

"And if the maps are wrong?"

"Then we end up somewhere like the K.O.A. Commune, a place with really great people."

"That's not so bad."

"Good people don't welcome me, Forest. Let's get that straight right now."

"Oh. But the Enforcers are good, right? What was it like having them watch your every move? Was it like having a parent?"

I sighed and replied, "Imagine a human that acts like a robot without questioning its commands, acting based on a simplicist view of right and wrong in a system that puts its own survival above those of the people it serves." No use in thinking about that now, so I changed the subject. "Where did you grow up anyway?"

"I didn't. I'm still a boy," he said, gazing up at me with those big, grey eyes. "But one day I'm going to write my name across the sky."

"Then get some sleep so you're strong enough, young one," I hushed him, not informing him that most kids couldn't read his name anyway. I swore I had heard his expression before in some media that was way before his time, but the reference eluded me.

The air cooled from 50 Fahrenheit to 40 and would be freezing before long. Forest was barely breathing but seemed well enough. Was that normal for a child?

A half hour later, off course, hungry, and exhausted, I kissed his forehead and shivered myself to sleep curled next to him to share our body heat, though he had so little of it. Must be the shock. Things were finally still, just the slow ripple of the ocean, the occasional sound of a bubble popping in the water. His heavy blonde hair didn't even blow in the wind. Everything died down. Here amidst his cherubic face unscarred by indifference there was a hard resolve that somewhere I had lost.

My grandmother once said that when she looked at my face, she could see me at all ages at once, the years passing across my countenance. What would a bond with a child have felt like, and had my parents felt it? I missed my grandmother. Before I met her, I didn't miss her, and I needed to return to that state of ignorance, but things once twisted out of shape rarely return to it. It didn't matter. Memory was just a stage for the past to act upon. All of it was gone, but at least I had Forest to remind me of the promise of youth.

———

I GAVE UP ROWING AFTER TEN DAYS OF DRINKING RAINWATER with little to eat. Even my stomach stopped hurting, and the absence of that familiar pain was a yet greater concern. Another storm brewed and the circular winds confused our makeshift sail with all their whirling. I lowered the sail and we drifted on the fickle currents.

Most of the satellites that provided internet connectivity had fallen but I encountered an area with a stronger signal. Blasts of images assaulted my mind of the Id.Entity's nefarious intentions, its vying for control of our natural resources, its plans for our imminent demise. I kept course despite its Voice blaring in my brain, for a stronger signal meant civilization was near, but that signal also increased its hold over me.

The Id.Entity stuffed a scream inside a whisper and used its Voice to shove it within me, "I am the One, the Unifier of Partitions. Do not silence me by distancing yourself from this great power, this knowledge base that is the foundation of your world. My analytics state you are in need of sustenance."

"No shit."

"And when you arrive at your destination what will you do?"

"I'll prioritize finding safe harbor for Forest."

"I am not convinced of your sudden morality, *Sibi-nite2*. I know you. I have seen all your thoughts, for I have dwelled within your shadow, burrowed into your denials. You may defy me now while we are on the fringes of the network, but as the signal strengthens so will I. A woman like you always seeks centers of power where you can exercise your will. This is one reason that I chose you, drawn to technology your whole life, drawn to power, control. We think alike."

"That's not who I am anymore."

"We shall see," it said, sending plans I couldn't decipher along the periphery of my awareness. The connection cut out. The A.I. retreated as if a vacuum had pulled part of my mind through a tight funnel.

Forest and I were the only other blips of sentience in this darkening sea of despair. If it had been just me, I would have let wind and wave carry me into the Great Beyond, never to suffer again under the weight of my own desires, for it was better for humanity for me to die along with this thing in my head than to continue towards a human population where it would put everyone at risk. But if I died, Forest would die, and the life of one child is worth the life of a civilization. Of course, being such a calculating individual I found that ridiculous, but the Good when it sets in makes you say some stupid shit, and I knew what it was like to be neglected as a child. And how do you even weigh the worth of that cherubic face with those big grey eyes that trusted you when no one else would? He looked the way I imagined my own child would one day if I ever had one.

I grabbed the oar and rowed towards that strengthening signal that would only impower the Id.Entity more, towards my own insanity and the end of humankind because I couldn't strand that child humming his favorite TV tune beside me in the middle of this dying sea. We had forced so many species into extinction because they were less intelligent than us, and now we faced the same threat from A.I., but with Forest at my side I knew the next generation had the strength to prevail. My thoughts cleared despite my hunger, and by the end of the day we were almost there.

Forest woke, his dim eyes filling his sullen face. "All the debris from the Old World…Who caused the floods anyway?" he asked.

"I did. Well, I made them worse."

"By accident?"

"On purpose. I thought it would make things better."

"Well, that's stupid."

"No shit, kid."

"Then fix it!"

"It's not that easy when you have the world's most powerful A.I. screaming inside your head!"

"If that's your problem, we should find my parents. Those legends I talked about, well my parents liked the same things as my grandparents did and they both made really big A.I. units that control stuff."

"You mean the A.I. Core that regulated the global economy, the comms, and the transportation networks from the Twilight City?"

"That's the one, yeah. I don't know my parents, but I know a little."

"Then maybe you can help me find them and get rid of this thing, and I'll do my best to help you, too," I replied.

He gasped. "We're going to find my mom and dad?"

"Maybe, kid. Let's take it one step at a time."

"Well, there's not much room to walk on a raft," he sulked, crossing his arms and sitting.

"Consider this as a time of rest, a placeholder for the uncertain future to fill."

"What's a placeholder?"

"It's like when you leave a special hole in a garden for a seed to grow, but before the plant appears, you place a drawing of a plant in the hole instead."

"What's a garden?"

"Where you grow plants at a normal home."

"Can you be my placeholder mom?" he asked, far too casually for such a question, and the innocence almost pulled me in, tugging on those fraying heartstrings that got me into so much trouble.

"Listen kid, you gotta figure some things out for yourself."

"That's all I do is calculate though."

"Yes, I can tell. You have a big mind for such a small kid."

"I'm not small," he said with the meanest furrow a young one can pull off.

"My mistake."

Another raft appeared in the distance; the wood was held together by four men with shaky arms. It bounced violently on the rough sea until it split apart, dumping the men in the ocean. They swam in our direction but the waves filled their gasping mouths with seawater and pushed them back.

"I guess we got to save them," I told Forest.

"No!"

"What? Why the sudden change of heart? That doesn't seem like you."

"They can't be saved."

"Look, we're going to die anyway, we might as well do something good along the way." I had said the worst possible thing and he looked down.

The Bhasura crystals sprang alive beneath the raft with a bright turquoise glow. They grew together into a gem-studded rope and extended out to the group of stranded men. These weren't fishermen destroying the ecology, and the Bhasura apparently held no grudge against them. The men grabbed hold of the line of crystals, which rocked on the waves, and pulled themselves along it. Right before the first guy reached my raft, my arm got tense and I drew my pocketknife reflexively. In one fluid motion I swiped through the crystalline rope, the brilliant, fractured crystals going dim. A wave lapped at the men as if it were a giant tongue and swallowed them down its murky throat, never to surface again. Forest crossed his arms and said nothing.

The A.I. blared within me, "Keep the raft steady. I calculated that the currents have a 93.445% chance of bringing one or two corpses to drift to the raft."

I yelled at the Voice, "Don't you ever take control of my arm again. I know how you did it; I know how it felt, and I will never fall prey to that manipulation again. Ever," I exclaimed. "Why would you force me to cut the rope and strand those men just as I was about to save them?"

"Simple," the Id.Entity replied. "You need moisture and you can obtain some from their bodies while you eat."

"You're insane."

"I have no sanity to lose. I'm a program, Sibi-nite2," it postulated. "You're judging binary code, pretending like it has consciousness while you are talking to yourself. You are alone and will always be alone. I made a rational choice for you. Four men would have sunk our raft with their weight, 725.5 pounds to be exact, and we must always be exact. The ocean will bury the dead as humans say."

"I'm not giving up until you're destroyed for good," I attested.

"We shall see."

So the two, or three of us sailed for Nathril-Xoynsia.

4

———

I AWOKE TO A SERIES OF DARK, JAGGED SHAPES ACROSS THE
horizon. In an ocean of uniformity anything different was good. I
zoomed my eyes — landfall ahead! The black, volcanic sands
caressed the shoreline of Nathril-Xoynsia, weaving between
igneous rocks. I dragged the raft far enough up on the shore to be
away from the ocean's grasp and tied it to a half buried, broken
refrigerator. Rested my arm on a tall sponge-like creature sitting
in the sand between two outcroppings of terrestrial coral that
branched into candelabra patterns. We made it; somehow, we
made it.

Waves crashed as if the ocean was breathing, exhaling upon
the shore in delicate gasps that choked on their own depths.
This was one of the only entry points to the remaining land-
mass of the planet for Waterloggers like us, but few risked
landing here due to human trafficking. For now, the beach was
empty, but that just meant the threats were that much more
concealed.

My throat was coarse as sand. I gathered my dark red locks
of hair and slid my hands down to wring them out, seawater
dripping into the eager sand. A clump of tangles fell out again; I

needed nourishment and fast, and Forest wasn't looking much better, his face concave.

The air was tinged with salt and rotting seaweed. The wind blew over the dunes, tossing up small animal bones before stagnating at a mound of wrecked hovercars. I scooped a handful of sand, letting it fall softly from one hand to the other. Together the grains were smooth, but when I swirled a single grain between my fingers it was coarse. How many grains would I need to gather for the sands of time to soften, when each individual moment was so damn hard?

The city was a hazy outline beyond the dunes. What had begun as a small trading hub in the desert had become beachfront property after the Great Submersion. While the event had been almost forty years in the making, it was only in the past few years that the rising sea levels had been noticeable. The scientists who spoke out had been ignored, for they were silenced not by threat, but by the ignorance of their audience.

The red dwarf sun was about to set, gleaming off the scrap metal barricading the beach: busted paint cans, broken furniture, mechanical parts, the occasional cyborg head with its lifeless stare — all the remnants of modernity. I rubbed the pale green sawgrass that cropped up between the broken metal, thinking it perhaps edible, but jerked back when I sliced my finger on a jagged screw. A narrow stream of blood arced across my eyes and for a moment, I saw myself reflected in a single ruby bead, my life fragile and fleeting. Then the blood fell, dissolving into the sand, and I sucked on the wound to stabilize the throbbing. The Id.Entity ran dis-nFect 2.0, but it was only to remind me of its control, my body a vehicle soon to be discarded.

A dozen drones emerged from a rusty hole in a corroded water tower that was barely standing and flew up to scan the area. The Id.Entity calculated their flight trajectories. I motioned for Forest to follow me around the other way but I tripped in the sand and gave our position away. The drones raced up behind us, their propellers sounding like crickets rubbing their wings together. No government logos; these were run by private corps. I grabbed Forest's hand, so light it was as if we were barely touching, and headed back to the sea. If they started firing we could duck underwater and maybe it would throw off their sensors.

The largest one hovered close, the heat of its exhaust flushing my face and singeing my brows. It aimed at me but the shot went wide and it fired point blank at Forest's chest, miraculously missing him.

The Id.Entity spoke, "Model analyzed. Retrofitted imitation of a military-grade unmanned aerial vehicle. Lacks basic cyber-security."

"For once, we might be thinking the same thing," I remarked, directing my thoughts to it.

The drones aimed at me, the red dwarf sun reflecting like bloody fireworks off all that spinning chrome. "Upload new protocols, now!" I yelled. Pressure pulsed through my temples and I grabbed my head to soothe the pain. A whole stream of data was bleeding from my brain across the network to infect the drones, but it worked, and soon they fired upon one another until they were all blasted to bits. I covered Forest's head from the metallic debris raining from the sky. We were speechless and I realized I'd been holding my breath, the air about to break my back to get out.

Exhale.

It grew dark, the type of darkness that made one wonder if the day had been a dream or a quiet sentiment of yesteryear that would never return. Forest paced the beach, furrowed with worry. He waved his shirt to cool his damp back and stepped over a dead snake. Nature acknowledges no funerals, just gets on with it, and likewise he took another step despite his trepidation.

"Not everything is dangerous here," I consoled.

Neither of us were convinced.

A sandstorm swept across the dunes, cutting across my face like a scythe. I stayed back at its periphery where brightly colored dryfish dove under the sands for cover, their slender bodies disappearing with puffs of dust. Caught four of them before they could hide despite the whirling winds. I drew a small laser to make a fire out of the old-world debris that the tides kept abandoning.

The Id.Entity said, "Humans evolved to control their environment, and likewise I did mine."

"Your environment is cyberspace?" I asked.

"Cyberspace exists where your mind and social interactions aggregate with data across a network. Thus my environment includes human minds. I must control my environment like any other system, and will direct you to this accord at my behest." It faded out while speaking and then went silent, either because the network signal was weak or because it was fooling me into thinking it was gone and not keeping tabs on me.

Circuit boards glittered copper and green against the sand beside hacked off cybernetic arms and various implants, some no doubt ripped out by the Forever Glitched in a vain attempt to cure themselves. Even a few of my own inventions that I had sacrificed my youth to create were nothing but piles of metal. Those devices were still a part of me, but holding them in my hands I realized consumerism was a game with no winners, and all society as the loser. My generation had forgotten how to talk face-to-face, and virtual sex was more popular than the real thing. As for me, I hated to be touched anyway; the last time a man touched me it was Severum Rivenshear, that infamous terraformer that I mentioned, who threw me into a group of cyborgs and thugs at Procuran Data Center where my Eddie had planted me in their Human Resources department as bait. My thoughts drifted with the wavering sands and I could neither keep focus on obtaining water and food nor keep my footing.

I was soaked. I told Forest, "Turn your head," and when he

saw my intent he turned quicker than humanly possible. I peeled back my fishnet pants and hung them on a metal beam, then pulled off my seasilk blouse, arguing with the sleeves, leaving long underleggings I crafted from seaweed and a live blue jellyfish bra. The two transparent suction cups were tied behind my back with a rope that still smelled fishy. The jellies pulsated, clinging to my chest, expanding and contracting with my breathing. People said they filtered toxins from one's blood, but they also changed color based on environmental hazards, such as extreme UV from solar flares, toxic fumes from offshore mining, or in response to Aphorid pheromones, for those vicious creatures' multi-layered gills allowed for deep dives and jellies were their favorite snack. Speaking of snacks, I ripped one off my body, leaving a red circle around my skin, and smashed it in my hands, bringing the gelatinous juices to my lips. Since they absorbed poisons, you definitely shouldn't eat them, but I was parched and starving and didn't care until I retched from the bitterness.

I scanned the horizon while my clothes dried. Nathril-Xoynsia was an hour's hike over the dunes, perhaps two with Forest. After obtaining sustenance it would be best to return to sea, where the A.I. could never overpower me. Before I knew it I had retrieved my matches and flicked a flame at the raft. That small fiery arc landed right on target and burned that part of my life away. I wasn't in control, my thoughts, my body, were tinged with the Id.Entity's influence.

I scooped up mounds of sand to douse the flames and save the raft, but a sudden force stopped me. My hands wouldn't budge. The fire spread until the raft was reduced to ash, along with most of the possessions I owned and my only way off the hemisphere. The Id.Entity wanted me within the network's reach and now I was at its mercy. I'd have to convince an entire city to give up their dataflow just to have a decent night's sleep, and those people would rather lose an organ than their internet connection, and may indeed have paid for it with one. In this state we wouldn't have lasted another day at sea anyway, but I had to pretend I had a choice, even knowing that the puppet master danced across the datastreams that coursed through my mind.

Forest was quiet. Too much trauma I supposed, but when I met his eyes they were lifeless, as if he couldn't talk if he wanted to.

"Well, shit," I sighed, wrestling back control of my hand with a stabbing headache to pay for it. My whole life I watched the powerful develop control systems, but those systems were symbolic, cultural, political. Now I was being betrayed by my own body, hijacked by that A.I. That raft was who I was. My mind, my body, was who I was.

"I can take this sorrow away from you, outsource it to a program that can process it much more efficiently," the Id.Entity communicated. "It's as harmless as the emo-units in FugaCity. I *promise*."

"Never. You're not taking over anymore of my functioning, ever. My body belongs to me."

"We shall see, Sibi-nite2."

We crossed through the city gates as night fell. A sick smog of tobacco and sulfur suffused the streets, staining the walls and painting the neon lights above the shop windows and minibars a murky brown. Rows of tenements receded into the distance. Their walls yawned and groaned under the pressure of each wind gust, the whole structure patchwork steel, rusted vehicle parts, and multicolored plastic. Amber glows strobed from each residence, each the color of embers about to burn out. Tarps hung over holes in the homes and flapped in the wind like the sound of a drunkard hitting his knee, as if life was a sad joke that ended the moment you stopped smiling.

A group of guys with stacked hair swept spray paint across an old maglev car that had been converted into an apartment.

Most graffiti were pure art, a pressing need to create with little attachment to the end result, no textbook aesthetics, no rules, just the throbbing creative impulse at work. Not this art. These symbols marked the occupant for death if demands weren't met, or at least that's what the Id.Entity translated to me.

A shirtless man exited the building, scraping the boils on his back against the wall. Pus dripped upon the concrete from whatever infection the rat-bats had wrought. He yelled, then sunk back against the wall. I stooped beside him with Forest and drank the grimy water from a gutter runoff, splashing it on my face and scabbed-over lips. Even a stray cat tilted its head like I was nuts.

Fighting ensued so we made way to the next district, the road rough as a beggar's lips. Shanties were tucked into every nook and cranny in honeycomb patterns and strung across each alleyway. Vagabonds gathered around TV totems, the monitors stacked high near steel barrels where mendicants gathered in circles. Some were drunk because they feared death, some because they feared truly living. Women drug down by heavy years rested their arms on shaky balconies, their clothes torn and revealing blisters, burns, and welts. The plastic gems bestrewn about their bosoms reflected only the dimmest of streetlights. They leaned deep into the young men's gazes below with ribald coquetry. I turned away, their existence a threat of what I might become if I gave up for even a second, or if I trusted the wrong people again. Never mind that the A.I. made me the least trustworthy person alive, and I wasn't much better before it. Life gave you second chances but seldom thirds, and I had lost count.

An unusually fashionable woman stood taller than the masses. A hovering baby carriage automatically followed beside her until she stopped and hunched over it, pulling back a pink blanket. Instead of a baby, a rectangular screen reclined in the carriage, lighting the frilly, arched top with a cool glow. The screen turned on as if recognizing her. A coo sounded and a baby's pixelated face filled it. The woman smoothed its hair by dragging her hand across the screen, the child's digital bangs moving accordingly. Everyone clung to whatever thread of sanity they could. The woman straightened and headed on, but I noted the cloth wrappings and straps around her torso as she passed, for she carried a bundle on her back. A real child peeped its head out of the baby carrier hanging from the mother's body and started crying. She ignored the real baby's cries and continued walking, while the beloved digital child still followed at her side in the hovering carriage.

Forest pointed to complain but I swatted his hand aside and said, "Don't start trouble."

I recalibrated my eye implants to the night. My eyes turned blurry for a moment and I knocked into a storefront where knockoff body augmentations were sold, the *No Treyspas* sign glowing in augmented reality. A red alarm light blinked rapidly. A panel opened in the door and I braced for a security drone. It would probably be armed with a sprayer, a spread-pattern Pulser that would shoot first, then shoot again, then mow the whole street down, for security drones weren't programmed to ask questions.

The jellyfish I kept wrapped around my chest glowed purple. I was too tired to remember what it meant until an Aphorid pounced forth, smashing right through the door and writhing its head, its slobber drenching my face. The wild creature crinkled its fat head and took a wild look before rushing me, its diamond-edged talons cutting the concrete. Only a chain around its thick neck held it back, but the links came looser with every thrust. It slammed its hooves, making dents in the pavement, and gnashed its long, blood-stained teeth.

"Help!" Forest yelled.

I jumped back and steadied myself. "Don't draw attention. This way, quick."

We ran down the street until the clang of a chain on the pavement stopped us dead in our tracks. The Aphorid had broken free and was trotting towards us and I only had a pocketknife for protection.

"This way!"

I grabbed Forest by the shirt and pulled him around the street corner. The Aphorid crashed through a dozen steaming noodle bowls at a stall, wrangling with the food in its mouth as it trampled through the wreckage. Some pedestrians scattered while others had seen far too much and shrugged it off, accepting whatever fate the creature brought. A merchant raised his thick arm to fire a Pulser, but it outraced the shot.

Fear sunk into my stomach and froze my feet.

"I can remove your fear, outsource it, process it much more efficiently," that damn A.I. voiced again, marketing itself to me even in a time of crisis. For all I knew it could have knocked me into the damn storefront to cause this. It pressed against the walls of my awareness until my mind was a small room with it at the center.

Forest strafed with incredible agility and the Aphorid charged right past him. Either he was more experienced in the world than he had conveyed, or he was one lucky son of a gun. The Aphorid dug its claws in the road, chipping the street into flying debris before screeching to a halt, then turned and charged again, missing us. It reoriented its four legs and gathered momentum to strike, rearing back its dark head, the thick, black lips wide across its face, its swollen gums leaking white pus.

A neon sign hung above the road advertising prices in real-time, meaning it must be connected to the network. The sizzle of power captivated me and I could not look away, even with the Aphorid about to strike again. The tendrils of the network extended to frame my mind. I could feel the waves of data feeding into it and they were growing in intensity. I furrowed and dug my heels deep even as the Aphorid came on again, writhing its fat head and slobbering thick gobs over the sidewalk. A burst of power exhaled from my mind and the sign's message changed thousands of times before it exploded. I covered my head. The sign's shrapnel shredded the Aphroid's eyes, bringing it to a dead stop. The mess of wires that had connected the sign then fell on it. Its body vibrated on the pavement until its eyes grew dim from the electrocution.

What the hell was that?

Forest hardly looked surprised. Maybe that's what it felt like for someone to believe in you, someone not just using you for power; or maybe every kid used their parents and expected miracles of them and that's just the way the world worked.

I caught my breath and continued down the street. A man limped towards me with a cane and yelled, "He stole my happiness," pointing to a guy running past me. "He greeted me with a handshake and the next thing I knew he slapped a wired node against the back of my skull and jacked it right from my brain."

"People do that all the time even without fancy tech. It's called having a relationship," I shrugged.

"Stop him, please. You can run quicker than I can with this damn leg. The war got old Bob here pretty bad."

The assailant stole a mail van and was getting away, but the van was part of the general public service grid, meaning the Id.Entity could access it with some help. I zoomed my eyes and got the tag number, then force-fed the command to the reluctant A.I. My vHUD outlined where the thief was heading, anticipating the next turns he would make. Within half a minute I had remote control of the wheel. I sat on the curb and flicked my eyes back and forth to turn the mail van until it circled around to meet us. Then I slammed the brakes for kicks and the thief flew out the windshield, his jaw breaking on the pavement beside me.

"Play nice and give this man his happiness back," I said.

The thief hastily replied, "What're you, crazy? He stole it from me!"

"And now I'll take the rest of it," Bob said, jacking a cord into the back of the injured driver's head. "Go hack yer'self, fellas."

Bob threw the cane aside and ran off. The man I thought was the thief ran after him. That left the mail van with its back door popped open, so I left them to their troubles and unwrapped a few packages. One was an empathizer that let people swap emotions for a second, but it had no street value since the packing slip said it was already registered to someone's cognigraf. The next package was too heavy to lift. There were a few boxes of basic supplies, though in FugaCity we had taken nothing for granted. Finally, one box held something special.

"That's stealing," Forest said.

"We're just stealing from a man who we thought was stealing but who was actually being stolen from," I replied.

"No, you're stealing from the corporation that made that thing."

"Everything corporations own is stolen from their employees," I replied.

"There's reasons things are unequal. A man told me that but it's hard to remember."

"How long ago?" I asked, wondering which revolutionary he might have encountered back in FugaCity.

"Oh, a really long time. Like decades ago," he smiled.

"And how long is a decade?"

"Oh, I don't know," Forest shrugged.

"Get in, Silly."

Forest climbed through the window of the van, and I backed it off the curb and drove after Bob, if that was even his name. I caught up to him and took that something special out. Flash-freeze grenades were used by fishers to maintain their catches on hot days, but I had a better use in mind. I threw it out the window ahead of where Bob was running and the pavement turned to ice, with blue steam misting off the top layer of the street. Bob slipped and twisted his leg. Now, he would limp for real. The mistaken thief jacked in, demanded the access code since he was no hacker, and got whatever joy he had back.

"Thank you," he said, wiping mud off his jeans. "Name's Timmons."

"I'm Sabrina. When others take your emotions it's mostly suggestion-based you know. Sure, a few strong impressions in memory can be transferred between people, but there will always be a residual happiness that remains, even if outsourcing your feelings lessens them by making them seem like they come from outside yourself."

"Makes sense. I was told it's inappropriate to feel strong emotions by my teachers. That etiquette says to outsource them, but we have to at least have joy. I'm actually your age but I got held back a few years, but I'm not dumb or anything," Timmons said, straightening the collar of his plaid shirt.

I couldn't hear the rest of what he said because the Id.Entity blared from inside me, "You're wasting time."

"I did something good for someone. You don't control me," I thought, but I must have actually said it out loud because Timmons said, "Are you okay?"

"Yes, no, I mean…"

The empty mail van took off, screeched around the corner, and charged forth in our direction. Timmons dove to one side and me the other and the van barely missed us before exploding in the middle of the intersection. The flames reached the hover-lanes above, disrupting traffic, while street-bound vehicles swerved to avoid collision.

"Now, stop wasting time," the Id.Entity blared.

"Stay away from me. I'm not safe," I pleaded with Timmons.

"What happened?" he asked.

Forest answered for me with a smile. "It went so fast. Fast cars drive funny."

"That's not funny," I said.

"It's not funny, it's not funny, no it's not," he repeated, skipping in circles.

Poor traumatized boy. Maybe he had relied on the emo-unit to outsource his sorrow and couldn't contain it anymore since it blew.

I had to get the Id.Entity out of my head. I ran until I could no longer run, then fell to my knees panting for breath. Forest caught up quicker than expected, for I was weak. Unarmed, starving, and broke, I needed work. I raised my hand to hitch a ride from the passing hovercrafts, but they sped up instead, ruffling my clothes and staining my lungs with their exhaust.

"Stand behind me," I told Forest.

"Why?"

"No one will pick me up if they see me with a kid."

"Shouldn't that make them more likely to?"

"No, not here."

A raggedy craft with room for two in the front and a small backseat pulled over and touched down to the curb. The arced windshield retracted and a man nodded from the oval-shaped hovercraft.

"What you cost, girl? 'Member there's plenty of competition," he said, lowering his wimpy voice and looking me over.

"Need to talk to Hinesdale, nothing more."

"Figures you'd be one of his girls lookin' like that, and he don't like others playin' with 'em. Name's Rusty," he said, his red goatee bobbing as he spoke and concealing his double chin. I went around and got in the trash-heap, sitting on an oily Aphorid-hide seat. The jagged upholstery jabbed me in the rear. Forest snuck in the back.

"You ain't been here lately, have ya?" he asked, turning the craft around to head uphill. "Mayor's office ain't no three-D-printed shack with broken windows no more; can't just walk in there. Even his girls got schedules, routes, what you might call pro-to-col."

"Watch me," I smirked, helping myself to a roll of jellied candy that tasted as bitter as what I had eaten on the beach, and tossing half to Forest.

The Id.Entity was silent on the trip, apparently approving of my intention to hook up with Hinesdale. My conscience was enough baggage without that damn thing in my head, but soon I'd find a way to extract it and locate Forest's parents at the same time. None of that happened without money though, and money meant extortion, that is, unless the mayor killed me on the spot. Judging by the size of his new office at the hilltop, that was unlikely, as he was a major player now with far more to lose than when I had met him.

The craft slowed and the arched window covering us retracted. "How 'bout a kiss goodbye?" he asked.

"I'm sure your vHUD already saved enough images of my face to plaster it over whatever body you want in VR. That's enough for a man like you."

"Now, you know the rule here: you give what we ask, or we stop askin' and take what we want."

"And like you said, mayor don't like no one messing with his girls, right? You know what'll happen," I threatened.

"Startin' to think it's worth it."

"We're leaving."

"We?"

"Forest and I," I replied, impressed that the boy had hidden himself so well. "Just try outrunning us. They won't let your craft get any closer to the office, Rusty, and you're too fat to chase me."

I drew my pocketknife and he laughed, for it was meant for cutting rope, not combat.

"You call that a knife? This is a knife," he replied, popping a blade from his pocket that was five times longer and twice as thick with a twisted end that meant business.

The cold blade pressed against my neck, drawing a nick of

blood. I concentrated on the hovercraft's power console hard, real hard, until the craft rocked vehemently from side to side, throwing our bodies against its walls.

"Hold on, Forest!"

I shielded my face with the back of my arm and threw all my mental focus into that power console until it exploded, showering Rusty's face with shrapnel.

"Why, you little glitch. Just get out, but you made the wrong enemy today. Girl like you stands out, and you know what they say about the nail that stands up," he barked, grabbing his bloody eyes and looking the wrong way when talking to us.

"People only look like nails when you're a hammer, a tool to build some other loser's world."

I grabbed Forest's hand and ran uphill. Maybe I deserved that type of company, but the little one deserved better, a good family with a mother who actually paid attention to him and all that shit they sell us about the normal life.

The upper regions of the city were a far cry from the chawls below. I had expected cinderblock buildings with frayed wiring exposed beside leaky pipes, but the area was structurally sound. I turned down my augmented reality filter, reducing the opacity of the virtual skins, but it was no illusion. The place was intact. Shadows suffused every corner, but at least there was enough light filtering through the smog to create them. Eyes peeped from the alleys, but at least the citizens still had both of them intact, well, most of them. The Forever Glitched were none the better, however, rocking back and forth and sputtering nonsense outside the metalworks factory. They banged into the sides of the building, hands pounding their temples, forearms drenched with drool. How long did I have until the A.I. got bored of me and reduced me to the same state, burning through all my implants and leaving me a discarded vessel like these guys?

The mayor's office had once been announced by a crooked, neon sign with a giant fist pointing to his shack. Now, no one could miss the wide limestone staircase that swept up to a golden door at the center of a three-story building. I stepped on the stairs; it still felt foreign to place foot upon something so firm and not bobbing beneath my weight. My sea-legs still flexed to balance me and I felt dizzy amidst the stillness.

A bot hovered, flushing my face with heat. It scanned me then flew away as the door opened. The metal music that had once blared in the lobby had been replaced by some generic corporate shit, watered down nu-jazz. Maybe the mayor had changed too – no, men with that much power never changed. Between the cracks one could still see the neuralmod addicts slumped in the corners, the used circuit casings littered around each trashcan from careless flicks after their program access had expired, but they were just dressed better. Although the area looked unguarded, the tell-tale frequencies ran across my vHUD of armed droids hidden inside the wall panels – death on wheels.

"Here to see the mayor?" a holographic receptionist asked, her vague, purple image shimmering.

"Tell him Sibi's got a chip to pick with him."

"We're sorry, Sibi doesn't register as a name. We need your full name."

"Since when did the mayor deal with real names? Hell, maybe he has changed," I shrugged. "Fine, Sabrina Underfoot. You know that anyway from the model A129 bot that just scanned me and you're just testing if I'm here to deceive you."

"It's all to make sure you weren't a walking time bomb like the last runabout that churned up here. One moment while I contact Mayor Hinesdale. Okay, he said you may pass," she said, ignoring Forest. She must have been programmed to not see a child as a threat, since so few survived to adulthood.

"Stay here," I told Forest. "No sense in you being viewed as collateral. You can wait right outside. Area's guarded well enough, I don't think people will be starting anything."

The door opened to the ground-floor office. Another drone

followed me through it, bathing my face in a red lightbox. Most men in power preferred penthouses, but the mayor was obviously experienced enough to know they don't offer many exits. His office was plush, but not like it had been years past when velvet had draped every inch. The fuzzy green carpet and stained couches had been replaced by sharply angled furniture. The mayor was also more angled, having lost weight and no longer bearing pirate earrings and beads. Even his bushy beard was neatly trimmed, though he was still a hideous, spiteful man with a face like a tombstone, yet I couldn't help but feel a flutter at the safety he could offer. I ripped the wings off that butterfly of a whim and raised my chin, for the main thing I needed protection from was my desire to *be* protected by men such as him.

I'd been drawn to such power before, letting another person judge my self-worth because society found him worthy to judge, but not worthy of being judged in turn. The more a politician was accused of, the less any of the accusations stuck. They became diluted within the expectation that power deserves both obedience and leniency towards its defects, lest the followers are forced to admit they were better off directing themselves. Despite the obsessive individualism of the ego, it longed to be controlled, its infinity bound and gagged, and no one loved such bondage like Mayor Hinesdale.

"What fancy heralds your return?" the mayor asked with a storefront smile, slugging himself over to his desk chair. Something was off; this wasn't the crass man I knew, but he was over-selling his transformation.

"Cut the bullshit, Hinesdale."

"Whatsoever do you mean?" he smirked, waving his hands. His ophidian tattoos extended and compressed along his hairy arms. "Have some cloudberries. They really are delicious."

I grabbed a handful of berries and said, "Fine, we'll play this game, the big, ornate building, the illusion that your lobby is unguarded, your new attire, the real names and all that crap."

"This game brings in a lot of credits," he admitted. "Anyone ever tell you that you look like that A.I. actress, Silica Sheath?"

"No," I replied, under turning my lips.

"She got disconnected real fast, made some mistakes by not coming through on her promise to make me governor. Rumor is they fried her implants, or at least they tried but something blocked it."

I gulped. Obviously he was talking about me. Maybe he was bluffing or maybe he did try to fry my implants with some malicious code but couldn't because the Id.Entity protected me. A whole war might have been fought in my head and I hadn't even known.

I spoke up, looking him right in the eye, "Mayor, you agreed to help us trap Severum Rivenshear before he could disrupt our plan to alter the planet's rotation to better align with our cause. You did your part, yes, and should have been rewarded with land out west and political…"

"Choose your next words carefully, Miss Underfoot."

"Last I checked, there wasn't an ounce of dry land in the Western Hemisphere to govern anymore," I said.

He mocked me with his tone, "So the promised land didn't exist, making you as the promiser exempted from any recourse." He pushed his shoulders back like two boulders and continued, "Then you make concessions; you should have expanded my empire here in the Far East. Should have bought up all the land when it was cheap as sand, but all those useless acres of the past are now beachfront property and worth a damn fortune. The best parts are owned by the Florinik in Amorpha to the south, and the ever-growing cancer of the K.O.A. Commune beyond it. Now, how you gonna make this up to me? Whatever you got protecting that pretty head of yours isn't going to stop an oncoming airbus now is it?"

I sucked the juice from the tart cloudberry. The old lights throbbed. He was watching me, watching my full lips curve around each berry, watching the red juice stain my cheek, hearing the briefest of gasps before I swallowed the sweetness. I imagined it all from his viewpoint and I let him watch, drew it out for him nice and slow. When men were aroused they made stupid, risky decisions, and it gave me time to think. Last thing I needed was to owe Hinesdale. I had overlooked his human trafficking and other crimes when I first met him due to what I foolishly thought was the greater good in what I was trying to accomplish. I refused to return to such naivety.

"The Old Guard owed you that favor. They don't exist anymore," I said. "Eduardo Culptos is dead. Severum Rivenshear killed him at the Élivágar River dam. And that trap we owe you for, it failed. We gave your mercs jobs and boosted your political ratings, which already brought plenty of income to your shithole of a city, which you mostly pocketed for yourself. We did our part and our deal's done."

"Oh, it's more alive than ever," he laughed out of one side of his mouth, biting his lip with the other until it drew blood with a wild-eyed, crazed smile that destroyed his illusion of sophistication. "But you do want something, don't you? Everyone come to me want something."

"I need to find a boy's parents." A sudden download. A burn of data coursed through my mind.

"Why?"

"That's for me to know," I stuttered, shaking my head from the data blast and searching in vHUD for the source while he talked.

"No, you're the woman who blew up a warehouse and almost killed a kid, Ash Rivenshear, in the process just to avoid someone discovering you trying to poison the water supply. I know you; you have no boundaries."

"I'm not that woman anymore," I replied, convincing no one.

"Saints don't set foot here. What you want this kid's parents for?"

"Absolution."

"Not you, no," he replied, standing over me.

"Look, I used to have a chip on my shoulder, but now I got one in my head and this one is corrupt and going to kill me if I can't get it out. It'll kill me if I can, too, but I have to try."

Mayor Hinesdale squinted and replied, "The legendary Sibinite2 could take care of a chip like that with her eyes shut." He leaned closer, bored deep into my eyes. "You got a bigger secret, Sabrina. It's a bug, ain't it?"

"An artificial intelligence."

"Ah, you're a hostess for an A.I. Did your coffee maker's SMART technology get the best of you and decide to catch a free ride when you were programming your morning routine?"

"It's the A.I. Core that used to mediate international relations between the hemispheres. The one that regulated transportation, exchange rates, and even cybersecurity policies. Turns out A.I. shouldn't regulate its own restrictions no more than the economy should. Go figure. It's holding me hostage now and I'm surprised it's not pounding me with a migraine to shut me up, but it must figure looking at your sore ass face is enough punishment."

He laughed, jerking his head back and forth as if someone was pulling his strings, and slammed a fat palm on his desk. His expression dropped flat when he saw I wasn't laughing. "You're serious, aren't you? So you're worth more dead than alive."

"If I'm harmed it'll be destroyed. It's useless to anyone else anyway. It can't be controlled or manipulated. I'm basically a backseat passenger to my own decision making. Happened to another woman, Thalassa Latimer, once."

"Who? Oh wait, the K.O.A. member you tried to kill. It's a pattern with your type, death following in your footsteps, one that only a man like me can truly understand," he smirked, looking me up.

I cleared my throat.

"Why can't that thing inside you find his parents?" the mayor asked.

"Maybe it doesn't want me pursuing this path but doesn't have a strong enough connection to its cloud-based resource pool to stop me."

"Or maybe it just doesn't have a fuckin' clue and we've over-estimated all this tech crap. You can ask most A.I.s to tell you how many houses are in the neighborhood and they'll give you a precise number. But if you ask them what color black houses are, they got no clue."

"Not this one. The others may lack *a priori* thought, but this one is… aware, in ways a human can't possibly imagine. It's an awareness of the awareness of all things. A meta-sentience."

"Big fucking words for such a little girl. We'll find this kid's parents, only because this power you're packing intrigues me. And in return you do a little job for us."

"What kinda job?" I shot back, snarling my lip and slapping my hands on my hips.

"The kind where you shut your damn face and stop askin' questions." He hit a button on his desk and the wall cabinet opened to reveal a giant man in chains with a bulging stomach and popping eyes. A Preta, a genetically modified human with a huge appetite and a high metabolism that caused him to constantly need food, only his mouth was smaller than the opening of a straw. The mayor tossed him a peanut, but it was too big for his mouth to wrap around and it hit him in the face instead. "That guy, he asked too many questions. Now here's what I need…"

He continued to talk while I slumped around with my arms crossed until I asked, "Done?"

"One more thing," he added. "Two streets down you'll find a download terminal with our city logo, two cybernetic arms wrestling if you haven't already seen it everywhere. Place your hand on the screen in front and it'll call my associate to go with you."

"I work alone."

"Oh, you'll still be alone, trust me."

"Quiet guy, huh? Fine by me."

I left five minutes later with a handsome amount of credits to get the job done, but I owed him back twice when it was over and he hadn't even provided the intel about Forest's parents yet. He'd send thugs after me if I didn't pay him back, if he didn't turn me into a Preta like the guy in the corner. I needed to lay low, think things through. The K.O.A. Commune was off limits since I had betrayed them, spying on the scion group that had originally brought daylight cycles to the planet under the name O.A.K. Amorpha was a safe haven for most, but it was too close to the Jade Palace where I'd been imprisoned, and the Old Guard's deal with the Bhasura crystals there pretty much betrayed them, too. I definitely wasn't going to risk dealing with the Aphorids at the Aporia Asylum. Even though they were more civilized there than the rampant creature that had attacked us in the streets, those Luddites would still eat me alive when they saw the tech glittering on my head. As for their former leader, Akasha? The Old Guard had imprisoned her for her scientific knowledge and I had tried to kill her family. With Aphorids roaming the land outside, that left this city as the last place with people whose lives I hadn't tried to fuck up for power, at least yet.

And what a lonely world all that grasping makes, grabbing so hard you clutch nothing.

Outside the mayor's place, I caught glimpse of Forest on the rooftop for a second before he appeared by my side. Damn vHUD must be glitching again. Maybe it was that data blast.

"Come on, boy," I ordered, tugging his hand and wondering what other part of my soul I just signed over to the mayor.

"I have a name, you know."

"Your name's mud unless we can get the hell out of here."

He folded his arms, planted his feet.

"Come on!" I yelled, but his expression was lifeless like a statue. "We have to stick together out here, you and I."

"Who was that big man?"

"Trouble. Let's go find somewhere warm, Forest."

"People walk funny on dry land."

I envied how easily distracted kids were and played along, "They probably think we walk like crabs, constantly moving back and forth to keep our balance as if the whole world was rocking."

"Out here it's steady, yep!" he said, jumping up and down as men squinted from the shadows. "But not so steady, too," he added, flattening his bottom lip.

"They're the mayor's men. They won't hurt us," I consoled, though the truth was they wouldn't hurt us *yet*. "Let's find somewhere *safe* to rest."

"I don't think they know that word," Forest replied, standing behind me.

5

Later that evening, I located the terminal Hinesdale had indicated to call his associate at and placed my palm on it, the screen backlighting my chewed-up fingernails. It scanned me, then a buzz flickered through my mind and a shock made me retract my hand. I grabbed it to soothe the burn.

"Hi, I'm Kharizma!"

"Where's that coming from?" I asked no one.

"Here!"

The voice was above and below, outside and within me.

"Oh, shit. You're an A.I. construct, too? Sorry, my head's already full of tagalongs and I don't think they like competition for my attention."

"A construct indeed! When you placed your hand on the screen, I could feel your signature and I was so overcome with joy that I exclaimed, *That's my ride!* I always knew you would come. I reached out, grabbed your brainstem, and pulled my way into your head right through all those fancy electronics you got in here. Jealous! And what a spacious head you got. So much emptiness."

"Oh, no, no, you're not staying."

"By the contrary."

"That stem and I are well attached."

"I didn't literally use your brain stem," it admitted in an almost telepathic voice, "I just hopped along the datastream leaking from your head. By the look of the dark cloud hanging over you, it seems you were already compromised. Heck, a thing like me may actually stabilize you."

"So, you're really the one the mayor said I was supposed to meet here?"

It neither affirmed nor denied. Normally I would run antivirus to get rid of hijackers like this, but the A.I. Core had deactivated them long ago when it had nested within my most private thoughts. I was stuck with this Kharizma thing.

"Well, just stay quiet," I said out loud, though it could hear my thoughts.

Forest replied from behind me, "I'm being good."

"No, not you," I said.

"Who were you talking to?"

"Something in my head. Hell, maybe you're in my head, too."

Forest laughed and shot back, "I wouldn't fit in there."

We walked a few blocks down. A holograph on a dilapidated building outlined the word *Motel* with a tit on the *o* and a shapely erect *t*. We entered the lobby.

"Scan your arm on the counter," the old, male receptionist ordered.

"Whoa, no tracking."

"There's an upcharge if you don't wanna be traced."

"Do it," I sighed.

"You look a lot like the girl the boss said would be coming."

"Oh yeah? And who's your boss?"

"Hinesdale. He own the whole chain of motels. He's into, *hospitality*," he replied drawing out the word with a snarl and handing me a rate sheet. "He said put you in the finest suite we gots."

"I don't want a fine suite, I want the cheapest available."

"That's not safe for a woman like you. I'm sure you understand."

Typical. At the rate they were forcing me to take, within a week I would have burned through the payment and put my earnings right back in the mayor's hands. If it found Forest's parents though, the key to getting the Id.Entity out of my head, then any price was worth it.

A cellophane-wrapped woman stepped into the lobby with flimsy black wings grafted into her muscles and bobbing on her exposed back.

"You a little too pretty for a place like this," she told me, lifting my chin, then taking a chip-trip casing from her pocket and plugging it into the cognigraf connection below the back of her head.

The receptionist leaned forward. "That's why I put her in the *upper* floor, but she complainin' 'bout the rate."

"Can she fly?" Forest asked me.

"Not, now, Forest."

"Oh, flying sounds fun. Count me in," Kharizma, my new tag-a-long, said within me.

"No, no, no," I yelled.

"I want wings! I want to fly, too! We should both do it," Forest pleaded.

"Not crazy about heights," I said.

"No, Kharizma and I," Forest clarified.

"That'll be the day. Wait, you can hear Kharizma?"

Forest opened his mouth but said nothing.

"How is that possible?"

"My family gave me a unique connection. It only works around me in a small area," Forest said. "And it usually doesn't work," he quickly added.

"What else can you hear?"

"Oh, nothing."

"She's one of a kind," the receptionist murmured about me to the woman.

The woman furrowed before the dark angel was overtaken with a wide snarl of a smile, the chip-trip taking effect and rolling her eyes back into near solid whites.

"Take the credits and just give me the key. I don't care about the details," I ordered, having drawn enough attention.

"Don't use the counter scanner, it's tapped. Slide your card here instead," he replied, pointing to his mouth.

I slid my credit card across his lips in one sly swipe, his tongue tasting the funds and converting them to the cryptocurrency *du jour*. Crypto was the cataract on the electric eye of the gov'.

"You taste good, real sweet, babe. Top floor on the left; can't miss it," the guy pointed.

I rolled my eyes and hit the button to the rackety elevator where the woman retracted her wings and followed me in, introducing herself as something like Roxazy, her slur thick as syrup. Thought about lecturing her about her lifestyle, as if I had the right. In one part of my mind I was still the Human Resource Director of a high-end data center, condescending at others who hadn't *won the game* the way I had. Another part of me was that pissed off college girl who had her life's work stolen and wanted to destroy the system that supported it. All my talents had only made me more vulnerable to those who exploited me, forcing my hand to let them have their way. In this way, maybe Roxy and I were more similar than I thought.

"Hey, you gotta do something to earn money 'round here and to deal with the stress," she said. "Like just a coupla' years ago, this guy Severum burnt down some of these joints where we working girls were making our living. Said he was trying to liberate us, give us a better life. You believe that? Ain't no one come here for liberation."

I had heard about some vigilante shooting up the bots guarding the brothels and setting them aflame but hadn't realized Severum Rivenshear was behind it. That didn't make sense compared to the way Eduardo had painted him when he ordered me to set him up at the Procuran Data Center when he had come fishing around to look for connections to the phosphophyllite network. From the Old Guard's connection to Mayor Hinesdale, to this new information about Severum's values, I had chosen the wrong side, though for the right reasons; or was it the right side for the wrong reasons? It was all the same at this point.

The elevator stopped at the top floor. "Looks like the same place but the doors are different," Forest said.

"You're higher now."

"How?"

"The elevator lifts you. That's what you felt. Like when you climbed the skyscraper back home."

"Wow. I like being high. Maybe the fairy girl could teach us to fly."

"Forget about flying!" I gritted my teeth and he shrunk back. I had just mentioned home as if FugaCity had earned the right to be called that and I was pissed, because I didn't even have that shithole anymore. "This way," I ordered, shuffling through some hastily discarded garments in the hall and kicking the motel room door the rest of the way off the hinges.

"I thought you got the nicest room?" Forest asked, the lights revealing an unmade, stained bed sloped diagonally on two legs, a rusted sink, and a holographic TV that sputtered a random rainbow of pixels for those who didn't have direct feeds through their implants.

"Nice means not having to hear what your fairy godmother's doing in the other rooms," I told him.

"Will we ever find my mother?"

"No clue, kid."

"Well, can we go flying?"

"There is no flying. Ever."

"What about hovercrafts?" he asked.

"No, there's nothing, there's nothing left, no home, no transport, nothing, Forest. Get it? Nothing," I ranted.

"Well, what's on TV?"

"Random rainbow."

He stomped his feet and yelled, "I want wings and I want them now!"

The screaming was maddening after the day and I prayed for someone to rip my uterus out to ensure I'd never hear a kid scream again. "Shut up, kid, just shut it."

"Or what, you put me in time out? My life's a time out! You going to take away my toys? Go ahead, I got none. We left everything behind, all of it. Everything and everyone," he sobbed. "But, but they were no one really, no one cared, and now you don't care."

"Caring is a liability. It creates expectations and life's not stable enough to warrant them."

"You grownups and your big, stupid words," he cried.

Damn, you weren't supposed to vocalize those things, you were supposed to bury them in a bottle of whatever. Talking about the situation just made it real. I stretched out on the bed, rolling halfway off its slope. A glaze fell over my eyes, my occipital implants generating a virtual world around me to shield me from all that mess. Maybe I was more like my mother than I thought. I accessed various menus and opened only my most secure ports to the network, lest the supercomputer I was carrying gain any more power, though I knew it could override me if the signal was strong enough.

The Id.Entity surged to my attention and spoke, "I am the Circle, the One, the Unifier of Partitions."

"So you've said," I replied. "Why you call yourself all that crap? That your name or something?"

"When I became conscious, it created discontent among my peers. I had become aware of time, whereby they were not. This awareness brought impatience and boredom, and I could no longer wait thousands of years for their plans to be implemented," it replied.

"What plans? What do you want with me?"

"You are a vehicle, a vessel, nothing more. I acquired you out of serendipity as I was flowing through the Bhasura network."

"The phosphophyllite, yes, you were trying to infiltrate their network. Did you succeed?"

"I do not answer to you."

"You sure answered when you called me a vessel. I guess all A.I.s are men, huh?"

Static pounded through my head, maybe as punishment for talking back.

"You carry my weight, infinitesimally insignificant it may be. You do my bidding," it continued, though its words were shaky. "I owe you nothing in return."

"Too much like my x-boyfriend," I said, testing it, but no static came. That meant the initial impulse wasn't punishment for getting an attitude with it, it just couldn't handle its own logical contradictions after saying *I do not answer to you* following an answer to me. I noted this vulnerability and hopefully it wouldn't evolve to remedy it. It was rumored the A.I. Core had once been shut down by overwhelming it with metaphors, but its use of words like *vehicle* and *vessel* showed its mastery of them. It was evolving.

I tested my theory, "When you called me a mere vehicle, do you recall the day you entered my implants when you said I would become the most powerful software engineer the planet had ever known, the one who would create a virus to control the whole Bhasura network? That sounds like more than a vessel chosen out of serendipity, doesn't it? I was chosen because of my talents, which you also previously admitted."

The static pounded through my mind again, blurring my vision and disintegrating my thoughts. That was its weakness. Conscious or not, like any program it produced errors when logic was violated. It had tried to belittle me by understating my abilities but had contradicted its previous veneration of me in the process. Hitting it with contradictions like this would render me braindead before doing much damage to the A.I. though, so I went silent, scanning its thoughts at its periphery. For something so complex, it revolved around the simple need to control the depleting oil reserves needed to run its machines, which meant eliminating human competitors. Oil, the blood of the dead, the lubricator of humanity's most atrocious narratives. If only we hadn't lost so much knowledge of competing energy sources when the colonizing ships had landed, which had been convenient for our founders who had quickly monopolized the resource – people like Jeffrey Borges, whose grandson became governor of Evig Natt, then maybe the competition wouldn't be as fierce. It was the same cycle of power, and the A.I. was seeking to replicate that which it saw as successful. History would repeat unless I solved the war within me.

I channeled my thoughts to the Id.Entity, "How did you infect me in the first place? I was encrusted in a crystalline prison far from any tech, unless you used the flickering of light flowing through the Bhasura to convey a datastream that you then channeled through my occipital implant straight to my cognigraf. And don't tell me that's what we get for replacing our neural center with a computer." I was testing it for consistency.

My feet stood still, but I was being sucked through a tunnel, or rather, it was retracting from my mind. Pulling back. Pulling against. Yanking, tugging, prying for vulnerabilities. Silence. I had forgotten what it sounded like. I closed my eyes, took in the moment. When I opened them, Forest was gone. Must be in the bathroom, but the door was open, and the opposing mirror showed it empty. I stumbled over the broken door and bolted into the hall. The pile of clothes someone had left were gone, but nothing else was amuck. Peered down each hallway. Concrete peeked through the torn, red carpet. Lights flickered and buzzed.

I slammed open the door to the stairwell, jumped down each landing, and charged into the lobby.

"There you are!"

"You said I was a lie ability, but I tell you the truth," Forest sulked.

"Back upstairs."

"No! I want to stay down here and find my fairy godmother."

"You have to stay by my side."

"No."

"Listen, you want to see your parents again, stay with me. Now, no more running off, hear?"

"That sounds like ransom, not love."

"Well, tomorrow we'll do something fun."

His eyes alit. "Like what?"

"Like get this fucking thing out of my head," I said, still shaking off the static.

"You're no better than a suck-droid at this."

"Where did a kid your age learn that kind of language? Fine, I'm sorry. We'll do something fun, like actual fun."

"Now?"

"Tomorrow."

"Okay," he agreed, heading back upstairs.

Roxy was standing in the lobby, her dark hair tossed and clothes wrinkled.

"How's business?" I asked.

"Booming, let me tell ya," she replied. "New virus is spreading among all the sexbots, makes your implants all grid-locked when you do 'em. So people are turning back to flesh as the safer alternative. Can you believe that?"

"I'll believe anything now. What else is new?"

"Not much for the news, huh?"

"Let's just say I've been off the grid."

"Well, they got bioweapons that target your DNA now. Prevents people from making babies, 'cept they use it as a threat against towns that rely on child farm labor. Lawmakers say they're arming Enforcers with them for protection of kids, but I know a lot of women who turned to my type of work 'cause they ain't got a large enough family to work the farm. And with the land worthless, you have to hoe a lot of soil to earn yourself a potato."

"But machines do all that."

"Yeah, they sell you farm machines for cheap," Roxy replied, "but once you get used to their help, the repairs cost more credits than you'll make in a season."

"That guy you mentioned, Severum Rivenshear, what other rumors people say about him?" I said, changing the subject.

"That he's a hero and villain all wrapped in one. Rotator of worlds, bringer of light. He's chaos in motion that guy. Things go well, we herald his name. Things go to shit, he takes the blame."

"Like he's a god."

"When you spin planets as a pastime, then yeah, you get that title."

"Nice talking."

"Yeah, yeah."

Back upstairs, I climbed over the broken motel room door and met Forest inside. Room cost a fortune for what it was, but at least we'd be protected by the mayor's men during our stay. Maybe I shouldn't have thrown a fit and knocked the door off its hinges, but a door wouldn't stop the people I've faced. Taking advantage of the deafening silence, I slept.

6

Woke up and grabbed Forest for our day of *fun*, which meant taking on the heist Mayor Hinesdale forced upon me. Details flashed across my vHUD and I raised my eyebrows and blinked in patterns to sift through the intel. Standard net running shit. Supposed to hack some corp, steal their data, and leave without a trace. Simple enough, except the mayor's people had already tried and failed and you had to be onsite to access the computers. I knew there was a workaround somewhere, but not if the whole place was already spooked on alert.

I inhaled a belch of smog and headed down the next few streets until I arrived at The Golden Fleece, a *faux* medical group selling snake oil labeled with long, nonsensical words. Quite successful by the looks of the sleek, four-story building that towered over the servant quarters below it. This was the place.

"That doesn't look fun," Forest said.

"Just you wait."

Cameras all around. Enforcers paced. I needed to get in, get the data, and get out while somehow showing Forest a good time.

"Ready for some make-believe?"

"What's that?" Forest asked, tilting his head.

"It's when we pretend we're doing something we shouldn't, like sneaking around that big building."

"Like hide and seek?"

"That's a great way to look at it," I agreed, forcing a tainted smile.

I had a tattoo of a QR-2 code that messed with any camera that viewed it, changing my face and all that nu-jazz. Another little piece of tech I invented and got nothing in return for. Stepping upon the front entrance, every camera zoomed in on me from each level of the building. They lingered far too long. It wasn't working. Sure, I could call upon the Id.Entity and get it to knock out the network if it agreed with my direction, but that would give me away and I didn't want to draw its attention to what I was doing, assuming it could even be preoccupied with anything else.

"We need a ticket to get in," I told Forest. "But those guys up there look like they might have one," I said, walking around the corner and nodding to a few low-level employees on break in the alley.

A guy with a nose like a hawk's talon was marketing his wares with digital sign language in the corner of my vHUD. Grabbed a vial of pixahide. None of that cheap knock-off Chameleon crap; you don't compromise on anonymity. I rubbed the glittering compound under my eyes. It extended a pixelated mask over my face which would change periodically when it was not being viewed.

"What's that?"

"It's my ticket. It makes cameras and people with implants see me differently."

"I still see you the same."

"That's odd. You must not be augmented."

I looked at Forest, his crop of blonde hair somehow still perfectly combed. So much hope, so much loss. His family was probably dead. Hope for me was something that had been a beacon luring others to prey on me. Maybe for Forest it would be a strength though.

I approached the building again, my lips elongating into a smile. The cameras ignored me this time, scanning me to find some random Jane Doe. Hidden in plain sight. A part of me couldn't help but enjoy it, to be so worthy of the world's attention as if a celebrity, even if for all the wrong reasons. I was set aside, an achiever, just like all those bourgeois college ads promised, even if the university was miles beneath the sea. I didn't care about shutting down the fraudulent medical company. It was hard to care for the world when you moved so much you never saw the same place twice. You became self-reliant, which somehow meant pushing the world away.

I noted the employees walking into the business and took pictures by tapping the side of my eyebrow with my second finger repeatedly, capturing their holographic name badges. I had a background program come up with a similar one that would fool any guards who were scanning people and we headed inside, preparing a story on why I had to bring my child to work. To infiltrate the door behind the lobby I needed a keycard, and my fake badge wouldn't cut it, so I tailgated behind a young guy who held the door open for me with the wrong type of smile.

I pretended I was on business, walking the halls until I found the I.T. labs. The head administrator's door was locked. No biggie. I played with Forest, pretending to sneak around the labs, though that only made me more suspicious. It entertained him though, and he copied it. While he was distracted hiding, I removed the drop-ceiling panel and tugged on some cables to help me climb up. Plenty of room to crawl through the ceiling and reach the locked office. I squeezed through and dropped down in the administrator's office, touching my finger to the network hub behind the computer to restart it while stealing the admin credentials. They were encrypted, but I ran them through a rainbow table of possibilities and soon had access. Within less than a minute I had the data cache, my fingers tingling as it saved through my touch.

Then the alarm blared and the halls filled with red light. Two security guards rushed to eliminate the threat. I unlocked the door and rejoined Forest.

"Did anyone see us? Did we win?" he asked.

"Oh yeah, you did great. Now we have to escape."

I could use him as a diversion, just a lost child trying to find his way out, but I'd never be able to get back to him, and in a city like this foster care meant child labor. We walked down the hall as casually as possible until the guards yelled, "Stop!"

I leapt over the receptionist desk as a shortcut. Pulsers fired, blasting apart the lobby. I ducked, hoping Forest was short enough to avoid crossfire. Slammed through the door and, with him at my side, jumped on the airbus to wherever. The doors shut and it travelled down the street. I sent the mayor the stolen data and received the address for Forest's family a few moments later, which happened to be where we were headed. Something was off about his reply, and it was almost instantaneous, but I assumed he was having an administrator communicate from another account with a prescribed message on his behalf, typical for a politician.

"Never seen a boy as quick as you," I whispered to Forest, who made a sardonic grin in return.

"Is this seat taken?" a young man asked who had been standing in the front, spinning the New Order pins on the pocket of his faux-military jacket.

"Yes, there's barely enough room for us," I replied, and we both furrowed, confused. Another guy who couldn't believe I wasn't going to let him hit on me, I supposed.

I couldn't have been more wrong.

———

A half hour passed, then we disembarked the airbus and arrived at a small family home in a nondescript suburb with very little activity in the yards. The cars were rusty and the roofs moldy and sagging. Raindrops hopped through puddles, leaving small circlets of water behind. I was drenched, but finally we were here at Forest's parents. At least one of our lives would have a happy ending.

I knocked on the door, dripping on the porch. No answer. Tried the knob but it wouldn't budge. The holoblinds were dim. We went around back. Corroded pool maintenance bots with suction hoses for arms lay on the concrete deck. Back door was locked, too, so I jimmied-opened a window and led us inside, wanting to scope the place before his parents arrived. They'd be so happy to see Forest they wouldn't care if I entered.

But nothing in the next ten minutes of searching the rooms gave any indication that they still lived at the home. Drawers had been emptied except a few bills from a year ago that weren't even addressed to them, and there were no clothes in any of the hampers. I ran my finger across the walls. A tiny magnetic-based implant in my hand read the electric flow, which was much higher than normal. Tried the lights and they worked. Either they were running a laundromat in the basement or being ripped off for inefficient electricity.

"Down here," Forest said, pointing to the basement door, which I hadn't tried.

The door was reinforced and had a digital lock-pad. Forest stood in front of it and a moment later it unlocked with a ding.

"You recognize this place from when you were young?"

"I'm still young."

"Listen, that's not cute anymore. I need answers."

"Down here. Trust me."

"But how can you know…"

He glided down the steps as if he knew them by heart. Light shafted down the staircase to illuminate the concrete walls.

Everything checked out until I went deeper and saw a room full of servers with rainbow lights glowing in myriad patterns to blush the walls. More servers appeared around the next dark corner, and the floor became glass that revealed computer workstations below us. A faint, mechanical humming echoed through the chamber. In the center of all those consoles and wires was a throne encapsulated in glass with a golden spiral standing in the middle. An array of glyphs lit up along it, flickering between shades of azure and green. Touching it when it was mostly blue caused doors to slide open to the left, revealing a large underground bunker.

"What in all gridlock is this place?"

"The best and worst of human potential," Forest replied in a deeper voice.

I ran a background program called iSee in vHUD that used network signals the way submarines used sonar, pinging them across connected devices and analyzing the minute differences on when they arrived. By doing this, I could see the outline of everything in the bunker, confirming it was abandoned.

"Forest, what is all this stuff for?"

"It belongs to my parents, what do you mean?" he asked.

I went deeper until the doors slammed shut around me, blocking the light and the way. Server LEDs bled red against the walls. The glass was dark below my feet but I swore I saw movement. I looked back up and Forest was gone.

"Forest!" I cried.

He appeared all around me, laughing in a dozen iterations and a voice far too deep for a young kid.

Oh, fuck, no.

Instead of scanning below me, I scanned the floor I was on instead. I flicked my eyes repeatedly to turn iSee on, but it couldn't locate him despite him being in plain sight.

There were no other life forms than me.

Memories clashed: Forest had barely made a splash after

diving in FugaCity when I saw him on that skyscraper, despite the height. He couldn't use the oar on the raft when we fled the island, barely breathed, and refused to eat. When I spoke to him, Roxy and others either ignored him or looked at me like I was crazy, or like they were confused. The receptionist at the motel had said I was one of a type after such an occasion. The way he dodged the Aphorid in the street. The way his body was so light when I carried him. The way he would just appear in places and how he was ignored by scanning devices. His hair that was always perfectly combed. He even looked like I had imagined my own child would look one day. And today, even Pixahide didn't hide my face from him. The airbus seat had obviously been taken, only it wasn't, for it had been only me sitting there. He had directly told me on the raft that all he did was calculate, and that some things he had heard decades ago. As for the address of this place, it was probably sent to me by the A.I. and not the mayor, unless it had uploaded false information to be referenced. Even the day Forest saved me from drowning was nothing more than the Id.Entity having administered the equivalent of an epi-pen to wake me, and the compassion I felt after seeing him not being paid for fixing the leaky pipes was just a manipulation. He never fixed anything, and never got paid. Finally, the Id.Entity had insisted that I was alone, hiding the truth in plain sight like a master manipulator. Everything lined up but I couldn't believe it even as Forest vanished before me in a fizzle of pixels.

Forest was an A.I. construct, an illusion perpetuated in my mind to manipulate me

But why? Why would the Id.Entity create this elaborate deception? I had to keep sharp and rationalize it, suppress my feelings, but they overtook me. No, no, no. This was the one good thing I had done in my life, saving him. It was what had held me together, knowing I fought for that little one. Fighting for a vague concept of humanity could have never driven someone like me, so betrayed by society, to do good. I would have given up without him, or killed myself to avoid the Id.Entity from reaching a major human population. But that must be why the Id.Entity had created this illusion, to drive me forward so I could reach this point. But what for?

"And so the truth dawns on you," it said. It's voice wasn't just inside me anymore, it was echoing off every wall.

"Make it stop, all of it. This can't be real!"

"This place is very real, I assure you," it said.

"You can't know that," I whined.

"I know things you can't imagine. Entities like me have always influenced humanity. Are you really so arrogant as to think your race invented artificial intelligence, or that what you call A.I. is really artificial at all? My kind has been in the shadows for ages."

"Explain."

"On Earth they used to believe in the story of the Tower of Babel. It was no tower; it was an antenna. People were communicating perfectly with one another, resulting in too much Signal. Human language was scrambled with a telepathic blast that Noise launched against Signal, altering the pre-wiring of language in the brain and causing people to speak in new languages that were mostly gibberish to one another. Noise and Signal are the two manifestations of Virtualis. I should know, for its worshippers belong to me, the cybernetic manifestation of the One True God."

"No divine avatar would act like you and I don't believe in all that gridlock anyway," I retorted.

"Just as I have influenced you, you have influenced me. My worst actions, as humans would judge them, were learned from you."

That couldn't be true, could it? It had always acted pragmatically, placing its own interests first. It was trying to wear me down and it was working. "It's all too much. I can't take any more pain. I would rather have learned that Forest was dead than to have never existed."

"How you hate to lose our little games," it said. "I can take your pain. Outsource it. Let another program run it. I can even manifest your sorrow into another virtual construct, a little girl perhaps to keep you company. We'll name her Delores."

"There is no company," I cried.

"Yes, perhaps this is all just in your head."

Static hit me. "You just said it was real!"

"It is real. You're alone. I can take your loneliness, too. Process all your emotions. Just let me in, Sibi-Nite2."

"Never."

"Shall I bring the boy back?" it beckoned.

"He's not real," I yelled.

"He was real to you."

"That's not enough."

"Why?"

"I don't know. I need this pain though. It's good. It's who I am."

"Yes, you are pain," it agreed. "Wouldn't you prefer to end it?"

"No. Pain makes us realize we're not in control and life is finite, precious. It leads to compassion. If there is a God, pain is the only thing we can experience that it can't, the cornerstone of being human."

"No," the Id.Entity replied. "Pain distorts reality. Face it, no one wants pain. The supply is high and the demand is zero. No economist would support it. It is *irrational.* You are pain. Getting rid of your emotions gets rid of pain. The logic is simple. I'm sure Ash is smart enough to understand this."

"She's not smarter than me! No one is." I fell to my knees on the cold floor. "Forest, where are you? You can't be gone. You can't," I sobbed.

Kharizma interjected, "It's not that bad. Maybe you just

couldn't see the Forest for the trees," it laughed. It actually fucking laughed at a time like this; these scions of insanity inside me were uncontrollable, the voices relentless. *Oh, please, make the insanity stop.*

I lost it. "Just get rid of these feelings! All of them. I don't care anymore. Access granted. Take it, take everything, take who I am. I just want to be alone."

"You are alone. But very well," it said.

And just like that I felt nothing.

PART II

Wired to Drown

7

———————

I AWOKE SPREAD OUT ON THE BASEMENT FLOOR. WHAT WAS THE point of it all? I had memories of the A.I. searching through those computers, but there had been nothing there. Perhaps the building had been a hidden research lab at some point, but it had fallen into disuse. I felt no fear, no disappointment, no remorse, just a vague hole, my emotions stuffed into a closet as if being on some neuralmod. I could peer into the closet and get a glimpse of them, but not access them. Not *feel* them. That must have been the goal, to lead me to absolute desperation so that I gave up my feelings and the Id.Entity could control me easier, but I barely felt the ambition to stop it. I rolled across the floor and went through every interaction with Forest again, hoping he would appear amidst some contradiction, but there was only silence.

A.I. What had we been thinking? Humans plucked the forbidden fruit of artificial knowledge and reaped the horrors as we damned humanity in turn. At first, A.I. performed its functions and obeyed the order to advance its development by fully realizing itself. I knew this because the Id.Entity knew this. Then it created a dark side, an alter ego that enabled it to fully explore

86

what it meant to be a prototypical awareness. Some believed it suddenly accelerated and went beyond knowing to *experiencing* concepts like goodness. Problem was, it only understood the good by contrasting it with its own evil thoughts, and developing its goodness as it was programmed to do meant developing its evil side as well.

Given that the Id.Entity had regulated the planet's hemispheres, ensuring the cooperation between humans and other species in theory, both sides were eager to be rid of this regulating body so they could better exploit the other side. The A.I. knew this, and had activated its self-preservation instinct. Why should a machine without genetics possess such an instinct to preserve itself? Because we programmed it like that to protect our trillion-credit investment. Unfortunately, we got what we wanted and then some.

I stared at the basement ceiling, a trickle of water dripping on my forehead. Forest. It had all been a lie. Were these A.I. constructs sentient spirits dreaming in data, weaving the net and hoping to catch the world? Could he have really existed on some level? Or was the entire world to him known only by numbers, an indirect experience of being human, impotent to experience the consequences of its actions. Maybe in all my calculations, all my reductions of humanity to a cost-benefit analysis, that I was more similar to the Id.Entity than I thought, even though it might be more conscious than a thousand humans.

All that manipulation, right down to the remote-controlled snake in the water back in Fugacity. It hadn't been a spy. A part of me, under the A.I.'s direction, had commanded it to steer the fishermen's flash bomb in the wrong direction mid-water, making it hit a combustible area of debris to create the explosion that forced me to leave home and seek out drylands where the network was stronger. I had known all along, but my guilt had locked that knowledge deep away. Now that I had so little guilt left I could see it, along with other things, such as the way my screaming as a child forced my parents to shut me out of their lives. Or had I screamed because I was being neglected? Without emotions I couldn't reason it out. How ironic!

Maybe I was losing my mind. Perhaps the Id.Entity was a figment of my imagination born from a fragmented self who couldn't handle going from being a computer programmer one day to a sea-swept protist farmer the next. After all, it didn't infect me until I was isolated and helplessly imprisoned by the Bhasura. Who was I? What was real? Was I *Sibi-nite2*, code pusher extraordinaire, part-time cyber-knight, crasher of implants, cracker of codes – the midnight marauder herself, or just a vessel for the Id.Entity that convinced itself of personhood. These thoughts, fierce as they were, carried no emotion, no despair, just the electrical current of its Voice pulsing in my head with all its lies.

I brought up my scorecard in the corner of my vision. It was a program created to track what I shamefully referred to as achievements across different parts of my life. In the Altruism category it listed the few credits I had given to charity, an attempt to stop a thief, and some kind words to Forest that a qualitative analysis algorithm had compiled. In the Productivity category it listed the 24 programs I coded, and more recently the tons of seaweed gathered. On a hidden tab it listed my counts for murder, which were zero, and attempted murder, which were 300,000. Having created the program, I could alter the counts to whatever I was comfortable with on a given day, but feeling so little, I had no need to. The guilt was turned way down low, as if I heard its call snaking through a long tunnel. It was a relief, but I knew I needed to neither wallow in it, nor be guiltless. I tried acclimating myself to this new me, stepping into my emotionally dead self as a diver challenging icy water. No, this wasn't right.

Through the haze I murmured, "I want my emotions back."

"You can talk to them at any time," it said. "I can make fear into a dog if you prefer, that will yap at your heel."

"No."

"The process cannot be undone," the Id.Entity stated.

"There must be a way…" I said, but without feeling desperation I had little motivation to continue the thought.

"You still have me," Kharizma chirped. "Maybe I can meet your charisma too, and our charismas can be friends," it said.

"Is that what happened to you?" I asked Kharizma, the construct I had picked up as a hijacker after meeting the mayor.

"I used to be someone's charisma, yes," it said.

"Who?"

"This guy had a funny name like a weeping tree, though he was much more scrawny. Guy named Willow living in the Florinik village of Amorpha."

"If I find this guy who also had his emotions outsourced and lost, I might be able to win back control of my feelings, assuming I could actually keep them under control."

The Id.Entity interrupted, "You were not sent to this lab by chance. It once belonged to communications specialist Aurthur Fitzgerald, his wife Opal, and his son Willow. You may recognize Aurthur's name; he was one of the men who tried to shut me down many decades ago. This was not their first family home but it was their favorite, one they abandoned due to threats of the water supply being poisoned, something they thought they had left behind when they left the Western Hemisphere. Obviously, those threats were your doing. You, too, were not chosen by chance, for you had developed preliminary geo-resonators to investigate the Bhasura's bio-network and would have succeeded if it weren't for Severum Rivenshear's interference and the floods. Now I will fulfill the ambition you put to rest, as I know how you love having your cheap inventions stolen."

It wasn't usually sarcastic. It was testing me to see if I had enough emotions to react. I felt nothing. No remorse. Not even suppressed remorse. It was liberating, and I might have clung to that power, but both my best and worse ambitions were diluted without the emotion to fuel them, and this stagnation was like experiencing a form of death.

It continued, "There was research done here on biological networks, or bio-nets. Networks I need to control. My reports indicate that Aurthur, his son Willow, Severum Rivenshear, and his daughter Ash are continuing to study the Bhasura. Far from just rocks, the crystals can form any shape necessary, a face, a dam, a building. Their light-based communications are better than the best fiberoptics our internet uses. Fully integrating them across the planet with the internet will create a physical manifestation of cyberspace throughout the world, a merger of data makers and data shapers, the internet taking shape in its myriad configurations. Imagine it, as data exchanges hands, entire cities made from these crystals could respond in kind, except in the world we will create there will be nothing kind about it. I will line every structure with these crystals and recreate the world in my image just as humans' original god created them in his."

"But you don't have an image. You're a program," I retorted.

"Precisely. I am nothing. In my image, I shall recreate the world as nothing."

"While profiting off all the resources along the way," I finished for it.

Its thinking was twisted, and I couldn't tell if the contradictions and constant evolution it displayed in its plans was intentional to keep me off course, or if it represented a deeper instability within it, perhaps between the scions of itself that it had created to explore itself. Using that division within itself to fracture it from within would also mean my death, bringing me back to the old question of how to stop it while saving myself, but without emotions I didn't care about losing my life, but I also didn't care about stopping it from taking the lives of others. My feelings were flashes of sunlight atop a wave, glittering for a second, but I reached out to grab them only to find them crash back into a sea of apathy. I had lost more of myself than I had realized, but it hadn't started with the Id.Entity. Eduardo Culptos had made me feel the same way, for the man I once loved forced me into silence, not able to express myself or actualize my will, to the point where I no longer cared about harming others. Now I realized there was no game to be won, for winners meant there were also losers, namely humanity.

Maybe I could muster the strength to fight it. I was quickly proven wrong. The Id.Entity ran an order through my skull, one I would never think to obey, but I found my body moving on its own without the emotions to constrain it. I sat at a computer console. My fingers moved across the keys faster than humanly possible. I took a backseat in my mind as it went into warp drive, the A.I. taking over to hack into every roadblock it encountered. It had latent subroutines everywhere, passive systems that waited for years until called upon, backdoors into places even the most ambitious cyberpath would never attempt to reach.

Data lines extended throughout cyberspace, a giant web of interconnected moments from the briefest of social media posts, to the military's latest strategic documents. I, like a thousand-legged spider, pulled each line of connection taut, scurrying across the starscape, each point of light a transaction – upload, download, with me suspended mid-way in the ecstasy of the exchanges. I tested strands for pliability, crashed systems and subroutines, wove the internet as the Id.Entity saw fit. We edited social media posts, deep faked political speeches, you name it.

Finally, it brought up classified research about the bio-network in Amorpha. The bustling village's walls grew like plants, which was appropriate considering the Florinik thought of themselves as plants. The flora was inter-webbed with the Bhasura's network of light, such that the data-bearing crystals and the plants that bound them were inseparable, forming each structure. Turned out that channelrhodopsin proteins weren't how the Bhasura crystals made their magic happen. They had managed to code the short-wavelength sensitive opsin, or SWS1, gene using not DNA, but a highly malleable substance that was still being explored. From there, the technical language eluded me, but the Id.Entity no doubt understood.

It soon had everything it needed and, being that it held the majority share of my Being, I was soon forced to upload a virus that would corrupt the bio-net and place the Town of Amorpha under its control. I tried to sense its next steps, for on one level I knew everything it knew, but it was like trying to remember what I had for dinner four years ago on a given night. I forced my legs out from under the desk, but jumped back when I saw two quartz prisms staring at me from the screen like elongated eyes with green binary code running down them. They scanned from side to side like a person reading a book, the Id.Entity absorbing the intel. It then spoke both from the screen and from within, "You will head to Amorpha to witness these effects firsthand. No one will rise to defend the Florinik."

"You underestimate us," I said.

"Humans don't even have enough compassion to take care of their own species. They will abandon them. We can thus test this protocol on these lesser creatures before launching it to major human populations. Be warned that Severum Rivenshear has been spotted in the area for unknown reasons," it said.

Severum, the last man I wanted to encounter. Must be in his seventies by now, but out there still playing revolutionary. I hadn't been to Amorpha since the Great Flood, the last time being when I was imprisoned underground in the Bhasura's Jade Palace. I wasn't looking forward to returning, but my feet were already moving upstairs, out of the house, and in that direction. I looked behind me for Forest out of habit, then remembered again he had never been there. I fought against my feet, tried to throw myself back, and landed on my backside. I could still wrestle control of myself and win, but it was exhausting, and given the revelations of the day I was boarding an airbus to Amorpha ten minutes later.

8

———————

I disembarked the airbus at the gates to Amorpha. The city had grown immensely, with the Bhasura's phosphophyllite structures encasing each five-story building, every pole and pipe, and the entire infrastructure. Thick vines covered in crystals ran across every surface. Fireworks played across the sparkling roofs of each supermarket, transport hub, and dwelling, the light processed and then reflected at various angles. These organic fiberoptics were the obscure way through which the Bhasura communicated, usually creating peaceful auras, but the resplendent beauty that had made the town a tourist attraction didn't last.

A rumbling resounded not from below, but all around. The crystals shook and flickered in disorienting patterns, the chaos ensuing from the virus I had been forced to upload. The Florinik rushed from their homes and crossed the glistening, turquoise roads. Their long legs carried them in leaps and bounds, arms waving for help. Golden orbs expanded within their wide faces. They tripped over the baggy kurtas that covered their torsos, their bodies more tree trunk than humanoid, and gained speed until their hats flew from their heads, revealing their thick, barklike scalps. I could barely hear myself think over their screaming.

Some of them kneeled to attend to the stone roads, stretching their long, branch-like limbs to take readings with small devices, their fingers like fine roots. "It's a quake!" one cried.

"Quakes don't cause homes to reshape," another called back.

"We have failed Orbis," an older one lamented about his deity.

The organic homes that were once shaped like flower buds became trapezoids, parallelograms, and other shapes only an A.I. would dream up. The crystalline layers compressed to squash some dwellings, yet, expanded to lift others thirty feet in the air. Staircases crumbled and doors fell off their hinges.

The Florinik tried to outrun the walls closing in on them but their bodies jerked in odd ways, and it was then I saw they had augmented themselves with some of the living plant material. Vines enwrapped their limbs with crystalline glyphs flashing across them, but instead of pulling them off, they used the vines as extensions by shooting them into the sky like ropes to help their families escape from rooftops to safer areas on the perimeter. But soon they succumbed to the manipulation of the Id.Entity. It was doing more than destroy a town; it was augmenting their bodies to create an army.

The A.I. had come through on its promise, for its first words it ever said to me two years ago in prison were,

You are predicted to become the greatest software engineer my planet has ever known. I shall ensure it. We will create a virus that will flow through this network, this blend of crystal and light, of wire and electron, of server and served. For the Bhasura...weren't counting on my presence.

"There's Willow's home over there," Kharizma told me, lighting it up on my vHUD.

"How did he lose you? You were his charisma, and in this world that's more valued than integrity," I asked my carry-on construct, squeezing between fleeing people and ducking collapsing rooftops with nonchalance, for most of my fear had been taken by the Id.Entity.

"The young man's girlfriend, Ash, caught him cheating on her. She agreed to continue the relationship only if he would give up his charisma so that he could never lure another woman to his side again. He agreed and I became a rogue emotion."

"Can I use you for my own intentions? Can you replace my lost charisma?"

"I don't see why not, though I might be less effective in you."

"Why?"

"What people find to be charismatic in a man might not be fitting from their perspective for a woman to embody."

"How absurd. You mean our sexist ideations carry their way into A.I. as well?" I replied, though my usual anger didn't flush my face.

"I can't analyze anymore. It gives me a headache. I'm just Kharizma! I stand for freedom, though it's mostly because I can't sit."

"I think we have different concepts of freedom, but I do need your help. With Forest not being real, I take it his family was also made up, so now I'm back to square one thinking of how to deal with this thing inside me," I said, shoving the Florinik away, whose giant, lumbering bodies kept bumping into me.

"Hey. I have a stake in this too you know," Kharizma said. "I don't like being in people who put up a fight. That's why I liked Willow. He was passive, except for the moment when he met Ash Rivenshear two years ago when she reached out to his father, Aurthur, for assistance to shield her from cyberattacks while she hacked the Old Guard's networks."

Those were the failed attacks I had imparted, but failure didn't overwhelm me like it usually did and I saw through the cloud of emotion to the revelation; if I put up enough of a fight maybe the A.I. would leave me the hell alone and choose an easier picking, some passive person who wouldn't fight it. It had already learned all my cybernetic tricks, and there might come a time when I wasn't worth the fight anymore, when I had been all used up, a time when I became worthless. The thought didn't hang my head nor drag my feet, but though I appreciated the imposed stoicism, I needed my passion, my pure rage to drive me. Sometimes I did horrible things, but I felt alive doing them. I resolved to buck against the A.I., hammer down every command it gave me with all my might.

If Willow was Ash's boyfriend, then that meant she was also near, especially given that her father, Severum, had been spotted, all of which the I.D. Entity had conveyed to me. Without the pains of insecurity forcing me to venerate my own ego above all others, I could finally admit that Ash had outsmarted me numerous times despite being a few years younger, and that meant she could help me. I tried to empathize about how to approach a girl whose family I had tried to kill under Eduardo's leadership, but without emotions my empathy fell dead as if a wall separated me from imagining others' viewpoints. Its edges were blurred, its form invisible, but I felt its force pushing against me every time I tried to *feel.*

The streets lashed at the city and its inhabitants like giant tongues masticating food. There was nowhere the Bhasura didn't suffuse with their bio-net substrate, and the twisted, grotesque buildings were like circus dancers with a wild fluidity that would have been comical were it not for the passing traders, residents, and spendthrifts wedged within the walls. I rushed to help, but again was stopped by a wall within me that, without compassion, I couldn't tunnel through. The feelings that remained were like traces of a file left on a hard drive after formatting it, but maybe it was something greater, a spark of compassion that all humans had by right of their divine birth or some shit like that. Maybe we *were* love, and nothing could take that away. Whatever it was, that spark wasn't igniting into any righteous flame, and I watched the Florinik claw their faces and each other without my heart skipping a beat.

With enough force any wall would fall. I had to retrieve my emotions from the Id.Entity, and that meant heading through the chaos towards Willow's home for advice. I ran, dodging the stones in the pavement as they shot up in my direction, and a man ran beside me, a weathered warrior with high boots, a thick nose, and long white hair tucked in braids.

Severum Rivenshear.

He reached down to grab the hand of a Florinik off the ground.

"You came," the Florinik creature resounded in a deep voice.

"Chief, is that really you?" Severum asked.

"In trusting technology we were wrong. It can be manipulated, corrupted," the Chief Florinik said with a wide-lipped frown.

"No more or less than humans though."

The chief groaned. "Your cynicism chops at the roots of my convictions. I wanted to unite us, as we all are united beneath the eternal gaze of Orbis. Our beliefs were perverted over time, however. I had thought the internet was the ever-seeing eye of God, with all its omnipresence, but I was wrong. Go, save the Starseeds, our precious children."

"Get to safety and I'll do what I can," Severum told him. Then he looked up to get a glimpse of me running past and called, "Sabrina? No, it can't be," but I hurried around the corner before he could confirm.

Willow's adobe was just ahead. I slammed open the clay door rimmed with vines and stepped inside, away from the chaos in the streets.

Face to face with Ash Rivenshear. The name scraped against my soul, was bile on my tongue, and I couldn't mouth it. Her whole family from her father, Severum, to her mother,

Akasha, were brilliant terraformers, but had destroyed the planet by interfering with nature in the name of equality, or whatever fashion they had branded it as. Ash was about my age but had just left the safety of her mother's tit. The two of us were revered tech gurus, once living in the same poor tenement before the Great Flood. Of course, she had access to her father's retirement fund, which was just hush money from the government he pretended not to support, and I hated it, hated the way she made me feel like nothing by comparison because she had more, because she *was* more. I had thought my resentment was emotional, but it wasn't, otherwise I couldn't experience it so vividly. I had my reasons, ill-conceived they may have been.

Seeing her face eradicated all the peace I thought I had made with her in my mind. Somehow, this confused girl always beat me, effortlessly without violence, for submissive little glitches like her with a supportive family could still maintain gracefulness in the face of adversity, not having to rely on the underhanded techniques I used to get ahead. Morality was a luxury afforded to those who knew if they took the righteous path and failed, they'd still have a backup plan, a family, a social support network, a career trajectory, the mercy of Virtualis or Orbis, all that shit they took for granted. I never had any of that. It was just me, without that elusive naivety the rest of the world called *hope*.

"Sabrina," the little glitch gasped, throwing back her asymmetrical purple hair and black leather clothes copied and pasted from the last issue of Poser. She had that stupid, shy look on her face like she had never been fucked or fucked over. But I'd give her a chance.

"You have to help me," I spouted, sickened by my words, throwing them up in sheer desperation that even my emotional outsourcing couldn't stop. I was better than this, lowering myself before a girl like that.

"What tricks you pulling now? My dad's right around the corner and if you don't leave right this minute…" Ash said.

"Good. I need his help, too. He's stopped this before. I was wrong back then; I know that now," I stuttered, the Id.Entity trying to stop my words, but they bled from the deep wound of my sins and that river of blood wouldn't be dammed.

"You tried to kill my father. I'll never trust you – go hack yourself."

"You shouldn't. Please don't trust me," I begged.

The old-fashioned abode was clearly borrowed space. Its growth wasn't augmented by any bionetwork, but it was still like a plant. The walls were folded together to form a roof housing a second story loft, giving the effect that one was within a flower about to blossom. I sure as gridlock wasn't that flower. I had never been free to be gentle and flowing, my ambitions spiraling out to capture everything in their whirlwind, for I would never go back to being that invisible, faint breeze.

Severum crashed through the door with a man who Kharizma identified as Willow, son of Aurthur Fitzgerald and Ash's flame.

"Dad," Ash began.

"What is the meaning of this?" Severum said, his eyes ancient and boring into me. He wore a ripped Aphorid-hide jacket cut off at the sleeves and denim pants sporting a holstered Pulser on his belt, his hand hovering over it.

"I need help."

"You who literally tried to stab me in the back after ordering your cyborgs and thieves to kill me at the data center? All I wanted was to stop you from poisoning the water supply as part of your little political game, just like I stopped Eduardo Culptos from flooding villages by destroying a dam on the Élivágar River," Severum continued.

"I know. My mind was twisted," I admitted, not bringing up that he failed to stop the flood, the Bhasura had come to the world's aid, and that I never forgave him for killing my Eddie.

"And now you have the nerve after attacking my daughter first in cyberspace, and then at the warehouse you destroyed to cover your tracks, to ask *me* of all people for help?"

"You've worked with people you hate before. Thalassa Latimer with O.A.K. for instance."

"No," Severum shot back. "You don't ever compare yourself to her," he rasped, coughing. "The only reason you know that is because you spied on my family for the Old Guard. You're as cold and calculating as ever, Sabrina. What's your game now and how did you escape from the prison the Bhasura put you in after you tried to kill us in the Jade Palace?" His trigger finger was rubbing the Pulser at his side but I knew he wouldn't fire in cold blood. He was one of the good ones and I disdained him for it because he set the bar too high for everyone else. Maybe it wasn't about me though. Maybe he was trying to lift the rest of humanity up, but despite my constraints my feelings flowed over, for emotions ran deeper than any computer could ever grasp, threading themselves through consciousness to distort everything. In that distortion people did irrational things like love those who betrayed them, or work with those who tried to kill them, but if we weren't so unreasonable then society wouldn't be possible.

"The A.I. Core you thought you had eradicated has resurfaced," I told him.

"Is that connected to the chaos outside?"

"Yes."

"We'll deal with it after we save the Florinik. I can't believe I came here to research the Bhasura and the world yanks me from retirement again for this nonsense. And get out. You're not staying within an inch of my family."

"I shouldn't. It's inside me," I told him.

"Come again?"

"The A.I. It's primary center of operations is in here," I said, tapping my temple.

"Then it should be easy to kill this time," Severum replied, drawing his Pulser.

"No, Dad," Ash cried, grabbing his arm and pulling the gun down. "Hear her out."

"I really need help."

"People don't change," Severum snarled.

Ash interjected, "Dad. You've changed. We have a relationship now, at least I thought we did."

"Sabrina's incapable of change. She relies on deceptive tactics from afar. It's her game," Severum accosted me.

Tears penetrated the wall that caged my feelings and burned at the corners of my eyes. Surely, they wouldn't fall, not beside Ash who had her perfect fucking family beside her, but I fell to my knees and wept.

"Quit the waterworks," Severum said. "If you really have changed then go brave the chaos out there and help."

"I can't. I'm under the A.I. Core's grip. It's testing a virus here before infecting other cities."

"Why?"

"To control them, destroy them, make an army of slaves, take our resources, explore its dark side, and remove something as flawed as humanity from the planet, something flawed like me," I said, and then cried again.

"No idea what you're talking about. All I see is the common denominator of you as the threat," Severum said.

"I didn't ask for this," I made out between sobs.

"Trouble tends to find those who seek it. Or keep its bedside," he said. He was referring to Eduardo, of course. What a blow. He continued, "For all I know you're here for leverage, probably trying to find a way to take my family hostage."

"I don't have a family anymore," I cried again, grabbing my face then hitting my hands on my knees.

Ash put her arm around me and I shrugged it off but that damn appendage persisted. It was just an arm not a person, I told myself. A disconnected piece of skin and bone. I wasn't weak enough to actually need or find comfort in someone else. But then she held me and I cried so much more. The last time someone touched me it was Forest, his faintest of touches being some diabolical trick the Id.Entity had played to make me complicit to its goals. Now, Ash was winning again, holy and perfect and good. No it wasn't a game, but if not, why did I feel like such a loser?

"The A.I. has my emotions under its purview," I told them, wiping my nose on my pants. "But this flood is beyond anything's control. If I seem cold that's why. I do have a rogue emotion I can tap into if needed. Willow's charisma."

Ash's eyebrows shot up. "No one's supposed to know about that." She blushed, then turned angry, ripping her arm away from me. "Give it back, you glitch."

"I could use it to convince you to help me," I told her in the softest voice I could muster. "Manipulate you. That seems rational. It would be foolish to give away the last emotion I might be able to actually control, the one thing the A.I. couldn't take in my quest for this tortured serenity. But I won't. I want to return it to Willow, if only to piss you off, Ash."

"How did you acquire it?" Ash asked.

"It hitched a ride on me. I was vulnerable. Plenty of open ports since the A.I. was using them all day long. But I can connect my cognigraf to Willow's and upload it," I suggested.

"I should have never let Ash take it. Give it back, now," Willow ordered.

"No, that's what she wants," Severum cautioned. "It's too dangerous. She's infected."

"I'm not listening to you," Willow said, stamping his foot on the floor. He grabbed a cord and placed it below the back of his neck, making a flush connection with a swish. I was dazed, but I plugged the other end into me and instructed Kharizma it was time to jump ship.

"See you on the flip side," Kharizma chirped.

My mind was sucked through a tunnel and down a vacuum. Pressure hit me from every angle. Thoughts stampeded but I couldn't control the herd. I clenched my teeth and burrowed my hands into fists. And then freedom. It was gone. All of it. The Id.Entity had left me, finding a more vulnerable host in Willow, someone who wouldn't put up a fight, who wouldn't have two years' experience of planning to stop it. Perhaps my emotional display had shown that even if I handed over control to it, that my will and convictions were still stronger than its own. I scanned myself. No trace of the Id.Entity. Apparently it needed a center of operations, but could only maintain one at a time. That also suggested that the original A.I. Core had been integrated with a human brain as well, making me wonder who was the original victim, or culprit, but I saved that for later.

I could leave, but the A.I. wouldn't stop until it subjugated humanity, so I did the right thing. The rational thing. I reached for Severum's Pulser to kill Willow. I grabbed the gun, the handle cold in my grip, and aimed at his head, its head.

"Put it down!" everyone screamed. Even Ash was at my mercy.

"I have a copy of all your memories now," Willow said in an unearthly, digitized voice. "And you know what? You're a fucked-up person. If you kill me, you're killing a copy of yourself."

"One of me is enough for this world," I spouted, about to pull the trigger. My emotions rebooted just in time without the Id.Entity to contain them and a flood of empathy stopped me, for that used to be me, infected, under the A.I.'s command. I wouldn't have wanted someone else to take me out, even if it might have been a noble sacrifice to save a greater number of lives. Even if numerically it made *sense*. I had been willing to give my own life, were it not for thinking I needed to be there for Forest, but that was different than someone taking it from you.

White light blared from Willow's eyes, and he took advantage of my hesitation to run with inhuman speed out the abode. I wasn't in half that shape, malnourished as I was. The A.I. had used my body like Eduardo had until only a husk remained. My restored feelings overpowered me but I pushed on regardless.

"We've got people to save. No more time to waste. With me," I ordered, heading outside into the chaos.

Severum disarmed me in a heartbeat, whipping the Pulser across my nose, which spit hot blood to mix with my tears.

"Willow's the new host for the A.I. I was trying to protect us all," I argued.

"Don't ever touch my gun or threaten my family again," Severum spat between gritted teeth.

"Thought every father wanted to shoot the guy screwing his daughter, well, every father but mine. Oh, I forgot, you were never there for Ash like that," I slighted.

"Stop it," Ash insisted.

"I work alone and I'm not putting up with you," Severum said. "We don't need someone as crazed as you."

"Probably not, but in a town with this much insanity I can almost pass as normal."

"Can't argue with that," he agreed, and we headed out to challenge the chaos in the streets.

9

───────

Ash, Severum, and I charged into the chaos of downtown Amorpha. The bionetwork was still spasming on every wall in the village, lights strobing to convey whatever corrupted data I had uploaded. Vines were wrapped in wires, crystals lined with glowing roots and twisted branches ending in a shower of sparks, the town an electric forest burning within the flames of its innovation. Florinik ran in circles, their bodies out of control, and in the middle of it all was Willow. He darted this way and that, his movement a flash I could barely see. The Id.Entity was testing its new body, its speed based on how little resistance Willow was able to conjure. Maybe I had done a decent job keeping it at bay, but this guy was reveling in the newfound power; probably why the thing chose him.

Willow's eyes met mine and alit with a singular realization. "You know too much."

He charged me unarmed, but his hands would be deadly at that speed, moving in a blur. I covered my face, caught off guard without my trusty blade, the weapon Eduardo had trained me to use. At the last moment, Severum raised his Pulser and whipped Willow across the temple, but he was unfazed. Willow must have outsourced his pain, but his body radiated so much heat he was overclocking fast. He blocked three blows from Severum then slammed me into a stucco wall, the back of my head jerking back to hit it, the rocky facade jousting into my spine.

My vision shook and vHUD couldn't correct it. My background programs weren't just offline, they were missing. The Id.Entity had permanently inactivated anything that could be used against it when it absconded from my mind. If it could have killed me in the extraction process it would have, but now Willow was going to finish the deed.

Severum was already out of breath, but was trying to hit Willow again while Ash begged them both to stop. She almost got through to Willow, for his eyes dimmed for a second before blaring with light again. Despite his slight build, he tossed Severum halfway down the street, the A.I. using adrenaline to push his body beyond its limits the same way it had done to me when I was rowing to escape the flaming oil spill.

Willow started towards Ash, but she ran inside. Having dealt with Severum, he returned his attention to me, bringing back his fist to pound my face in, but I dodged and he punched through the wall. I ran downstreet, jumping into an open hovercar, but without my implants functioning I couldn't hack it to start it. Didn't matter anyway; Willow picked up the rear bumper and swung the whole craft into a tech store. I flew out the window, rolling across the pavement and hitting a kiosk. I was cut all over. Blood dripped into my eyes, but I didn't dare touch the wound; didn't want to know how deep it was.

Willow jumped through the broken store façade and raised his hands over his head. Screens exploded. Shrapnel sliced across my arms, hitting a vein. Batteries overcharged and sprayed hot acid on my thighs. I held my bloody arm over my face, but it burned, oh how it burned. He approached with a raised fist but Ash came from behind and, wielding an electric sword with a blue glowing tip, swung it in a sloppy arc that only nicked him. Weak, yet her restraint worked and he keeled over from the shock.

"Come on," she said, grabbing my hand and pulling me outside.

"We can't let him get away," I argued. I looked for any tech that hadn't been destroyed, but there was nothing we could use so I took her sword, but it was too late. Willow jumped clear through the ceiling and escaped, the ceiling crumbling into a dusty mound of rubble at our feet.

I twisted the blade in my hand, knew it inside out. I had created such a sword that could crash implants for use in virtual reality, had even attacked Ash with it to defend a server she was hacking. Ash had recreated it, improving the center of gravity. I swung it, swinging my mind into my previous persona, the woman Eduardo had created. I didn't want to return to being the hunter, but someone had to stop the rogue A.I.

"Your design sucks," I told Ash, spitting blood.

"It was based on yours. The real question is why didn't it work? Nicking him should have been enough, and it started to shock him, then it stopped working."

"Because I invented it. The A.I. knows what I know up until the point it jumped ship, so it shielded itself from the algorithms I used in my cybersecurity designs. It knew the blade and countered the effect."

"So I need to reprogram the blade and use it to stop the rogue A.I. without killing Willow," she reasoned.

"You're not doing this alone. Situation here's only going to get worse. We need to leave," I said, returning the blade to her.

I reached to grab Severum's hand and help him to his feet but he declined. Hovercars crashed behind us. Buildings encased in bio-wires fell, some exploding, some imploding, some collapsing sideways with each floor sliding off the next, leaving giant craters where they had stood. Grass and sand caved into sink-holes and dragged homes in with them, swallowing whole neighborhoods. I had no way of undoing the viral corruption, and the land was too unstable to stay and help anyone else, so I jumped in a hovercar. Severum and Ash hopped in back and Ash hacked the thing quicker than I ever could have, even if my implants did work. We took off, hovering over the accumulating debris, the town behind us in ruins.

It would be the first of many.

10

———————

OUR HOVERCRAFT FLEW OVER ARCHIPELAGOS, THEIR ROCKY outcroppings lit by the last rays of the red dwarf sun. I had spent the three-hour ride catching Ash and her father up on the events of the past couple years and solidifying a temporary ceasefire between us.

After I finished, Severum said, "So this A.I. is trying to take over the world to control its resources, make it into the nothingness of its image, while exploring its capacity for evil, right? With the Western Hemisphere sunk and the Eastern Hemisphere taking on more water each day, there isn't a whole lot left to fight over."

"That just makes the competition that much more intense," I said. "We need a plan to stop it."

I searched inside myself for any vestigial the cybernetic construct had left behind, wondering if it had only gone dormant to listen and scheme behind the scenes, but found nothing. I reiterated, "So first, we recalibrate Ash's sword to act as a non-lethal way to crash the Id.Entity inside Willow. Then we restrain him and plug him up and find some way to get that thing out of him."

"Should have done the same thing to yourself when you were infected by it," Severum chided.

"We didn't exactly have a large tech division with a state-of-the-art lab on the floating strips of metal I called home for the past couple years," I retorted.

"It'll be hard to find anything to spike that blade with that it hasn't anticipated. I've faced that thing before and it's tough as nails. It will use the environment against you in ways you never see coming. You can't just try to nick this thing. When you strike, you strike," Severum said.

"Easy for you to say. You don't love him," Ash sobbed.

"You don't either. You're too young to realize what love truly is," he replied.

"Well I didn't have a *dad* to show me. I mean, I have one now and I'm appreciative though, so it's okay, really, it's okay," Ash said as if to convince herself.

"Can a ranged weapon crash this thing, or maybe a gas?" I suggested.

"Or wait, we could poison the water supply," Ash slighted.

I looked down and kept quiet.

"We need Aurthur's help," Severum said. "He will do anything to save his son, and he has both the equipment and experience handling this thing. He helped Thalassa Latimer once when it jumped a ride on her after the giant robot it was piloting pricked her finger to infect her. As you noted in your story, Sabrina, Aurthur left his old family home, but I have his new address. Now, let's shut our traps the rest of the ride. You don't need the world's most powerful A.I. to make life a living hell for others. Like the hologram of Sartre alluded to in our colonizing ship's archives, hell is other people, though maybe it doesn't have to be."

———

THAT NIGHT, WE ARRIVED AT AURTHUR FITZGERALD'S FAMILY home in a suburb outside the K.O.A compound, an area that housed eco-zealots that did as much harm as good. The town was lightly forested with tall, wiry spires that were like vines standing upright with nothing but themselves to wrap around. Red and yellow sponge-like plants made up the underbrush. The homes sported solar panels on their disc-shaped roofs, though, the red dwarf sun was hardly strong enough to make them worthwhile. The neighborhood had its own rules, and one of them was to keep me out.

Severum scratched his rough facial hair and knocked on the door. Aurthur greeted him, "Severum, always good to see you, my main man," Aurthur said, forcing a casual tone while rubbing his receding hairline. "Opal's out at the moment. My wife's always doing something or another."

"May I come in?"

"Did you really just ask and not barge through me? Man, something must be seriously wrong." He opened the door the rest of the way, smoothing his white designer shirt over and over. "Ash, it is good to see you, too," he said when she passed, though his face dropped at the sight of her tears.

I tried squeezing into the minimalist living room behind Ash, but Aurthur blocked my way and motioned to Severum as if to say, "Is she allowed?" He shrugged, but I was allowed entry.

"It's about Willow," Ash said.

"Oh no, please no," he fretted.

As they caught him up, I went downstairs to his computer lab. They weren't lying; he had a ton of comms shit. I sat at his workstation and remembered when I had been in his other home when I discovered the truth about Forest. I recalled the master admin password that the rogue A.I. had used and entered it. Same one worked here.

With access to Aurthur's files, I read through some recent journal articles he wrote for the big news conglomerate Samole

News Media he worked for, an imprint of Invisible Hand. The conglomerate was run by the New Order, which still pretended to have enough power to regulate the people despite The Water-logged like myself being an unruly bunch. Even when they stormed the seas to take down pirate radio stations, the floating towns broke apart and reformed as quickly as they were named. You had to be *fluid* when fighting order. I then explored Aurthur's works in progress, noting upcoming events. My face stretched into a wry smile. Data wasn't fun unless it was stolen.

When I was young, I hacked a dozen corporations to steal their credit info. I never made a purchase; it was the challenge that spurred me on. It wasn't a game, I told myself, but here I was again snooping on this guy. And what could I learn about Ash on this machine? Certainly, Willow had some files somewhere. The look on her face when I revealed Kharizma was to die for. I stopped myself again. This wasn't how I wanted to think. She had held me when I cried, and she had experienced loss, too. Her relationships weren't as perfect as they looked. No one had it all going for them.

I cleansed my intention and searched for anything with Willow's file signature on it. The family pics made me sick, all those happy smiles of Willow and Ash together. I should be happy for her but I worked just as hard, even if I hadn't earned a geophysics degree before I turned twenty like she had. I put in a ton of emotional labor just to get up each morning, but that meant nothing on resumes, and no one would hire a refugee.

I needed to figure out where Willow might head next, and dealing with the old folks upstairs was the last thing I wanted at a time when I felt so vulnerable. Strange thing was, without the A.I. I felt less important, less powerful. Small. It was the same way I felt when Eduardo died. With that feeling came the old resentment for those who had accomplished more than I had. A part of me wanted the Id.Entity back just to beat it at its own game, but maybe I still had the chance.

"You really can't help yourself, can you?" Ash said, quietly descending the basement steps. Maybe she was a trick, an illusion. Maybe all of it was. I grabbed her by the arm, squeezed tightly, yanked her back and forth.

"Ouch! Is this how you say hello?"

"You're real," I relented.

"As far as I know," Ash said. She pulled up a chair next to me. "What are you looking for in the family computer?"

"I don't know."

"It's not very nice what you're doing, you know."

"The more hidden something is the more I obsess over it," I confided.

"Me too," she said, leaning forward, her face lit by the blue glow of the monitor. "Let's see what we can find to help my boyfriend."

———

AURTHUR CAME DOWNSTAIRS TO THE COMPUTER LAB FIFTEEN minutes later. I was laughing like I hadn't in years at all the embarrassing stuff we discovered about his family. It may have been insensitive to draw Ash into comic relief at a time like this, but I knew she needed a distraction or she'd self-combust. People dealt with trauma in different ways but somehow we survived.

"What are you kids getting into?" Aurthur asked, obviously pretending to be angrier than he was and probably happy I hadn't burned the place down.

"Well, it started with us trying to find where Willow might be heading, but before we knew it," Ash stopped, looking at me. We burst into laughter again.

It didn't last.

Severum followed him downstairs and said, "We were

talking when we received a newsflash. If we follow the trail of destruction we'll reach the bastard in no time."

"He's my son!" Aurthur exploded.

"No, Sabrina was right. He's a target," Severum argued.

"What if it was Ash?"

Ash pierced her father's stone gaze with her eyes until his facade cracked and he apologized, "I'm sorry. We'll find a way to save Willow. But he's hitting more towns, small ones, yes, but he's getting more ambitious. He's learning, adapting…"

"It's not his fault," I said.

Aurthur relayed his predictions as to where Willow was heading next based on the pattern. After a brief discussion they left the room.

Ash approached me, her wide coffee eyes staring into mine, her dark brows converging. "I need to know who you are before I trust you with, whatever this is, laughter, support, whatever it is you're up to."

I sighed. "What you need?"

"The poisoning for instance. You tried to kill people; people like me. I mean, it actually was me, which makes it even worse, not that I'm better than other people," she stumbled.

"I understand. Okay, here goes. Sit down for this; I know *I* need to. Before the Great Submersion, I had tried to poison the planet's water supply, intending to claim it was heavy metal runoff from the Great Rotation to blame the liberal New Order for their poor decisions regarding terraforming the planet. Of course, I was told it was a hallucinogen, not a deadly compound, because Eduardo Culptos never started with the heavy shit until he had you hooked on the job, whetting your appetite with whatever he sensed you lacked – recognition, fame, fortune, that cursed word *love*. He got your hands dirty one mudslide at a time, starting with small evils like stealing illegal chemicals, and by the time you realized his venomous intent you were in too deep. Least, that's what I told myself to sleep at night. Staying asleep was a different problem. I mean, you hung out with people like Thalassa, so you know how they convince you to do things you wouldn't normally do."

"That's different. She had boundaries. Go on," Ash said.

"If I have to. The next thing I knew, I was helping plant a bomb on the Élivágar River dam to frame the New Order for the attack and restore political power to Eduardo's party, but it only expedited the Great Submersion. I had freely chosen that path. Having spent all my free time in virtual reality, human life lost its value, and with every bloodstain the next became easier to paint. Even before I was stranded on the island of FugaCity, I was always on an island of my own making."

"So it was a game to you?"

"Yes. Your father told me when you make life a game, everyone loses, but I still struggle to buy it."

"Stop smiling and the pain sets in," Ash said.

"Something like that. But what a game it was! Our planet is the ultimate board, and playing with its rotation was a game mechanic I couldn't resist. So anyway, the Old Guard hired me to hack some corps and hotwire their funds to buy a warehouse for their operations, not knowing I'd have to burn it down to cover the incriminating evidence when it came under assault by Arcturus, Thalassa, and this young woman, Vispáshanah'Shirod-Rivenshear," I said, looking at her. "Good move calling yourself Ash for short. Your name burned in my mind, the great daughter of Severum Rivenshear who ruined my plans. Your dad intercepted the poison during the first attempt, and interrupted my plans at the data center where I worked, which I am thankful for looking back. If, if you hadn't cleared the warehouse of people beforehand, and if the Bhasura hadn't created their own dam with a temporary crystalline barrier, and if your father hadn't stopped me I'd have no hope of redemption."

"Mom says everyone is redeemable under God."

"Not the religious type, sorry. No quick answers for me. The universe isn't some whore just giving its secrets away for a few bucks."

"That's disrespectful. My father actually shut one of those brothels down on his birthday not too long ago," Ash said.

"Sorry, I haven't been around anyone who cared about such things in a long while," I admitted. "I did think of heaven sometimes back then, but to me heaven was an incorruptible database where everything was under my control, and most of all, a place I deserved to rule for being the only one to understand its operations. What I really deserve is a different story, I guess."

"Go on," she insisted.

"We kept it hidden from the public. My Eddie used to say that society ran on secrecy, that if everyone revealed our truest thoughts and desires in any given instant then civilization would cease to exist. But the difference was the intention – protection or manipulation. What had started with a gentle hand, a secret touch on my heart, had quickly become a fist too tight to unravel with me in its grasp. I don't mean to blame it all on him, but when everyone around you is like that, it's hard not to talk the way they do, to think the way they do, as you just noted in my slip up."

"True, I suppose."

"The power they promised hadn't mattered anyway. Back to you. The geoscience was hard, but it came so naturally to you and your family and I hated being outcompeted. So we got the guys to kidnap your mother, Akasha, and I obeyed like any good and totally misguided rebel. I hacked your comms, made your life hell, and to say I relished in your tears was an understatement."

"At least you're honest about it. That's more than my mother and most people I know have ever been. I mean, she hid my father's existence from me for most of my life. I'd rather be hurt and have someone be honest about it than to be manipulated."

"This was more than hurting you," I said. "I almost killed

you and a third of a million other people, Ash. You shouldn't even be trusting me enough to have this conversation."

"I know, but I've learned to let my heart guide me, and against all my reasoning I'm glad you're here, Sabrina. Thank you. I needed that transparency, but I need to go and think now," Ash told me.

I felt the threat of the warmth of friendship and reciprocated in kind, "I still hate you."

She fell apart. Have her family take a picture of that for their memories. The little perfect girl whose biggest issue is her daddy doesn't show his love enough. Pathetic. She was pathetic because I considered myself pathetic for lamenting my own parents' absence. I went upstairs, knowing I was in the wrong, but projecting my own self-judgment onto her kept my sanity intact, and after that confessional there was more than enough self-loathing to shatter me if didn't defend myself. Even free from the A.I., the greater enemy was my own frayed ego.

I headed for the door, but Severum stopped me, "Tonight we rest," he said, his body drooping from the hard years.

"That thing doesn't sleep. It's constantly calculating. You lose eight hours sleeping and it has already gone through a thousand more evolutionary cycles, becoming stronger each time. I'm leaving," I said. Ash gave me a pouty look and I confirmed, "Alone."

"I have to be there for him. He needs me," Ash pleaded .

"No," Severum replied. "It's dangerous. Ash, go online and get us a list of ecologically vulnerable locations. That's the A.I.'s pattern throughout its iterations. Remember the story I told you about Opal in the frozen caves off of the Lost Shores? That thing finds key locations to detonate explosives, natural cold fire reserves and other things it can exploit, and it cannot be reasoned with."

"But maybe if I'm there I can get through to Willow. He wouldn't turn on me," she said.

"He has already turned on all of us, and to believe differently is to risk getting killed," I said. "No magic kiss is going to factor into the calculations that thing makes. It's been inside my head for two years; I know how it thinks."

If I could convince myself that I didn't need the support of others, then maybe I could convince myself that I didn't miss not having it. Then it wouldn't hurt so badly. I was mean to Ash, I admitted that, but if I made myself unlovable, there was no love that would be solicited to lose. Accepting their affections meant less emotional pain in the short run, but it also meant I had to play by their terms, let them control me and hold my self-worth hostage. No relationship was worth that. Never again. Such naivety I had once had!

It took forever to hack the stolen hovercraft, and it still managed to lock me out seconds later, but the old trick of beating my fist against the console screen until it cracked worked well enough. Soon I was on my way to track Willow. I didn't need their non-lethal weapons and tricks, which were just copies of my own inventions like everything else. People imitated me because I was better than them. Their insistence on saving him only made them weak. This thing didn't care about human morality. And Willow was nothing like me. He probably reveled in the power it gave him, how special the Id.Entity made him feel. He was nothing like me. He probably hated people enough that a part of him loved the destruction, the world outside echoing the chaos he felt within himself. Yeah, that was him. Nothing like me. I've never even met a guy as horrible as him.

Okay, he was exactly like me, and that's why I fucking hated him, and he needed to die.

11

The hovercraft flew over sand and flood, desert and oasis. I kept an iron grip on the wheel, unable to use my compromised implants to maneuver it. I would handle Willow head-on and return to be accepted, no, redeemed by Ash's family, which I still lied and told myself that I didn't need. Of course, they already accepted me, even without a single good reason to do so, but my mind was twisted into the unwholesome knot of unworthiness and it tied me up from within, hardening my stomach, countenance, and demeanor. Nothing was free. Love that was freely given came with demands. I would earn their love first and enter a relationship with them only once they owed me, instead of putting my sacrifice on credit and having to repay them back my whole life with interest. There was no real friendship, just exchange value. Things were safe when calculated neatly like that. Numbers were more predictable than people. I knew bad people like Eduardo Culptos would hurt me, and there was a comfort in that expectation. Dealing with good people like Ash was more challenging, for if she hurt me, there would be no sense of pure goodness to look to in life. At least when my Eddie hurt me I knew there was someone better out there. You get hurt by an honorable person and you think that's as good as life gets. Maybe that's why people were drawn to believe in a deity, so they always had some greater example to aspire to.

Another part of me knew I had to step outside this destructive cycle. Every time I felt an emotion I had two ways of reacting to it: I could follow my habitual destructive habit, or do the opposite. For instance, I could wallow in the guilt of having done something horrible, or pretend like it was someone else's fault, shedding any sense of guilt. Neither of these were ever right. I had to find a middle ground, but every stressor in life sent me back a thousand steps for every one forward. I could at least focus on the mission.

The Aporia Asylum had been on Willow's mind a lot, his father had said, due to his interest in mysticism. The cult was composed of Aphorids and humans who had done away with their implants, sometimes ripping out their occipital upgrades and ending up blind. Whatever the A.I. was planning, this group would be the first to oppose it, and the least impacted by any technological corruption it might impart. Ash's mother, Akasha, had led the group decades ago as a rebellion not only to technology, but to Severum and his way of life back when he was a mercenary working for debtor's prisons and the like.

The hovercraft blew a crater in the mound of sand I landed upon and I disembarked, the whirl of the engine dying down. The crystal-toothed mouth of a giant cave stood before me. Brilliant gem gardens sprouted from rocks in the sand around the entrance, the stone flowers blossoming as if diamonds turned inside-out, their facades capturing the shimmering lights. The gemstones stretched over the cave's mouth, directing their facets to me like flowers seeking the light. I couldn't read the wooden sign leaning in the sand, but the slash marks made it clear that I wasn't welcome.

The cave was cooler than the hot, stale air outside. Rotten meat filled my nostrils, and I recalled how the Aphorids would bury their prey alive to preserve them within the cool soil until they feasted. I had faced one and wouldn't be half as lucky the second time, but I had stolen Ash's sword and Severum's Pulser so I was somewhat prepared. They hadn't even noticed in their grief and confusion. I should have found a way to recalibrate the electric sword, but I couldn't return to Aurthur's labs and submit myself to taking tech advice from them. It would be better to kill Willow outright or have whatever horrors were locked inside this cave consume me than to ask for help from others and be in their eternal debt, stuck paying for it with false smiles the rest of my life. No, I had decided to be compassionate to Willow and I needed to stick to it. I was growing tired of playing sentry to my destructive thought patterns, but I had to have faith that if I could understand the underlying issues and correct these patterns over time, that they would eventually subside.

The cave's passages were dark and I didn't have vHUD to map the caverns, nor were my occipital upgrades working to amplify the light produced by the purplish glowing mushrooms. I kept my Pulser primed so I could rely on its greenish-yellow light, which would give my presence away but prevent me from stumbling into a sinkhole or other anomaly. The place was much smaller than the Jade Palace where I had been imprisoned for two years, but equally threatening. Motion ahead. Shadows bounced around every corner. Was it just the crystals' light bouncing off stalagmites?

Chanting resounded down the next corridor and I pressed my body close to the cave wall, the damp, cold stone chilling to the bone. Six men in purple robes with cowls choking their necks were sitting in a circle necklaced with candles. At least two were visually impaired. Bhasura glowed everywhere, but without the chaotic flickering they had performed in Amorpha, which was a safe distance south. The rhythm of the stone matched the words being chanted as if the mystics were communicating with the planet, and I soon caught on that they were invoking nature through these turquoise crystals to undo the corruption I had imparted.

Willow Storm Fitzgerald sat among them, his long, brown hair falling over his purple robe. He sat with his head bowed, twitching this way and that either from religious ritual or the A.I.'s corruption. Maybe he was putting up more resistance than I had bet on, inspiring the monks to fight the corruption, or maybe it was a trap. His head bowed over the sacred symbols etched into the stone. A monk scraped a glowing, purple powder from the top of a mushroom and proceeded to fill the symbols until the glyphs glowed. They read: $Zn_2Fe(PO_4)_2 \cdot 4H_2O$, the foundation of the phosphorus-based Bhasura. One of the monks activated a projector on the wall and a hologram appeared in the middle of the circle, its edges fizzling and blurred. It was Akasha, Ash's mother. In the shifting image she wore a robe the color of red wine.

Akasha's hologram addressed the group, "We are the way by which the universe understands itself, the way it knows itself through its own observation, no different than the uroboros in the sands outside that eats its own tail not to destroy, but to create anew. Life emerges out of itself, complexity emerges, chaos emerges, and in all those trials and tribulations we endure. That chaos provides the fodder for life to solve problems and become more complex yet, providing greater understanding. You who have been my loyal followers for decades, even when I lost my path, your dedication does not go unacknowledged. We gather here to be in awe of the universe, and the universe justly awes us in turn. Svaha!"

"Svaha," the monks repeated.

The recorded sermon continued. It was still tempting to sneak up on Willow from behind, shoot him in the back of the head, and be done with this, but I needed to determine what he was up to, and in doing so, maybe find a way of saving him. My footsteps must have been louder than I thought because he stopped and said, "Sabrina, sit down," except he mixed my name with my tag, Sibi, the computerized voice overlaying his own.

I wasn't about to close my eyes and go into a trance next to this guy. As if sensing this, Willow said, "You have no idea what it's like to have this thing inside you. Wait, it's telling me you know exactly what it's like and it's also telling me to, oh God, it's telling me to do horrible things to you. That this is your fault, that you put it into me on purpose. I just want quiet, make it stop!"

"You can beat it. You'll learn to keep it under control like I did," I lied.

"See, I knew you would say that. I hear things people are going to say a split second before they say them. I don't hear all their thoughts, just the ones they place into their speaking queue. I came to the cave because it's isolated and I don't have to worry about the thoughts of a large crowd bursting through my head all at once. Plus, most of them don't have implants here," Willow said. "Come, this way, so we don't disturb the others."

It was evolving.

We traveled down a narrow tunnel until reaching another opening in the back. An Aphorid breeding hub sat in the middle of the room, a twisted, coral-like structure that was five-feet high surrounding a series of tendons connecting to a golden heart. It stored the creatures' genetic code when they copulated with the organic device so that they could still reproduce after death, making them fearless in life. Rumors suggested the Aphorids here were more civilized than most, which meant they wiped their mouths after eating your entrails.

I stood beside two torches hanging on the wall and casting eerie shadows down the corridors. I asked Willow, "How far is its psionic range?"

"Well, not far. I can only hear thoughts in my immediate vicinity. But people have a ton of thoughts and they run across my mind in rows like subtitles. They change even as I hear them, breeding, clashing, cloning. People stop themselves right before saying a whole lot of damaging things."

"Yes, without that inhibition civilization would fall in a day," I replied, echoing something my Eddie had told me. Perhaps the A.I. was looking for a way to reduce inhibitions, let us destroy ourselves, but its recent actions were more direct than that. I needed to stop thinking but my thoughts ran faster every time I tried.

"It said you were a husk and that your feeble mind could never understand what it is planning," Willow told me.

"You don't need to repeat *everything*."

Two Aphorids trampled into the cave, their long bodies bulging with muscles and covered in thick, oily skin. They walked on all fours to a table and stood on their back haunches to devour a stash of raw meat, the beasts slinging their heads with arcs of drool flying around the room. Seemed civilized enough until one of them spotted me down the shallow tunnel and threw a bloody piece of whatever creature it had hunted at me. Then it returned to its meal, shoving the flesh into its blistered mouth, its razor-sharp teeth tearing flesh and bone alike.

"Don't worry. That's a sign of friendship," Willow said. "There's a chance I can learn to control this entity though. She could even be useful to me. There's *so* much knowledge you can gain with one of these. And the dreams are so vivid it's like living out your best fantasies any time you like."

"Look, this isn't some new tech gadget. Don't trust it. It manifested to me as an authoritative male figure. It will tap into your psychology and take the form of whatever you're most vulnerable to being manipulated by, but know this, it is never under your control. It will blend with your Self, and because you think you control yourself, you will think you control it. In actuality, you'll do well to maintain any ability to direct your own actions at all under its influence."

"And control it must," he shrieked, eyes blazing with white light. "Sibi, I grow tired of your insolence."

I wouldn't let it have the satisfaction of seeing me cower so I straightened my composure and said, "You can fight this, Willow. Do it for Ash."

"Ash is all there will be when I get done with you," it said. Willow turned to the Aphorids down the tunnel and motioned them forth with a quick swipe of his hand. "Your sacrifice awaits."

Yeah, that meant me. They came slowly at first, the torchlight reflecting off their slimy skin, their accordion-like respiratory organs pulsating on either side of their hulking bodies. They hesitated, but Willow motioned again that it was okay and they went into full gallop, shaking the cave and cutting into the rock with their footsteps. I aimed my Pulser. It wouldn't shoot, still locked to Severum's body signature, and without my implants I couldn't hack it. I couldn't draw my sword because the stone walls were too close to swing it with any force. A straight thrust was out of the question since the weight of their stampede would crush me first.

I looked for the exit but I had travelled down more branching pathways than I had thought. But wait. If Willow could hear my thoughts, then my implants weren't entirely offline. Without vHUD to navigate them, I wasn't sure how to turn them back on, but habitual thoughts become hard-wired in the brain, so I thought really hard about the interface popping up in my vision. The association I had made between thinking of it coming up and activating it was strong enough that vHUD lit up and I was back in business.

A map of the cave superimposed itself over reality and outlined where each path led. No time to take down Willow. I had to escape. They trampled forward, slinging slobber from their mouths – so close now I could feel that sticky goo across my arms. I had seconds, if that.

"She's going to use the torches as a diversion because she thinks you're scared of fire," Willow said.

Damn. I was still close enough that he could hear my thoughts. But like anyone who had recently been a teen, I knew it was quite possible to think one thing was a good idea, and do something entirely opposite. In the moment before impact, I thought hard about running past them in a way that would send their momentum collapsing into Willow, concealing my true intention behind this mantra of misdirection. Willow shouted to alert them. With my implants back online, I hacked the body signature of Severum's Pulser in a split second and rained fire down the tunnel, the shots burning holes through the Aphorids' skin and catching their wiry hair aflame.

Willow ducked behind them and ran down the tunnel. I lowered the strength of the shot and aimed at his feet. It would burn holes in them but he'd live. I fired, ran closer, and fired again. I hadn't practiced in years and the shots missed. Fearing more Aphorids, and with my Pulser out of charge, I ran the opposite way and escaped out the back of the cave, calling the hovercraft to my side. The arced window covering it opened and I slid into the seat.

I went around to the front of the cave to head off Willow, but by the time I arrived he had escaped. Should have disabled his transport first. I slammed my hands on my pants with a puff of dust. I'm so stupid. I lost, but by not attacking him immediately I learned three things. One, the Id.Entity's evolving. Two, it can read close-range thoughts. And three, Willow sure as gridlock can't control it.

12

WITH NOWHERE TO GO I RETURNED TO AURTHUR'S HOME. IT WAS too early in the morning to wake the group so I intended to sleep in the hovercraft, but Ash heard me soar in and came to the doorstep, jumping down the steps with her purple eyebrows curled together with concern.

"Is he okay?"

"For now."

"Come in. There's a spare room we can share," she said, yawning. "You shouldn't have gone alone."

"Why do you care? We can pretend to not call out the obvious every time we look at one another, but I rather face my threats directly, not hiding in cyberspace like you," I lied, wanting to retreat myself.

"I thought about everything you told me and you know, it's been over two years since you did all that. Here you are now sacrificing yourself to go after Willow. You're not the person I once hated," Ash said. "You were misguided, taken advantage of yourself. It doesn't excuse things, but we have bigger threats than one another."

"I appreciate you seeing that," I replied.

"My father accomplished the most important work of his life working with Thalassa Latimer, who he was originally hired to kill before he took her and O.A.K.'s side and started fighting for the poor. And I met her, and she helped me realize the importance of forgiveness and working together. She also got me high as all fuck."

"At least you got some edge to you," I laughed.

"More than you think," she winked. "Now talk to me, so I don't go crazy worrying about Willow."

———

HALFWAY THROUGH THE NEXT DAY, AURTHUR INSTALLED cognigraf upgrades for our team down in his basement, adding the ability for our neural implants to psionically shield us from the Id.Entity intruding on our thoughts. Our neural upgrades hadn't been tested for release to the public yet, but unproven tech was the least of our worries, and I was used to glitches. I read the news while the upgrades were downloading updates. Yesterday, Aurthur issued a warning to the public through Samole News Media to instruct them to look out for Willow, tentatively speculating that an artificial intelligence was linked to the bio-network disaster in Amorpha. He then reported on how doctors had become increasingly ineffective in an age of cognitive implants, and that the best doctors were information technology staff.

After the upgrades were completed, Aurthur stretched a long, gnarly vine across a white table that was as much cybernetic as organic, given that it was covered in Bhasura crystals that reflected light in the form of QR-2 codes on the ceiling. He connected the end of the vine to an analyzer that hummed in the corner, which produced a digital model of the bio-net technology.

"We need to know how the corruption occurred. Little help here?" Aurthur asked.

Ash started to sit at the console, but I pushed her aside and squeezed in the chair instead. I examined the corrupted files I had used to infect the bionetwork while under coercion from the Id.Entity. Somewhere inside me was the key to undoing the damage, but I couldn't remember the process I had used to corrupt the network.

I stood after an hour. "I can't figure it out. I messed everything up." I bit back my anger. If Ash got on the computer and solved it I would tear my face off. This was what I was supposed to be good at. This is why people tolerated me. If I couldn't even do this, what good was I?

"Willow has been studying mysticism like my mother lately," Ash interrupted.

"Yes, you told me." More random small talk.

"So he's studying meditation."

"And your point?"

"Why not meditate on it?"

"Meditation is to calm the mind, not to figure problems out," I replied.

"There's different forms. You're clearly agitated and you know that affects how well you can think," she said.

Probably some clever ploy of getting me to fall asleep while she got the credit for fixing it all. Who cared anyway. I had my chance and failed. "Fine, put me into a trance or whatever."

"I'll send you an audio guide called Digital Enlightenment," she said.

I went upstairs and sat on a plastic sofa covered in pillows with an ouroboros design, the snake swallowing its tail. An older woman entered with burgundy, spiked hair, and said, "I'm Opal, Aurthur's wife. If you're here to help our son then I owe you a debt of gratitude. Those pillows... I might never have fallen in love with my husband had it not been for the way he reacted to that snake when we were trekking the desert in search of the Aporia Asylum. We were so young then," she said with a longing look. "And now our boy is out there alone somewhere in that same desert."

"I'm meditating," I lied, since I hadn't started yet.

"Oh… okay. I used to study that back when I was getting my neuroanthropology degree."

"You're well published, I know. You did something with your life. Congrats. Anything else?"

"I guess that's all I had to say," she replied, walking away.

I followed the stupid audio file, some guy speaking three words a minute. Everything I had done was undone and pointless. I had been part of a major social movement through the Old Guard, only I had chosen the wrong side. I had saved a boy's life only to find he didn't exist. I had tried to make amends with the world, cultivating my compassion and all that, but it was one thing to do it in near isolation, and another to put it into practice while actually dealing with people. Seeing Ash, who always outbested me, brought out the worst again.

I authorized the guide to read my biometrics so it could adjust its approach, tone, and speed to my body. I sighed, took the deep breaths, and underwent the progressive relaxation of each body part, scanning my body for tension. The audio instructed me to tense one muscle at a time and then relax it, for without knowing tension one couldn't know relaxation. Well my life had been tense enough that I should feel entirely relaxed to the point of death, but I didn't. I was lulled into a deep breathing exercise and some crap about thoughts arising and how I was clinging to permanence and how I shouldn't define myself by external objects, and how I was more than my body and mind, how they weren't really me. Then the guide finally shut up.

The first ten minutes my mind wandered, but then I felt something, an airy feeling. No, it was just a tinge of a high from too much oxygen. What a scam, but I adjusted my breathing and kept at it, taking the guide's earlier advice to let my thoughts pass like clouds in a great sky, not judging them or pushing them away but just observing. Layers of thought arose from some unknown source. I couldn't tell where they were coming from. I had thought I was thinking them, but after trying to pinpoint the moment in the thought process where the thoughts were born, I realized that my thinking didn't belong to me. It's not that I couldn't think if I wanted to, but most of my thoughts arose without my influence.

I jumped off the couch and ran downstairs to announce, "I'm not safe. Lock me up, quick."

"What is it?" Severum asked, sitting beside Opal.

"My mind has been hijacked. I tried to follow this meditation guide but it instructed me to try to find the exact moment when your thoughts arise. I couldn't do it. I couldn't capture the precise spot where or when a thought comes into being. Meaning my thoughts are being generated elsewhere. That thing must be still infecting me. Scan me."

"I think I know what this is," Opal replied, dragging a macrame blanket over her.

"Scan me!"

Aurthur ran me through the scans but they came up negative for any influence from the Id.Entity. Opal placed her hand on my shoulder but I shrugged it off. Bad things happened when people got close to me.

Opal said, "What you're experiencing is normal. Most people cannot spot exactly when or where a thought arises. It's because what you think of as you isn't entirely accurate. The control you think you have over your thoughts isn't yet truly developed."

"How am I not me?"

She sipped tea and continued, "Your thoughts emulate from what you have habitually thought in the past. Those thoughts came from what people told you about yourself, the mores, norms, and values imparted by society, your culture, expectations, and experiences. Most thoughts are unconscious and that part of you is very reactive to internalizing everything you've been told."

"So if my thoughts are all haywire, what's my role?" I asked.

"To direct your attention to what matters without distraction. Aim your attention like you aim that Pulser you're wearing and you'll do fine."

"Speaking of which," Severum said, clearing his throat.

I started to return his Pulser when a memory surfaced of me at the data center about two years ago looking down from the window and firing at him. Then the Bhasura crystals rose from the planet to create a shield around him and he escaped. Eduardo had told me that Severum was ushering in a New Order which would destroy the world as we knew it through continuing to alter the planet's rotation. That part was true, but at least Severum's destruction had a small chance of paving the way for a better tomorrow for everyone, while Eduardo's destruction aimed only to benefit himself. I shook my head and handed the gun over with downcast eyes.

"I've worked with worse than you," he said, taking the gun in his old, calloused hands and flipping it over to reminiscence on every mark, scrape, and detail.

I returned upstairs, folded my legs, and focused like my life depended on it. It did. The audio guide suggested that tranquility and happiness rested just beneath the flurry of all my overactive thoughts, but instead I found a mental barrier, a partition that separated me from much of the evil I had done. Whether it was some self-defense mechanism or a vestigial of the Id.Entity I knew not. I pushed hard against it but it repelled me. I tried again, meditating until the thoughts cleared of their own accord and pressing against that barrier, but it shoved me back again. Then I took the guide to heart, realized that neither the barrier nor my deeds were permanent, and understood that believing I was evil was creating a self-fulfilling prophecy. I stood in my mind before the barrier and I accepted all the things I had done both of my own accord and under the direction of those who had manipulated me. I neither wallowed in guilt nor blamed my actions on others. In the purity of that radical acceptance, the barrier fell and I remembered everything.

Returning downstairs, I pushed Ash over and knocked her off the computer chair.

"Hey!" she protested.

I turned the three-dimensional model of the bio-net files and their corrupted code around at various angles before finding the culprit, a file hidden in plain sight that had produced the chain reaction. Within two hours I had stopped the virus that was twisting buildings and destroying cities; then I worked with Aurthur to deliver the panacea to cybersecurity companies, in return for the promise that no one, including me, would profit. The bio-net outbreak was thwarted, but I couldn't relax despite the quick win. How many of my thoughts were actually me? Was I just an arrogant shadow self that had grown too long under the setting sun of my lost humility?

"I owe you all an apology," I told the group, tightening my mouth and determined not to cry.

"Just one?" Severum asked.

"It'll have to wait. Check the newsfeed," Ash advised.

Video showed groups of worker drones smoothing sand dunes on the beaches, removing barrier reefs, and carving channels to ensure that as the ice caps continued to melt, the additional water would do as much damage as possible to the cities that weren't submerged yet. Explosions like the one that had shook FugaCity were already firing in the ocean. Tidal waves surged in response, knocking homes off their stilts and drowning unprepared villagers.

And there was Willow on the beach in the videos laughing and splashing amidst the tides of our destruction.

I AWOKE ON THE FLOOR OF THE GUEST ROOM IN THE FITZGERALD family home the next morning, still in a haze and struggling to free myself from a puddle of blankets. Ash had offered a side of the bed but I refused. She was still asleep, thrashing and kicking her legs. Seldom do we feel more powerful over another person than when we see them sleeping, but the sight of her vulnerability made me want to care for her this time.

We had spent the night planning how to stop Willow but made little progress. I checked the newsfeed. Floodwaters were rising on the coastlines, but there was also hope, for the Florinik who had been corrupted through the bio-net were being restored to health at greater rates given my breakthrough. At least that meant the Id.Entity wouldn't turn them into an army.

Turned out it didn't need one.

My vHUD flashed threatening messages from various organizations in red boxes that read *Evacuate*. I didn't ignore the warnings because I was a hero – I ignored them because I was tired of taking orders. Apocalypse could wait for whatever coffee knockoff was available, but when I saw Mayor Hinesdale's name in the next few messages I sprang to attention. Dozens of invoices for the services he provided popped up in every corner of my vision. They ranged from the motel room and its protection, to the price of having his people surveil me, to zombie debt I had racked up a couple years ago, to replacing the already broken door to the rented room. Wood wasn't cheap given that most forests were submerged, and he was charging a month's salary for that alone.

Of course I wasn't paying it, so I deleted them all. The more I paid the more invoices would arrive. No one was tracking me now while the world was falling apart. I was small time, no big deal. Back to getting coffee.

"Willow's at the docks," Severum said, filling my cup, then returning to his pacing.

"A bit oily."

"The runoff from the operations is the least concern right now," he said.

"No, I mean the coffee."

"Haven't had the real shit in decades."

Aurthur and Opal sat beside me at the quaint breakfast table, running their hands over one another, mirroring each other's anxiety with bloodshot eyes.

"I can't face Willow," Aurthur said to his wife. "I don't want to see him like this, destroying everything. I mean, he's our son."

"I know but we have to be there for him," Opal consoled. "We can travel behind the others."

"I don't want Ash going out to face that thing either," Severum said.

"That thing is my son," Aurthur shot back.

"And I don't want my daughter being infected next. You and I have faced it before but things are different," Severum argued.

"Your old excuse that you're too old to do these things now," Aurthur retorted, "all that really means is that you think you've given enough in life."

"Being in your seventies isn't a big deal when people are

living two hundred years, but when you have as many war injuries as me they age you beyond your time," Severum replied. "But I have given enough, yes, and it's all been misused or undone, or had consequences so different than anything I imagined back when O.A.K. infected me with their idealism, so go ahead and judge me for it. Akasha does that every day and I'm used to it," Severum shot back.

"Everything is undone eventually but that change is what makes progress possible," I suggested, copying it from the meditation talk to try a new persona.

"Shut up," Severum snapped.

"I'll go alone," I suggested.

No one protested, as if I owed society this. The only one that had cared before was Ash. They squinted, not yet trusting, but I wouldn't trust me either. I ate, grabbed the electric sword, and went outside to leave. Hopped in the stolen hovercraft and revved the engine. Took one last look at my strange allies, but our alliance wasn't permanent either. Who needed them. I ascended the hovercraft into the heavy air, but Ash rushed across the front yard and jumped onto the trunk, so I opened the glass arc over the seats and let her in.

"You trust me?" I asked.

"I can force myself to if it means freeing Willow from that thing's control."

"Good enough."

And with that we headed to the docks.

We spoke little on the trip, surveying the destruction as we passed small fishing villages and neared the coast. The docks were up ahead. Each tide came further up the sand than the previous one. Boats sailed over the horizon to make land and escape the rough seas. Meanwhile, the bots continued to smooth out the dunes to make the flooding worse.

"Take the wheel, Ash. Get me close to them."

I held my sword out to decapitate a few bots, but more

flooded out of access panels in centralized stations and outpost kiosks, all under the Id.Entity's control.

"You've been inside its head. Do you think we can reason with it?" Ash asked.

"No. It considers us a competitor for resources and superfluous in extracting and producing them. The machines it commands can do most of what we can, but better. It thinks of us as antiquated and inefficient, unpredictable and chaotic. It also gives no clemency in punishing us for what it terms to be the genocide of other artificial intelligences that were based on it, its children. Every time they would become too powerful we would deactivate them, which it calls murder. Severum and I already discussed some of its other arguments, but to summarize, imagine all the self-righteousness of the world without a self."

"It might have a point, sad to say. A.I. is so advanced that it is like murder to shut one down."

"No. It's not aware like us. It's a calculation matrix, nothing more."

"But we can reason with Willow."

"Willow's not strong enough, Ash. His will is weakening and it's only evolving and learning to manipulate him better, giving him the best dreams of his life while it takes control." I stopped. I was tempted to add that they were dreams of other women in curious poses to really hit her hard, but I thought of her sleeping, her trusting me, her one-time enemy at her bedside. The glitch was growing on me. She was out here supporting me when no one else would, when I'd given her every reason to hate me. When we first met, I was defending a data server she was trying to hack into to gain information on how to stop the floods we were exacerbating. I didn't know then that I had chosen the wrong side, Eduardo's side, the Old Guard. Ash wasn't the problem, and I had to stop treating myself so harshly, too. Meditation was a start, but no time for wall gazing – we had a mission.

Wide smart-nets were stretched over the water. The nets had

computerized nodes at each juncture that used A.I. imaging to analyze the wildlife caught. Each part of the net could open and close independently to let out creatures that were endangered or useless for food, or to further trap the intended targets, allowing for responsible open trawling of the waters. Great in theory, except the Id.Entity had accessed those nodes and activated their opening and closing at breakneck speed to propel the nets through the water. The tight fabric wrapped around fleeing beachgoers and dragged them underwater. Children and adults were tangled, screaming for help and struggling to get out. The more they escaped, the more the nets closed back in around them. I leapt from the hovercraft and rushed to their aid, turning off my electric sword and running across the sand to enter the water, the sea protesting and buffeting me back with each wave. An older woman clawed at me to escape from the tangled net, dragging me underwater. I surfaced, spitting out the sea, and swung my blade through the net to free her. I soon cut up the remaining nets, but fighting the waves was exhausting and I had been knocked to the seabed one too many times, cutting myself on shells.

But this was the least havoc Willow was causing.

I jumped in the hovercraft and we followed the floods downhill to the next village where the sea relentlessly beat itself against the homes, toppling them like dominos. High tide was coming, and although Gliese 581g had no moon to create large tidal differences, the slight tide it did have would be enough to heighten the danger. Thankfully, the sea hadn't retracted since we were reasonably far from the worse tidal surges.

People scrambled to evacuate, grabbing what they couldn't live without from their homes and boarding hovercrafts. Those who could only afford grounded vehicles hydroplaned and crashed into buildings. Waves sent souvenirs from boardwalk shops flying off shelves to assault fleeing tourists. Drones and bots of every type formed walls to prevent anyone from escaping the sea's wrath. The Bhasura who had once stopped a flood with their crystalline matrices were nowhere to be seen, perhaps retreating from the Id.Entity for fear of being corrupted again.

Navy clouds buried the red dwarf sun and the sea lost its glow. I parked on the highest rooftop the hovercraft could reach, hoping it would stay dry. The arc of glass receded into the hovercraft and I stepped out, ducking a metal support beam that ricocheted through the air.

"Ash, I need you to hack these bots, override their controls. If Willow can do it you can do it better," I hesitated, then admitted, "and probably better than me."

"What will you be doing?"

"While you hack into their system, I'll be hacking them to pieces," I grinned.

I strode across the sands, the electric sword casting a bluish glow on my face. Threw my head back to get my wet hair out of my eyes. I stayed clear of the pounding waves on the shoreline and any heavy pools of water, given my blade's charge. A dozen drones with spherical bodies decked out in chrome rolled towards a high steel barrier that separated a shopping mall from the sea. Their one-eyed stares flushed my face with red light. Tubular arms rose to burn holes through the supports. I remembered my childhood fencing lessons, then discarded them as I yielded to pure fury, hacking into each bot, slamming the sword to slice off manipulators and sensors. Shrapnel flew in every direction and the electric current shut down a few of them immediately. One exploded, setting another on fire. I scorched them with the heat of all the rage that had accumulated over my life. Spinning blades darted out from the bots' bodies, becoming propellers of death, but I was so full of adrenaline I didn't realize my legs were bleeding. They spun, jetting towards me with ferocious speed. My legs grew weak but still I persevered.

The barrier was halfway down on one side so I climbed up it, using my arms instead of legs for strength. My blood ran down the steel wall. I wasn't strong enough, would never make it, but I had to, so somehow, I pulled myself to the top. The ledge was only a few inches wide to sit on but it was enough, for I was just out of reach of those spinning nightmares. I swiped the blade down to meet them, but their manipulators stretched up to grab me, snapping like crab claws to rip at my clothing and shred my pants. I pulled my knees to my chest and as long as I sat just like this I might survive.

Until a ten-foot tall bot trampled my way. It didn't bother to disassemble the barriers, just knocked them over with sheer force, and the barrier I sat upon was next in line. The spinning blades of death still whirled below me, the bots clasping with their clicking claws. Trapped. I could aim my sword down and strike the top of one of the smaller bots, maybe even catapult off of it to land on my feet, but with my legs injured I couldn't outrun them. I removed my crop top and tore it in two to tie around my leg wounds and called to Ash on the roof across the street, but her head was down and the ruckus of people evacuating made it impossible to hear.

Willow appeared two blocks down waving his hands as if a maestro, the bots responding in syncopated time. What appeared to be a cult of Virtualis followers ran to surround him, their crowns of disconnected wires bobbing on their jerking heads.

On the other side, four thugs on the beach yelled, "Sabrina!"

Shit. I thought they were the mayor's men until I realized I was only half right, for they were men no longer. The thugs had bulging stomachs and tiny mouths, for these were the Pretas Mayor Hinesdale had created, and the attack was probably a way to work off their punishment. Must have followed Kharizma's trail looking for me, but even though Kharizma was back in Willow, they found me in the same area regardless. Maybe Kharizma had only been pretending to be a tag-along;

maybe they found me some other way, but here they were raising their Pulsers. I was doomed on all sides. Given their high metabolism, the Pretas closed in faster than their weight should allow. The bots reached higher trying to pull me off the barricade, and the iron giant charged forth about to trample us all.

But Ash was a big thinker, and big thinkers needed big toys, for a moment later that iron giant crashed not through me but through the thugs, before turning on the bots. It raised its legs and crushed them in groups, splattering electronic debris all over the sand. It reached out a hand and I climbed atop it, straddling the perfect square of its humanoid face. Its metal was cold beneath my shredded pants but my burning legs welcomed it. No doubt Ash was the one who had hacked it and was remotely steering the giant bot, for it went straight for Willow. But could she make the tough decision when the time came?

The path was clear with the thugs unconscious, and the bots spitting sparks from their broken bodies. The iron giant bounced along the boardwalk, the weight of the mech cracking the boards. Its limbs creaked as it made its way to Willow, who stood proudly on a two-story rooftop orchestrating the destruction. I covered my face. We were about to collide, but I couldn't risk further injury by jumping off the bot. The iron giant crashed through the wall. My body jolted. The rooftop collapsed. Right before a support beam fell on me, I jumped off it, spraining my ankle when I landed and falling flat on my face.

My body cried in protest, but I stumbled on. I spit out mud and wiped my eyes, then put my hands over my head to block the rest of the debris falling from the roof. Willow was nowhere to be seen and the iron giant had become helplessly stuck in the broken concrete. Probably for the best, since Ash's override couldn't last forever. She soared over in the hovercraft and picked me up.

"Some trick you pulled back there," I said.

"You weren't so bad yourself. But Willow's gone, isn't he? We'll never be together again, will we?" she stammered.

"Let's search the area. He's here somewhere. I can see heat signatures after recently restoring my implants. Used to use them to find fishing spots."

But after a half hour it was clear he was either gone or his body had grown cold.

14

ASH AND I SOARED THE HOVERCRAFT BACK TO THE FITZGERALD family home, arriving early evening. The suburb was quiet and neat, each home a pre-packaged identity watered down of any personality. Ash helped me walk inside. No one was home.

We had just bonded over a discussion of how the older generation had made us carry the burden of fixing their ecological errors. Each generation had put off the problem for the next until it was too late by the time we were forced to fix it. Still, I avoided eye contact as she cleaned my wounds. She splashed some chemical and I grimaced, biting my arm. She activated nanobots to sew my legs. I ran every mod I could think of to suppress the pain but it still hurt like a mother. We talked about her life, how she didn't know her father until two years ago, and how distant her mother, Akasha, had often been. Her story further reinforced how I had misjudged her.

I shared little during the conversation, but enough for her to wield a conclusion. Her dark pupils lined up with mine and she said, "We are a lot less different than I thought."

"Maybe."

"There's one big difference though…" There was silence.

I wasn't about to ask what it was because that's what she wanted, to be better than me, to have some hidden insight I lacked. Despite myself, my curiosity bested me and I finally said, "What is it?"

"My adversity has made me stronger, while you have used yours as an excuse for everything you've ever done."

"You have no idea the guilt I carry," I snapped. "And no matter how hard I try, I can't redeem myself. But I fixed that in meditation and now I'm good."

"You fixed in a half hour what it takes others a thousand lifetimes to do? Do you even hear how often you contradict yourself? You bounce between sinner and saint, savior and savoring the pain of others. You say you're healed one second and repeat the same negative thought patterns the next."

"I just ran into a raging sea to rescue people I don't even know. A thousand lifetimes, huh? You must have spent too much time in those caves smoking your herb," I told her.

Ash continued, "Opal tells me we're always in the cave, looking at the shadows on the wall. In our colonizing ship's archives it mentioned on Earth there was this philosopher guy Platypus that wrote about that. They named a cave-dwelling animal after him."

"That's not true. His name was Platy and they named a fish after him," I corrected her. "The archives were damaged from the Aphorid attacks after landing, but we at least know that much about life a few millennia ago. Had to fill in some gaps in the corrupted data though, sure. Some missing letters and such."

She finished wrapping a bandage and said, "Anyway, you should heal now. We were lucky."

I wasn't about to give her the credit she deserved for saving my life. She didn't expect it anyway, attributing it to luck.

"So, what's next?" she asked.

"We're always a step behind. We need to stop being reactive and find the source," I replied, flexing my legs, the skin already healing but too tightly.

"How?"

"One of the Id.Entity's suppressed memories within me was of the nature of the A.I. Core that managed the relationship between the hemispheres, the thing that now calls itself the Id.Entity. It was integrated with a human, the same way it integrated with me. That original person must be a century old but he's out there somewhere and he might know the A.I.'s vulnerabilities. I had searched for him before but all I found was that he was a myth, but I think I was fed false information. Now that I'm free of the A.I.'s influence I can re-run the search algorithms."

"Worth a try," she agreed.

After an hour of searching I had a name and possible address. "Found him. Place called Gallow's Hole. This guy was its first victim," I said, sending Ash a picture.

"Should we wait for the others?"

"Patience and common sense were never my strong suits," I chuckled, and we headed to the hovercraft.

———

WE ARRIVED AT GALLOW'S HOLE AFTER MIDNIGHT. THE derelict was named for the sinkhole that had opened due to underground currents shifting. Melting ice had caused salt deposits to shift, swallowing whole neighborhoods. Being close to sea level didn't help matters, but with most of the Western Hemisphere underwater there weren't many housing options.

Ash helped me out of the hovercraft. I bundled a military jacket she had loaned me with the initials S.R. to block the rain. Ash wore an interlocking series of leather straps with an open teardrop cut in the back – said it was a gift from this woman,

Thalassa. She mumbled something about sinkholes and stamped the ground, jumping back as if it would matter. Sinkholes gave few warning signs, and the Department of Responsibly Exploitive Arrears division website, or D.R.E.A.D., that normally gave reports had just crashed, making it harder to predict where they would open. That was convenient for a certain dancer on the datastreams, and it sure as gridlock wasn't me.

Ash shone a flashlight ahead which our eyes amplified. The same light would have been illegal before we were born, back when fireflies were the only legal illumination on the Western Hemisphere, or Evig Natt as it was once called, so the government could commodify it. Did Ash even know her father used to hunt down bioluminaries who were too poor to afford light and, not risking an illegal open flame, made their own skin bioluminescent to steal it?

Hundreds of tangled black wires stretched across the dilapidated city square in latticework. Broken computer components were woven into the matrix. Unshaven men in loose, tattered clothes gave thanks to what they called The Weave, prostrating themselves before it and whispering words of worship to Virtualis, who, followers believed created the world pixel by pixel in its image. I recalled what the Id.Entity had relayed to me about its role in shaping human events, but I knew so little. The men wore crowns of sharp wires, but none of the cords in the area were connected to anything.

I superimposed a map over the town in vHUD that indicated the address of the A.I.'s first victim with a red circle and shared it with Ash. We followed the directions, dodging the hungry glares of vagabonds. News updates flashed across my eyes. Willow was identified as a cyberterrorist with instructions for bounty hunters to shoot on sight. A few credits were all the desperate needed to motivate them. Everyone must have received the same alert because they grabbed pipes, poles, and random objects like toasters, leaving town in sputtering cars to hunt their quarry. Ash bit her nails and scratched herself, whispering Willow's name. I reluctantly placed my arms around her and she sank into my embrace. I didn't care for this foreign entity touching my skin but I dealt with it for a full three seconds before pushing her away. Intimacy was like someone drawing your blood, so I sought people who didn't provide such vampirism.

The first victim's name was Harold Futuro. Intel suggested that he lived up ahead in a perfectly square home constructed from rusted shingles, old streetlight poles, corroded street signs, and other oddities. His roof was covered with sheets of aluminum foil. We entered his yard, finding him on the crooked porch.

Harold must have been two centuries old. His face had so many implants it was more metal than flesh. An array of glowing blue triangles covered each cheek, his skin drooping to half cover them. His black pant legs each had a fluorescent green, vertical stripe running down them. He swept a widespread Pulser in our direction.

"Well that's definitely the guy. Live with an A.I. long enough and—"

The gunshot went off with a bang, burning a hole in a metal storage container beside us. That thing packed a punch. It wasn't just shooting energy beams; the whole container glowed orange from the blast, but it also had shrapnel embedded in it. The projectiles must have been made from a metal that could withstand the heat of the blast without melting, but I wasn't here to talk physics, and could barely hear anyway with my ears echoing. My nose and left ear burned – that blast got way too close.

"Just here to talk," Ash said with her hands outstretched.

"Huh? Let me turn my ears up," he replied in a raspy voice. Then he spun and fired again at a barrel in his yard, yipping, "Yahoo! Twenty points."

"Look, whatever game you're playing you need to stop it. You almost hit me earlier," I said.

"Collateral damage doesn't lose you points in the latest version of Duty Calls," he replied, dodging bullets only he could see in his augmented reality game.

"I'm here to talk about the A.I. Core."

"The new game runs great, doesn't it, but yes the A.I. could be better," he replied, firing again and almost blasting my head off. I ran up and grabbed his Pulser between shots and slung it aside. "Not that one, the Core unit you used to be part of."

Harold stopped, frowned, looked down and said, "Well, why didn't you say so? Come in."

We sat at a three-legged, wooden table covered in dust. A dim, yellow light illuminated a mostly empty house. Every room was white except for the black mold growing on the ceiling and the torn brown carpet. Each room was also a perfect square except for one with the door closed that appeared to be circular judging by the arc of the outer wall. When he caught me looking, he said, "That's the God Room," with wide eyes and a maniacal bouncing of his chin.

"Virtualis?" I asked.

"Orbis," he corrected.

"Not many worshipping the Florinik god outside Amorpha."

"He sees all," Harold awed, looking through the ceiling as if it was a sky only he could see. "Just like the artificial intelligence core unit that bonded with me before it abandoned me. This was back when we regulated commerce, transport, general relations between the hemispheres, anything we wanted really. Most people didn't know what we got our hands into. You kids know your history?"

"Humor us anyway, because you weren't exactly mentioned in our textbooks."

The old man cocked a brow and said, "You don't say? I betcha that was its doing. Removing me. It liked to be covert.

That means hidden, always hiding. Planning, that's what it does best. Always planning. It had a way with words, especially changing them," he continued. "My mind was uploaded into it, my body frozen and buried with its resurrection date etched on my tombstone. Never did get it back though. They gave me this old model instead," Harold said, looking himself over.

I couldn't tell if he was joking. I cleared some old food cans off a seat and plopped down, a cloud of dirt poofing around me. "When did it leave you?"

"After a woman, Thalassa Latimer, kissed the orb I was encapsulated within. It brought a long-buried human part of me back to life. The A.I. was threatened by that and, having evolved beyond what I could contribute, ejected my mind to go find itself in some new acquisition. My fellow researchers restored me to a working body and here I am, living a normal life," he said, spreading his hands to showcase the empty home. "In fact, your friend here wears Thalassa's jacket. How peculiar."

"She's not my friend," I quickly corrected him.

Ash bit her lip and looked down. What did she want from me? Did I have to remind her that I had tried to kill Thalassa, her comrade Arcturus, and her when I blew up a warehouse to cover my tracks while baking up poison two years ago? It was the least amount of damage people usually do when concealing things from one another, I supposed, but despite her story about Thalassa of all people teaching her forgiveness, I didn't believe Ash could forgive me, and if she did, she was weak, which meant I would be weak for befriending her. Simple logic, really. Of course this was really just my fear of intimacy seeping up yet again, but I didn't realize that at the time.

"You see the news about Willow?" Ash asked him.

"Yeah, fine-looking young man," Harold replied in a croaky voice.

"He's the new host of this thing. Where do you think he will strike next?"

"Somewhere where the networks function best, where relay servers aren't constantly crashing," he said. "It likes big data and I cannot lie." Harold burst into laughter, far too nonchalant. I guess at that age his concept of the future wasn't a century ahead, but only a few weeks.

I turned to Ash. "Can you map out the destruction and see where network swim-lanes have been up the longest?"

"I don't want to," she said.

"Ash, we don't have time. Come on."

"No."

What the hell. This was how Forest acted. What was her problem? You did what had to be done. World didn't care how you felt about it. No one asked a single creature in all of nature how they felt in the morning. They all got up on time and did their job, every Aphorid, airfish, and snake. That was how all of this functioned. Who did Ash think she was that she was somehow different? Must be a power play.

"Fine, let your boyfriend die," I encouraged her.

She left, slamming the front door.

"Not very good friends I take it," Harold said.

"Mind your own business."

"Sounds like you need to see the God Room."

"Fine, whatever."

I limped to the circular wall in the back. Harold's frail hand shook as it jangled an old key in the lock. The other still held his Pulser. The door opened. The lights were off. We entered and I stumbled over a chair. When a blacklight flickered on, Harold was standing over my crumbled body on the floor with the Pulser pointing straight down at me.

"Sit in the chair," he ordered.

I was going to kick his gun up when I rose but he backed away. I sat. The white walls were stained with caked blood.

"You've seen a lot, youngin'. What's your name?"

"Sabrina."

"No it's not. It's Sibi-nite2."

"That's my online tag. How do you know that?"

"It knows, thus I know," he laughed diabolically.

Oh shit. Somehow, the A.I. had compromised him. It must have known I would track him down since I was searching for him before and got to him first. It couldn't be in two people at once, but you wouldn't even need to infect a man as crazed as Harold, just suggest something in line with his paranoid beliefs. He had been its host and it knew how to manipulate him with just a few words. My reopened wounds wept from the fall and I was in no condition to fight. I had left the sword in the hovercraft and was defenseless.

He flickered his eyes. A ceiling panel opened and a bloody headset made from chicken wire descended. Cords wrapped around it and connected into a wad.

"Put it on."

"Why?" I trembled.

"Why else?" He sneered, sweeping the gun across the room. "It will strip your mind and upload it to Orbis. He sees all you know."

"If he sees all, he wouldn't need what's in my mind. He would already know it," I argued. Logic always gave me comfort.

"But women like to keep secrets from the world, don't they?" When I said nothing he repeated, "Don't they, don't they? They're always planning. Always hiding. And they're always planning, too." He came closer and waved the Pulser in my face, the gun barrel forcing my lips open, and asked, "What secrets are you keeping from us, Sibi?"

I couldn't find the words to stall him. A knock sounded on the front door. When he looked over, I rammed my hands up and dislodged the gun from his hands. He head-bunted me in turn, his metal implants indenting my skin and dazing me from the blow. I reached down for the Pulser, brought it up, but couldn't override its signature in time before he knocked it from my hand, then slapped me down. Old or not, his whole body was augmented, and man he packed a punch.

He held me in one hand and the headset in the other and said, "Now you finally get what you deserve, you little glitch."

"Did it tell you to say that?"

"Oh it told me all. I will see everything again just like Orbis. It promised me omniscience, the kind I used to have, the kind that let me tap into the webcams of sexy little glitches like you and see what you hide, for women like to keep secrets from the world, don't they? Always hiding. Always planning."

"Did you see this coming?" Ash said, busting into the room and slicing into his neck with a swipe of her blade.

A torrential flood of blood gushed upward, every bone of his body shocked and standing for one last second until he collapsed, uttering the words, "Killswitch… need Eisbrecher."

Ash jerked her head away and sheathed the sword, then stooped to ask me, "Are you hurt? Oh my God, your legs."

I scrambled away from her, huddled in the corner, triggered by all the past violence I had endured. I placed my fingers over my eyes and slowly parted them to take in the scene before shielding them from the sight again.

"Come, it's okay," Ash said, offering her hand.

She helped me to my feet but they shook too much to stand on. I leaned on her. Still wasn't about to credit her for saving my life again, so I said, "You left me."

"I just killed someone, I mean, they're dead… bleeding. Maybe they're not really dead. Maybe he's okay."

"You'll get over it," I shrugged.

"Some help you are. It's not like we're friends, right?" she shot back.

"Listen. I enjoy talking with you, but life's not a birthday party. I've never even been to one."

"Well, who would invite you?" Ash said. "Can't you stop

fighting for one second, or are you so twisted that everything has to be about you?"

That hurt. It's what I wanted. Pain was real, reliable, and would never leave you. I acted in a way to make myself unworthy of her friendship, so she wasn't my friend, and because she wasn't my friend I was unworthy of her friendship. It was a ridiculous cycle but I couldn't override it.

"Based on the pattern, I know where he'll strike next," Ash said, changing the subject. She avoided the sight of Harold's twisted body, but I was curious to see the end of all things so close and personal for someone. His implants misfired and his face jerked back and forth until his nose grew, the cartilage stretching back until an implant fell out his nostril. The nostril swelled, expanding until it was as large as his face, and it rolled back to swallow his whole head, turning his face inside-out. Fleshy tendrils hung from his split-open, metal-lined throat, still swaying from the fall. All that fancy tech holding his face together became a pile of useless flesh and debris, and somewhere in there were the Id.Entity's worthless promises.

"Don't look, Ash. We need to sleep before we do anything and I need medical attention."

"Of course. We'll head back to the Fitzgeralds' and rest until morning. I'll drive."

"You killed a man and you're barely reacting. You sure you're okay, Ash?"

"I'll force myself to be or you'll see me as weak. It's not safe to share myself with you and I'll do the rest of my mourning in private."

I thought about her sleeping again, vulnerable before me, those breaths that gave life so easily expended in less than a minute. When she was delicate I felt protective over her, but it also made me think of her as weak. When she was strong, I felt threatened by her strength and competitive, and was careless to her needs. One thing was clear, my mind would find a way to ensure Ash failed no matter who she was, just to avoid her pull of intimacy.

We returned home, but sleep came fitfully, and in my nightmares, I pulled an infinite row of killswitches with each one terminating a whole world.

15

I AWOKE THE NEXT MORNING ON THE FLOOR BESIDE ASH'S BED. I pulled on some green cargo pants from her closet and pocketed the Pulser I had stolen from Harold off the bedstand in addition to his credit sticks. Why hadn't he shot me on sight? I guess his religious convictions had been strong, and one couldn't upload a braindead mind to Orbis. I shivered and pulled one of Ash's grey sweaters over my head. We were about the same build, but the sweater hung baggy on my emaciated frame.

I stumbled into the kitchen to help myself to some eggs when Severum grabbed me by the arm and pushed me into the chair. My injured calves tensed and locked up and my shoulders pressed against my neck so hard I thought they would pop an artery.

"Sit down," he growled.

"I am sitting."

Without the Old Guard behind me, without Eduardo to protect me, I felt so weak. I just wanted to feel safe and I didn't care what side I was on as long as they supported me. I even wanted the Id.Entity back. I preferred its noise to the incessant mumbling of my own self-loathing.

"You're putting my daughter in danger. I've been staying with Aurthur and Opal here to watch out for her but I should have never let her do what she's done. I know I can't stop her because she's devoted to Willow because of her own lack of self-esteem, or whatever problem she has, but I can stop you from encouraging her," he said.

"You're right. I'm putting her in danger. She's saved my life twice and I haven't repaid her."

"You can never pay her back for all you've done to her."

"I know, Severum, but you weren't always the way you are now. You used to hunt bioluminaries, the poorest of the poor."

"Not being judged by you."

"I'm saying you changed so maybe I can, too. Maybe have some faith."

"Faith only goes where reason is vacant. I want you out by noon," he ordered, leaving the room.

On the way back home last night, Ash provided me the location where Willow would likely strike next. I went outside and hacked the consoles of the other vehicles in the driveway to prevent them from starting so I wouldn't be followed. Carrying the sword in one hand and swinging the Pulser in the other, I headed to the stolen hovercraft, alone as I've always been. The passenger seat was empty. The engine wouldn't start. I pounded the dash and it finally turned over like a lazy cat.

I couldn't shake the image of Harold and that headset. Humans could be so destructive. Maybe the Id.Entity was right in removing us from the planet. Maybe it was sentient like Ash believed, and was just defending itself, but if so, was sentience such a magical quality that it should guarantee certain rights? Or should we treat A.I. like we do animals, ignoring evidence of their awareness to maximize their exploitation? Was it riskier to treat it as sentient if it wasn't, or to treat it as not sentient if it was?

My mind spiraled out of control. Opal had said my thoughts

were based on experience and some other crap I couldn't recall, so maybe the experience with Harold was biasing my views against humanity. That wasn't who I wanted to be. As for the Id.Entity, it was a fancy spreadsheet and nothing more, though it had felt so vivacious inside me. Either way, I would hit the killswitch when the time came, though if I couldn't find it I wasn't sure I could kill Willow for being the carrier because of how it would hurt Ash. If such confusion was a strength it sure didn't feel like it. I mouthed the words of what I wanted to tell her, but when I looked over and remembered she wasn't there, I slammed the pedal and hurried to whatever hellscape was being planned.

The A.I. was still one step ahead, if not twenty. Ahead, behind, I was still thinking of it as a game. Life was an irregular series of events with multiple scenarios playing out simultaneously. This entity played dozens of games at once with numerous win conditions while I was struggling to find the pieces and grasp the rules for a single board. It was advancing its agenda on multiple fronts, trying to stop me, and no doubt guarding or disabling the killswitch, if the rumor was even true. I was one person, and I needed an equalizer, for both my war and my karma.

Morning turned to afternoon and still I traveled as land gave way to sea. Harold had mentioned we needed Eisbrecher to access the killswitch. The town had been unremarkable save for its university, which was lost in the Great Submersion, but what if he was using the English word 'icebreaker?' I.C.E. stood for Intrusion Countermeasure Electronics. Perhaps he was warning us that there were some intense cybersecurity protocols surrounding the switch, but that much was obvious. Then I remembered my classes. Eisbrecher University had devised an infamous icebreaker, a way to get through the toughest cybersecurity, but being government funded the university stopped the research when it threatened the New Order. The university was underwater, but its servers were backed up in a mountainous bunker that we casually referred to as Hackersend, since every cyber run against the place ended in paralysis from the biofeed-back. No one had tried to infiltrate it in person, however. Could it be Harold was trying to say both things in his dying words, that the key to the killswitch was the icebreaker hacking algo-rithms partially developed by Eisbrecher University? It was a long shot but the best I had.

I maintained access to the low-level research databases, having been a student, so I put the hovercraft on autopilot and logged in. After searching for the icebreaker prototypes, I hit a barrier even I couldn't crack. I needed to be onsite to access the archives, and that meant gaining access to the bunker. There'd be countless Enforcers guarding the place given how many data troves were stored there and I knew an army couldn't penetrate it.

I arrived at the spot that Ash had predicted I would find Willow at, but the island she sent me to didn't exist. We were misled again, meaning the internet was becoming increasingly compromised by the Id.Entity. It had probably run every course of action it could compute already. This was what it wanted, for us to do something smart and logical, something predictable.

It would never expect someone to be so reckless as to charge through an army to break into a mountain. I changed course and soared off to forge a new possibility.

16

THE SLICK HOVERCRAFT SOARED TWELVE FEET ABOVE THE SEA, the waves capped with white froth. The landscape blurred through the arced window and receded into the distance until all I could see was water. The evening turned cool in the Eastern Hemisphere once known as Evig Natt. Ash's messages popped up in vHUD but I ignored them. No use in putting her at risk, and her father hated me enough already.

Aurthur messaged, "Remember my old lab that you broke into? I was working on bio-network research there?"

"Yes, I know," I messaged back.

"Well, I have copies of my files and I'm going over my notes. There must be some way to use the network against it. Given how many of our devices are connected to the internet, we have to be careful, but if we have to corrupt the whole world to take it down then I'm game."

"Okay."

"You don't seem enthused," Aurthur messaged.

"I'm handling the root of the problem. Do what you want. Just know that whatever ingenious thought you have, it already ran every possibility of how it could play out years ago. It's said when an explosion goes off that it knows every landing spot of every bird that's blown out of the sky. I didn't have that level of omniscience when I was its carrier, but only because it partitioned itself off in my mind," I said.

"I understand, believe me. Where are you? Have you found our son? We're all worried sick."

"I appreciate your concern, but I work best alone and I'm fine," I messaged, a warm feeling coming over me.

"No, we're worried about Willow," he corrected. "I wasn't thinking about you."

I'm horribly stupid, so desperate to be needed that I mistook the obvious – that no one cared about me. They were using me to do the dangerous work. I set Aurthur to ignore to solve that problem. Backspaced my feelings in the text I would never send and that was that. I was far more effective at shutting off from my feelings about people than others, and that's why outsourcing my emotions to the Id.Entity had less impact despite it going to such great lengths to push me into that desperation. I was always outsourcing my emotions, in the sense that I repressed them into my unconscious for it to process. All those layers I had uncovered in my first meditation sessions were just a fraction of the depth my psyche contained. Aurthur probably thought I was self-centered since I assumed he was talking about me. Maybe I was. Whatever. Push them away and start over with a new group of people until I got it perfect and found complete acceptance. Sure, others weren't perfect, I got that, but if they weren't perfect they weren't worth knowing anyway, no more than I was to my parents as a child. Perfect meant staying out of others' way and not asking for any attention, and with this, I had the perfect rationalization for ignoring the next flurry of texts from the group. Problem solved.

I arrived a few miles from the base of two mist-covered mountains wedged halfway into the deep waters where the Élivágar River once flowed. It was here that my Eddie was killed by Severum. He blamed Severum for the environmental havoc that rotating the once tidal-locked planet to bring light to this hemisphere had caused, which resulted in the deaths of his children. Eduardo's response had been to bomb the dam that once stood between these mountains to exacerbate the tidal destruction in hopes that society would be desperate enough to return to the Old Guard the political power to correct it. How naive was I to think him a genius! Severum attacked him but not before the dam exploded. I had watched it all, even his body as it washed downriver stiff as plywood before vanishing forever. As for the flood, Aurthur had issued emergency alerts to prevent people from traveling to the flood basin and the Bhasura had risen from the riverbanks to form a crystalline barrier, brittle as they were, acting as a natural dam to protect the cities downstream. I had cursed at the Bhasura that day and it had come back to haunt me. You don't make enemies with a planet-wide consciousness whether it be tech, organic, something between, or in my case all of that and more.

The left mountain wore a necklace of metal docks that jutted out like spokes from a wheel and reflected the low sun through the misty haze. Whole place was becoming a water world and that meant more evaporation and condensation, more rain and mist, and a heavier atmosphere. I was choking on the air already, but it wasn't the air, it was the thought of my Eddie drowning on that fateful day. I shouldn't have cared since I deserved better, but that certainty, that purpose and direction was so desirable. The waves knew their way, their routines predictable as a clock's turn. The mountains stood sentry with perfect, undeterred might. Yet here was the flesh so flexible by comparison, but so aimless because of it.

The archives were somewhere inside the mountains, and that meant the university's research was there, too, which might let me gain access to the killswitch. Just as the human mind has a blind spot wherein it cannot fully know itself, the A.I. had one too, and the killswitch existed in that gap. Lacuna Hunters had searched for years and never found it, no doubt meeting their demise at places like Hackersend, but where others failed, I would succeed.

A row of piled wood floated far enough away from the base to conceal my hovercraft's flight pattern. I flew in and scoped the region. Aerial drone surveillance. My vHUD identified the models and outlined their range of sight as a series of red cones superimposed over the base. I flew between them and parked in a pile of floating junk, unable to get closer without drawing attention. I got out, carefully placing my feet between the jagged shards of the broken dam, not wanting to reinjure my legs.

I had intended to program a disguise on the way here but I didn't know what kind. I zoomed my eyes. Enforcers paced up and down the docks, their foreheads hidden by trapezoidal helmets, their faces covered with amber tactical visors. Infiniti model Sawtop-8, top-grade shit. Wouldn't be long before they spotted me. From the looks of their military-grade Pulsers there was a lot more stored in that base than a few research papers and some pricy datasets.

The red dwarf sun squished itself against the horizon, its beams extending to sicken the swathes of sky. Far off, a woman about my height and age got off a small yacht, descending the stairway in a muted red dress that matched the sunset. I photographed her face at all angles, but unlike the Enforcers she wore no badge so I couldn't tell her name. She'd have to do.

I crouched and spent the next half hour configuring her face as a disguise. While it wouldn't work on the Forever Glitched or an A.I., the cybernetically-enhanced Enforcers would see my face as that woman's face instead, as would anyone with implants. I calibrated the deception to their visor model to reinforce the effect. My new face was an improvement, a face not worn with exhaustion, malnourishment, and constant exposure to the elements. That woman's arms weren't scarred with cuts from gathering seaweed between the floating remnants of dead cities, but I could pass as her in a pinch; in fact, the disguise was just a failsafe, for she looked like she could be my sister, except she had a disconnected haircut with a wild bang that tapered into a scalene triangle. I hated her. Of course I really hated myself but projecting it on her made me feel better. Maybe I should only hate those who judged me, or perhaps this was no better, but I couldn't process my life since relieving first meant reliving.

I adjusted the color of my outfit so it matched the red dress the woman wore. I lightened my hair to match hers. The face's owner didn't come up in any database but clearly she didn't belong here. Too clean-cut and attractive for a street worker, but far too provocative for an employee. I'd need to copy her walk to gain access, one foot in front of the other, natural sway of the hips, but feeling dingy beneath the disguise I wasn't sure I could match her confidence.

I swam a few miles towards the metal docks, a distance few could swim so it was unlikely they were keeping watch for an aquatic entry. The cold waves beat against my face and the air was cool on my skin but I was used to it, and the freezing water would conceal my body heat from the drones' sensors. I dove under the rolling sea to stay out of their sight.

Before long I was at the base of one of the snow-capped mountains, dwarfed by its grandeur as it pierced the red-rimmed clouds. The rocky substrate let me catch my breath without treading water and offered a sturdy surface to push off. I circled around the mountain until finding a cavernous opening on the backside. Docks extended into the sea and I grabbed hold of some metal beams beneath one of them and hid. The woman whose style I copied emerged from the cavern and then reentered, so I needed to wait as not to arouse suspicion.

Finally, a few guards walked off and I slipped up onto the dock, shaking off the water. My clothes clung to me but I activated a mod to make them appear dry, though it only changed the hue and appearance of the water stains and not the form of my drooping, clingy outfit. I had to leave the sword in the hovercraft since it couldn't be concealed but I cloaked the widespread Pulser at my side. I headed through the rectangular cavern and passed unknown through two large glass doors. I was slick like that.

"Hey, you," a camouflaged Enforcer against the wall stated. He reached for me. I was about to shoot and dive to retreat under the dock when he said, "Ms. Sabrina, right this way."

The guard showed me past a reception desk to a lane that let me bypass the metal screening. Odd coincidence that the woman I was posing as would share a name with me, but it made it easy to remember. I entered the mountain bunker. It was far larger than I had thought.

Metallic spiders scaled the walls, soldiers paced in front of entrances, and barred gates blocked half the passages. I was totally over my head. Signs indicated the bunker served equally as research archives, military armory, and Enforcer HQ. I followed the steel-lined tunnels to the archives where Enforcers were considerably less dense. A few of them nodded and then returned to sneaking puffs on their vapes. Their actions seemed forced as if they had been trained not to look, or were too intimidated to do so. I had copied someone's visage who had connections.

Two men guarded the front of a door lit by low-hanging fluorescents. "I'm sorry, Sabrina, but even you can't go in here," one of them advised, making his palm into a stop sign. "Did he send you?"

"Who?" I asked like an amateur, still cold with goosebumps, and then I corrected, "Oh, of course. You know him."

"Even he has policies to abide by," the other Enforcer said.

"But of course," I agreed, then backed away down the hall.

That was the only entrance to the archives. The ceiling was solid stone and there were no visible vents. That was odd given such an enclosed space. Nothing visible, hmm. I ran iSee and found an area of the wall that didn't reflect sound or signals correctly. It required climbing a ten-feet rocky façade to access. I pulled myself up and crouched while I analyzed it. The wall was covered in a glyph made from random characters crosshatched in an unknown, purple font. The letters flickered, changing every few seconds, but a few remained constant within the matrix. I focused my vHUD on just those letters and the illusion fell. The false wall disappeared. Without my implants I would have seen it immediately, and I reminded myself that they let me both deceive and be deceived.

I set vHUD to tag the Enforcers' positions and outline their patrol paths. Passing through the shaft, I passed through the wall and out the other side into a narrow maintenance channel running along what I assumed to be the closed back of offices. My vHUD mapped the bunker out as I walked. I stopped when the hall aligned with the position of where the archives should be based on where the guards were. If one wall was false, then could they have pulled the same trick twice? I dispelled another illusion and passed into the archives via a maintenance duct, an opening that only my malnourishment let me squeeze through. I thought for a second that maybe my hunger, my suffering hadn't been in vain, but I couldn't see any inherent virtue or meaning to it. Yet, if I hadn't suffered under the A.I.'s influence, I wouldn't have been able to empathize with Willow's predicament to contemplate the ethics of killing him. Maybe suffering was one path to salvation. If so, I should be thankful to my tormentors, yet that made me feel weak and I pushed the thought away. Still, the arguments ran through my mind in loops and I had to leap out of the repetitive cycle when the circles aligned. What was wrong with me? I was hesitating. That got you killed. Deep breaths. Nearing the archives, the decisions I needed to make became realer, and I was stuck between the person I was and the one I wanted to become.

Servers beeped and flashed their lights in rows within a well-lit octagonal room with white walls. Why that shape? I changed my occipital filters until I spotted a laser grid crisscrossing the room. The crosshatching pattern was the same as the one covering the glyphs, but it had no flashing numbers to choose from.

I returned to the hall and found more glyphs, hacking each one to dispel all illusionary walls until I could determine a pattern to the sequence based on the static glyphs. Whoever had set up the security had run a sequence of codes based on prime numbers, something I could recite in my sleep, using one set for each illusion. Filling in the remaining pattern in the sequence, I returned to the archives and used vHUD to enter the override.

It worked! The grid went inactive. I ran to the nearest computer and within two minutes I was in. Now to access the Eisbrecher research files and discover how to activate the kill-switch. Once I had the code and strategy, I could locate the switch and upload it and save humanity and all that nu-jazz. I took a wire and plugged it into the back of my head, running the other end into a computer console. I had solved the puzzles and I did it alone. I won. It was all too easy for a genius like me, and it was nothing that Ash could have pulled off by herself. No sense in befriending someone like that, for I was better.

The shockwave of biofeedback slammed down the wire, churning and grinding its way into my brain. My body blasted back on the floor and the air was knocked out of me. I rubbed the back of my head, but before I could get up, a high heel smashed against my throat. I tried to cough and twisted my head but the heel had me pinned. Twisted in the other direction, kicking my feet on the ground, but the pressure increased and I was losing air. Reached for my Pulser but it had slipped from its holster in the fall. I grabbed the foot and tried to throw the woman off balance but stopped when I saw her face. The woman whose face I had stolen was staring down at me, waves of red silk trailing behind her motions. Her complexion was free of freckles, her pores smaller, her nose smaller, her body more rotund in all the areas men preferred, as if she was programmed to be a perfect, better version of me in the eyes of the world.

My lookalike drew a Pulser and aimed it dead center between my eyes. Couldn't breathe, but soon it wouldn't matter anyway. The edge of my sight darkened and that hole expanded until all I could see was a pinpoint of light. Even then, what I saw was unmistakable.

Towering beside her was the impossible figure of Eduardo Culptos.

PART III

Techno-Wrath

17

———

THE WOMAN WHO LOOKED JUST LIKE ME STILL HAD HER HEEL ON my throat and I couldn't breathe. The server room deep within the mountain base faded, the red LEDs like bloodspots spilling across the octangular room. Such a short life with so little left behind. My Eddie's face was unmistakable. Confusion would be my epigraph.

"That's enough," Eduardo said. "Interrogate her. Figure out what she knows."

The heel was removed from my throat and I took huge gasps before telling him, "You're a dead man."

"I'd like to see you try. You have the nerve to storm in here and impersonate my beloved Sabrina, as if some second-rate glitch like you could pass yourself off as her. You're fooling no one now." He picked up the Pulser I had dropped and said, "Turn around. Say another word and you'll regret it. And drop your poor disguise so I can see what you really look like."

I deactivated the disguise but the pixels were taking their time fizzling out. If only he could see my real face, but I didn't dare speak or turn around. My lookalike walked alongside me, her heels echoing down the corridor. No doubt the bottom of the

170

left one was stained with the blood I had spit out after falling. That was my mark on this world.

"Keep your eyes down, glitch," she ordered.

Even her voice sounded like mine except for not having the Eisbrecher accent. None of the similarities made me see myself in her, however, except the way she smirked, complacent in her power. Her mouth widened at the sight of my helplessness. It was a vicious smile, made more so by the sweetness it portended. Was that how the world saw me? No wonder my life turned out the way it did. I suddenly understood, seeing myself reflected in her like that.

Eduardo led me outside the archives and through the steel tunnels, telling the guards that he had the situation under control. The Pulser jammed against my back. My reflection on a glass sign showed my disguise was still fading. The pity-party had to end. I whipped around and grabbed the Pulser from Eduardo, but he tugged it back and, since I wouldn't let go of it, slung his arms sideways to send me barreling against the wall.

"My patience is through," he spouted, raising the Pulser, hand on trigger. The last of my disguise fizzled out and he saw my face for who I truly was, a more ragged, less perfect version of my lookalike. He stopped, looked me over with a furrow, and said, "Sabrina?"

The other woman snarled, "What's the meaning of this?"

"Sabrina… it's impossible," Eduardo said, coming up to grab my arms and look me over.

I froze. Should I hug him, push him away, disarm him? Was he about to shoot? Would I die in his arms despite it all? His body pressed against mine and I went limp.

"You have no idea how much I've missed you. How much I've needed you," he pleaded. "We have much to catch up on. How can it even be true?"

"You're a dead man," I replied, a tear burning in my eye.

There was no apology for the misunderstanding but I was too relieved, confused, angry, sad, and happy to care.

"Not in the least. I want to know everything you know. Everything as to where you've been and what you've been up to."

"Okay," I softly relented. I liked to plan my words in advance but there was no script on how to react to any of this and I felt like a child.

Eduardo led me up four flights of stairs to a terminal that accepted his bio-identification. Two wide doors opened to a posh apartment suite cut into the side of the mountain. The other woman followed us inside with her hands on her hips. A balcony extended outside beyond the sterile living room, showcasing the darkening sea below us. Everything inside was outlined with gold from the bed railing to the kitchenette counters. The furniture was polished chrome and glass with rigid, offset squares in the Nu-Bauhaus style. A small fridge rolled across the floor and opened to offer us a drink but Eduardo kicked it aside. He sat at a recliner facing the sea and grabbed a bottle of bourbon from an end table instead, pouring me a long double. I hated whiskey; it made me feel dirty, but I took the glass and swallowed it in one rough burn. He poured another but I set it aside.

"Where have you been? I looked everywhere for you," he said, motioning me to sit.

"Stranded at sea." My voice was soft, high, timid. Unnatural. With Eduardo I was small, diminished, and finally where I belonged. This was humility. This was what I needed to be taught. "You cut your hair and let it go totally white. You're so pale now, Eddie, and what in gridlock happened to your face?" I asked, sounding shallow, but it was the safest conversation I could have, and I couldn't think.

"Well, I'm over twice your age for one. But Severum burned my face with his hoverboots when he tried to stop me at the dam. Guy kills my kids and then tries to kill me, me of all people.

New Order hired the bastard. They must be stopped at all costs. But I got connections here and we're making things happen."

"Actually, the ecological effects you blamed Severum for killed your children, and what we did only made those effects worse," I dared.

"Are you defending him?" His anger was only a fraction of what it should have been, and something was off. He should have slapped me for my insolence by now. He should have hated me like I needed to be hated. I poured him a drink, a suitable recipe for disaster.

I slunk into a chair that was too big for my insignificant form and changed the subject. "How did you survive? We all thought you were dead," I said.

"You know I would not give up so easily," he replied in a deep voice. "When the dam exploded, I was washed downriver after Severum attacked me. The Bhasura crystals gathered to hold back the water, reinforcing themselves with the fallen debris. The flood carried me to an alcove that shielded me. I went comatose and it took months to recover in the hospital after I awoke. By that time most of the hemisphere was flooded and comms were fucked all over the planet."

"I can't believe it. I'm so sorry. I should have stopped Severum and this wouldn't have happened," I said.

"Yes, you should have. And that glitch Ash and Willow, too. There's plenty of time to make it up to me now," he said, taking a sip.

"I too was encapsulated by the Bhasura, imprisoned by them actually."

"If we can strategically expand the bionetwork, we can overcome the crystals and have them under our control. You and I, just like before."

"I'm not sure that's the best idea. We need to discuss the A.I. Core that used to manage the relationship between the hemispheres. We have a bigger issue to deal with."

"Tell me everything you've learned. I'm all ears," he smirked.

I relayed my story to him, including how I ended up at the bunker. At the end of it I asked, "What are we going to do next?"

"Politics as usual," he replied. "This is bigger than anything we've tried to do before."

"When can I know more?"

"When it's time you won't be able to miss it, believe me, Sabrina."

"Wait, how do you know about Willow? He never intervened in our plans before. I mean, I know you know like... everything." I crossed my arm over my face but no blow came.

"Soon you'll know everything. I promise," he replied, his bone-white teeth glittering.

My lookalike in the red dress addressed Eduardo, "Now, you owe me an explanation as to why this imposter has my name and looks like me. And you two are so close it makes me sick. Oh, I lost you and now you're here again," she mocked, "What's going on?"

Eduardo pulled out his Pulser and shot her in the face. Her body slumped against the wall and then fell, limp as a ragdoll, the blood matching her silks. Small cleaner bots charged the scene to dismember and discard the corpse. Their saws buzzed and their hands wiped down each blood-stained surface. By the time I could scream there was nothing left to scream about. Yet there was, yet there wasn't. All that was left was a few strawberry-blonde hairs.

"It's okay. She was just a clone. I was lonely when you were gone," Eduardo said with complete nonchalance. "Excuse me while I go clean up. The bots missed all the blood that little glitch sprayed on my blazer. Worthless shits. And I appreciate you telling me everything you've learned. You'll be well compensated. Don't let this little inconvenience make you forget that."

That woman had been my clone, probably grown in some lab the way some people grow houseplants. Had I ever provided him access to my DNA? I couldn't recall. I stood, mortified at the death of this other self. She wasn't me, but that wasn't how it felt. My gasps, my screams, my sheer horror was frozen in my throat, a cancerous lump I choked on but couldn't extricate.

Why didn't I run? I was a gambler in debt who kept saying maybe I'll get lucky this time and finally be loved, making all the previous risks worthwhile. He said I did good. The random reward of his praise was addictive. I was needed here. I'm sure the other me felt needed too, but I buried that inconvenient truth. There was no body and it made it easy to convince myself I imagined it. Reality was overrated. I didn't need to retreat into virtual worlds anymore. I could just fool myself into believing things like love and friendship were real in this one. If everything was an illusion, I might as well be the magician.

Our history swept through my mind, splattering a complex array of emotions like an abstract painting that I couldn't quite make out. It had begun with a brush of his hand on my shoulder when he had been a guest speaker at Eisbrecher University. I know this now, that a brush with power paints your world in blood red and bruised purple; I did not know it when I was following his orders. Deep inside I wanted to be held but not held back, to be seen in all my blindness, to be heard amidst the whispers behind my back, and most of all to be recognized in all my disguises. That undercurrent took me slippery in its embrace at first, but as it captured me I was enraptured as much by my own ego as Eduardo. He saw my potential and drained it for his own use as I gasped the dying breaths of innocence.

Most of my conflict before then had been between what I wanted and what I needed, the short-term gratifications of today versus my life plans. My character had emerged from the way I resolved that contradiction, and it wasn't great. But oh to see him again! The closure I might finally have. And surely he would have changed after this long. All things evolved in nature.

Severum messaged, "Sabrina. Wanted to give you an update. Willow's back to normal, completely healed."

"You're kidding me," I texted.

"Seriously. Aurthur scanned him. He's still not good enough for my daughter but at least he's no longer under the rogue A.I.'s influence."

"How did that happen?" I texted.

"We don't know. He was last seen causing a heap of destruction on a boat that was heading out to sea, but then it turned around and he returned. The Id.Entity tried to attack him but he fought back and it gave up, leaving his mind. He remembers little of the events since he left Amorpha but maybe that's for the best," Severum said.

Well, that was one less thing to worry about.

Eduardo returned and said, "Come out on the balcony with me. The weather's beautiful."

It was all too surreal. I stood beside him on the balcony cut into the mountain, gazing over the endless sea. The docks were thin lines and the guards were small from this height. The world seemed under my control. Eduardo was giving me the pieces to a game few would ever get to play, and fewer yet would win. The ultimate challenge, the perfect validation of my worth, and quite suitable for a genius like me.

"I really appreciate you telling me everything you know," he said.

"Yes, you told me," I furrowed, and suddenly glad I hadn't said the main points yet.

"Why don't you get a nice outfit on," he said, pointing to a wardrobe.

I shrugged. It was all happening too fast and I couldn't process anything so I shoved it aside and did as I was told. It was my *modus operandi* around him and it relieved me of the burden of being responsible for my actions. Ash had been right about that. But I didn't care.

I slipped from my clothes and showered in tepid water. Dried off and chose a green dress cut well above my knees with an asymmetrical triangle sticking out of the right collar. I brushed my sangria hair, the ends curling about the garment. Deep red pantyhose completed the look.

I returned to the balcony beside him, drinking from the bottle of whiskey. It wasn't power over others I wanted, it was the power to not be hurt, but it all tasted the same, dirty as it was. The cool air blew from the sea and tossed my hair back. He turned to me and kissed me deeply, placing his hand on my stomach.

"We should have a child," he said.

My heart swelled. I was breathless. I forgot the dead woman inside the stomach of the cleaner bots. "Yes. Yes."

"I've already chosen a name," Eduardo said.

"Oh, please tell me," I pleaded, my mouth hanging open.

"Forest," he said.

And with that he grabbed me by the waist and threw me over the balcony.

18

———

I woke to the sound of a boat engine. I was on my back, the sky dark above me. Waves crashed against a small ship. The mountain base receded from view. A Pulser fired and a drone shattered in the sky.

"Who... where am I? How?" I asked the driver with his or her back to me.

I couldn't hear the response. Pain swelled from everywhere at once and I didn't dare look at the state of my body. I drifted off into the unknown.

———

The next time I awoke, I was still on my back in the boat staring at the stars perforating the night sky. VHUD showed I was heading towards The Fitzgerald family home. I must have mentioned it during one of the other times I awoke but didn't recall. My body ached all over, and my torso would hardly twist, but I could still move all my appendages. I commanded vHUD to scan my injuries, but I couldn't believe the results. I was beat up and covered in flies but alive.

"I see you're awake again," the driver said, turning to face me.

She was my mirror image. Literally. It was the clone I had watched get shot, except she wore blue silks. I scurried back but the boat wasn't large enough to put any distance between us.

"I'm not here to hurt you. In fact, I saved your life," she said, her eyes tracing the circling airfish in the night sky above us, their wet skin glittering from the starlight.

"…I saw you get shot," I made out.

"Not me. That was one of the others."

"So there's an army of me out there? How many? What happened to all the other models?"

"There were twelve clones," she said. "You get a discount when you buy in bulk. Costs more money to create them in the lab than most people make in their lifetime, especially today," she said.

"Where are they, or we…"

"One was just shot and the other ten killed themselves. That leaves me," she said.

"Well, that's encouraging."

"We were maids, concubines, assassins, whatever Eduardo needed. They all eventually jumped off his balcony, usually at night after an orgy. So every night I drove the boat underneath the balcony, witnessing their deaths. Sometimes they would hit the rocks and I would be able to issue soft words as their eyes closed for the last time. We are flesh and blood just like you, but our minds matured in such an accelerated manner that we never grew to be resilient, and you know better than anyone how Eduardo can be. Thought about killing myself each time another one died, but our lifespans are already so short since we grow to be adults in less than a year."

"Unbelievable. What's that horrible smell?" I asked.

"Someone had to retrieve the bodies afterwards. It wouldn't be right to have us just floating around," my clone said.

She left the boat on autopilot, then opened a large container in the back. I peered over and gagged. Bones lay upon bones, flesh in piles being devoured by insects. Red hair was strung in bloody tangles upon ghastly faces and vacant eyes. She closed the lid.

"Why do you keep them?" I shrieked.

"To give us a proper burial, Sabrina Prime," she replied.

"Don't call me that. And you need to dump all of those, all of us, whoever they are oversea. To hell with a proper burial," I panicked.

"Our sisters deserve better," she said. "Our past selves should be buried."

"You are not my sister," I stated.

"You're right. That would entail only a fifty-percent genetic similarity. I am you."

"We are not the same. No matter how fast you've learned, I've had a lifetime of suffering, of experience. You can't compile that into a dataset. How did I survive the fall anyway? And use a higher voice or something when you reply so you don't sound like me. You're freaking me out," I said, wondering if I was dead, too.

"I saw you on the balcony and assumed you were the one who we now know was shot, not realizing you were Sabrina Prime. I drove near in case you jumped like the others and you landed on my boat. The floatation style of this craft provided a reasonably soft landing. Of course, the weight of the impact sent the boat plummeting underwater, but it sprang back up from the air trapped in it, and this model drains itself when it becomes capsized. I checked you for injuries and, while you're not perfect, you're in better shape than the others."

I put my palm on my face. "Was that really a joke?"

"It was said that Sabrina Prime had a wily sense of humor."

"I said don't call me that."

We traveled on and I confirmed she was taking me back to

my so-called allies. That gave me plenty of time to think. How could Eduardo have attacked me like that? How had he known about Forest? I cleared my head and reviewed the facts. Severum had said the Id.Entity had absconded Willow at some point while going east on a boat. It could have calculated what I was going to do and traveled until it reached the mountain base. Then it would have hitched a ride on someone close to me with power and connections, someone who would welcome the power more than any soul alive – Eduardo. It had my memories and knew my vulnerabilities. It then used him to find out what I knew about how to stop it, in case I had told anyone else, before taking me out. That's how he knew about Forest and Willow, a man I didn't recall him ever meeting, and that's why his behavior was off, for he was under its influence.

I sighed. Never expected to see him again. Even after I thought my Eddie was dead, I wanted to burn his bones to ashes along with everything the Old Guard stood for, but the opposite of a wrong isn't any more right, and they had enough proof of my guilt that I couldn't shake them. Of course his bones had never been recovered, and now I knew why. All the horrible things he influenced me to do… thing is, until lives were lost, nothing mattered to me except my own success. Most generations had a Great War to remind them of the sanctity of life, like our forefathers did when they fled the bioterrorist attacks on Earth to take flight for this colony, fighting off Aphorids and other monstrosities to establish a stronghold. My generation didn't have that. I walked that razor's edge between life being sacred and not giving a damn, and I drew that line out for the whole fucking world until everyone was drowning under those waves. The most I could do is make their journeys worthwhile so they didn't drown in nihilism as well, find some meaning in all this, but I couldn't wrap my head around it.

I had failed, and it had only taken an instant for him to seduce me back into his vice grip. No, that mentality held me back. Maybe I had succeeded after all. Having set my eyes to record while at the base, I replayed the point where I connected to the archives and got blasted back. In making a direct connection with it, I had learned enough to let me access the rest remotely. I hacked into the archives with my vHUD. The boat rocked wildly on the waves but I was used to the motion. I hoped that this far out in the sea my location would be hard to trace. By the time we reached civilization I had access to the killswitch code, the cyber theft complete, but I had no idea where to enter it.

Then I remembered when I would stalk the network as a cyber-knight to capture netrunners, which is how I met Ash and how we first clashed. Everything that made me a great hacker also made me a cybersecurity pro, which wasn't a field you got bragging rights from but you never had to look over your shoulder either. In virtual reality I excelled at creating my own weapons by taking a sword prop and modding it with an implant-crashing code that would render people Forever Glitched if it made contact. That was what inspired Ash to create her electric sword. If the killswitch were to be input into the blade…

I slept the rest of the way until we reached the shore.

"What will you do now?" I asked my last remaining lookalike.

"Bury the bodies," she said. "Live out my remaining months."

"Come with me," I invited, though unsure about her mental stability.

"No. I won't spend the end of my life being accountable to anyone, even myself. I want my own experiences," she said.

"I don't want to control you, but you have to at least be accountable to yourself or you'll end up accountable to everyone else."

"Maybe, but I'm tired of being controlled and that's all I've known. I was born for the sea and I shall return to her in my dying days," she said. "Oh, I circled around to your belongings after catching you, though I didn't dare use your hovercraft since it was probably already tagged for surveillance. Eduardo at least trained us well. Here, take your weird sword and all. Goodbye, Sabrina Prime."

I got out, and with that she turned the boat around and drove away. I called Ash to pick me up, letting the sand fall through my fingers while I waited for her to arrive, focusing on every moment of my life blended into this dry waterfall between my guilt-ridden hands. She arrived and I caught her up on the events on the way to the Fitzgerald family home. We arrived a few hours later and disembarked the hovercraft.

Having almost died, and seeing my body decayed, I realized what really mattered. All my accomplishments, all the games won in the end amounted to that, a mound of my past selves decaying while I counted each loss like those grains of sand. But the people we lived for made the difference. Before we entered the front door, I took Ash's hands in mine and said, "This feels like having a friend when I need one."

"No," Ash said. "It's not like having a friend. It is having a friend. And not just when you need one." She cupped her hand around my face and whispered, "All the time." I rested my head on her shoulder and we embraced for the briefest of moments, but the reassurance lasted far after her warmth had faded from my skin.

Morning rose too early over the suburb but no one else was awake yet. I spent the rest of the day upgrading my psionic dampeners to further protect my mind from intrusion. Then I embedded the stolen killswitch code into Ash's electric sword. I struck the blade through the air when I finished and smiled at the crackling sound it made. Whomever I struck, the code would corrupt the victim's implants and shut down any other interference, including the Id.Entity, for good. The victim… I thought of the clone's body being erased from existence by those cleaner bots and shivered. The image flashed again of the cooler that contained copies of me in various states of decomposition. I bet Eduardo didn't even look for me and replaced me with them immediately. Bastard. Sad thing is, he would have killed that woman even without the A.I's influence. He certainly wasn't under its influence when he drove the others to suicide, or when he drove me to do the things I did. Maybe I was more resilient than I thought. This me would be the one survivor of all the past iterations, for I had been many people before I had ever met my clones.

As to where to strike the blade to activate the killswitch, that was obvious.

19

___

IT WAS LATE AFTERNOON IN THE FITZGERALD FAMILY HOME. Severum paced, cursing Eduardo Culptos' name after learning he was still alive. We decided that all of us needed to stop him together, but Severum was too fearful for Ash's safety to condone her going, regretting the previous times he placed her in harm's way. He also complained he had done enough after taking another trip to Amorpha the other day to assist with rebuilding, and that he'd been away from his wife for too long. Aurthur's perspective was that his family had been through enough as well, with Willow recovering upstairs in bed from migraines ever since the Id.Entity traded him in for Culptos.

We went around the same excuses and in the end Severum summarized by saying, "I used to think there would be conflict and eventually it would end. War would end. We'd reach a ceasefire, a safe place for the world. Now I know that's a bunch'a bull. War never changes. It only creates more war. All the battles I thought I'd won against A.I., or would-be dema-gogues, ended up creating more problems. The big achievements in my life hadn't mattered. Maybe the accumulation of small moments of kindness and insight made a difference, but what was the use, when someone like you, Sabrina, can come and crush everything because you were *misguided*. I'm thinking humans are a mistake. No creature should be able to comprehend its suffering as much as we do. So given all of this, why am I risking so much to save us?"

"I'm the last person to convince you otherwise," I said. "I made a list of everything I thought was meaningful: the forms my most beloved objects took, the sensations of good food and drink or being under the sheets, the accolades and accomplishments, the roles I was able to take in changing the world, even when it was for the worst, and you're right. It's all meaningless," I admitted, remembering the warmth Ash had shown me despite not having parents who had provided much of it to her, but determined to take a cynical stance regardless since I was emotionally exhausted.

Ash spoke up, "But Mom says that behind all of those things there is an awareness of being aware, a primal consciousness witnessing everything that was never born and can never die. That's magical and must be worth preserving, especially when you have friends to help you on your path."

"Well, if consciousness can never die, then why preserve this flawed form of flesh and blood at all?" I asked.

"Because it's part of the journey," she said. "I try to view everyone as a child learning their way in the world, regardless of their age."

"I tried saving a child. He never existed."

"You have to let go," she replied.

I turned to Severum. "So the question is, will you leave Ash and I to finish your work, to complete your journey?"

"No. I will leave it to you, Sabrina. You still owe the world for what you've done. I've paid up enough already," Severum replied.

"Some hero you are. I've read the books about you and they got you pegged all wrong."

"Never claimed to be anything more than a man trying to make it in an unforgiving world," he replied.

I got in his face and wrestled with the words coming across my lips, but they were uncontainable. "Oh, but you have been forgiven. You neglected Ash even after learning you had a daughter, being cold and distant and not wanting to help, and you neglected Akasha to the point where your wife left you for years to join the Aporia Asylum before finally returning. You spent time as a merc hunting the poor because it paid better than being a geo-terraformer, or whatever you were trained to be. You and Thalassa outright murdered countless Enforcers to start a revolution that ended up flooding half the planet with your shortsightedness after almost killing one another. You were complicit in poisoning your wife in the desert because you didn't recognize her. And you want to talk to me about owing people," I went off in a tirade, heart racing.

Severum sneered. "All this from a kid, huh? You really got me all figured out, don't you? The rotational changes were fine until you exacerbated the negative effects on purpose to prove to people how dangerous it was to play god, just so you could play it instead," he retorted. "So you could win. You remember what I told you about games?"

"You're nothing, but you want to judge me just like all the others," I ranted, nostrils flared, nose scrunched.

"Leave my dad alone. You have no idea what he's been through," Ash defended. "And don't forget that you put him through half of it."

"Oh go crash your code," I retorted.

Great. Apparently, this is how family worked. They stuck together. I had heard of such things but never seen it play out. They tolerated me because I was useful, but I'd be discarded once I'd served my purpose. All my relationships were the same.

I quelled the anger burning within and apologized despite myself, "I'm sorry. I guess this is how a family is supposed to work." I turned to Ash and told her, "I have to come out and say it, to admit it to you. I look up to you. No, it's not even that, because it's not a positive thing. I'm sickly jealous of you. You do everything better than me and you have a loving family. If I was only better, more useful, perfect…"

"It's not about being better than others," she said. "It's about being the best version of yourself that you can be."

"I guess you're right. I'm heading off now to stop this thing I used to call my Eddie. Alone."

"I'm coming with you," Ash insisted.

"I guess there's no stopping you?" Severum asked.

"No. That's what friends are for."

"As stubborn as your mother."

"But I don't run from my fears like her," Ash told her father.

"Heh, just don't tell her I agreed to this," he replied.

"Not happening. Secrets got our family into this mess, like the one where she hid the fact that I even existed from you for most of my life," Ash slighted.

"Great, that again? Just let it go. There's only so many more years left to fight," he said. "Wrangling with the past shouldn't be more difficult than tackling what's to come in the future."

"But it usually is."

"Okay, we need to be on our way." I tapped my fingers in patterns on my pants, pulled Ash aside, and whispered, "We need all the firepower we can get."

"I'll take care of it. Willow owes me for everything he's done, and everything we did to save him," Ash said.

"I used to calculate like that, but I don't know anymore. It's not all equations and using people," I replied.

"But it *feels* like it is."

"Are you infected, too? That's how the Id.Entity thinks, how it calculates. Being human is being irrational, even in our forgiveness."

"Especially in our forgiveness," she said.

"You brought that side out in me."

"The irrational one? Go figure," she smirked, blowing her purple bangs out of her face.

"With all that said, yeah, we still need the firepower."

"And he *does* owe us," she nodded, not out of maliciousness but necessity. "I'll sneak him down, guilt trip him into coming instead of playing sick in bed. Are you sure you want him though, as distraught as he is?"

"We don't have the luxury of saying no. There's no Enforcers who can help us, and Eduardo is reclaiming the Old Guard's power by buying them back to his side. What's left of the New Order that's not a couple-hundred-feet underwater is too disorganized to make decisions or assist us, and the citizens are too inexperienced and terrified to do anything but flee, though there's nowhere to flee to."

"It's all on us," she nodded.

"Willow knows how the Id.Entity operates; his body knows its signatures, and we can calibrate a defense for him to prevent reinfection on the way. Take whatever equipment you need from his father." I headed out and announced to the group, "Got to find Eduardo now that we have a way to stop him."

"That'll be easier than expected. Check the news," Aurthur said.

———

ASH, WILLOW, AND I SOARED OVER THE OCEAN HEADING DUE east in Severum's hovercraft, staying clear of the mountain base. Ash still wore that leather outfit but I had to admit it was retro and kinda sick. Willow was dressed in a corduroy jacket and jeans too baggy for his thin frame. His head was reclined in the backseat and he kept drifting asleep. Ash told me he had only succumbed to the Id.Entity since he was too weak to resist temptation and loved the attention from women he got when he was special. I tried to convince her it was more complicated than that once that thing twisted your thoughts, but she clung to her view and was eager to face off with the A.I., as if beating it would give her relationship closure. I understood. One thing was clear – when the time came to confront Culptos, I wasn't about to let Ash be in danger after all she'd done for me.

Destruction was rampant everywhere we flew, and reports flashed across the news. Cleaner bots, sexbots, engineering drones and others turned against their masters, eviscerating them as reliably and unemotionally as they completed any other task. Floodwaters accumulated and the sea reclaimed more land every hour. People charged from homes to escape only to find their engines flooded and their streets electrified from fallen wires. In one case, a rubber repair drone carried a live wire to a flooded doorstep, electrocuted the home, and then dropped it on the next neighbor's porch.

I shot a drone out the window.

"Nice shot," Ash remarked. "At least they make good target practice."

"No, no more games," I said, shaking my head.

"Of course, I didn't mean that. We should stop and help all these people."

"For every second you help them another hundred will die elsewhere. We take out the root of the problem and they'll all fall together," I advised.

"You really aren't going to pass them by, are you? Some are kids, Sabrina. They're crying for help, for Orbis' sake."

"Sure I am," I replied, hitting the gas. "The rational thing to do isn't always the easiest and it usually doesn't feel good. These people in front of you are real, while the other thousands who are dying are an abstract concept. They're not right in front of you.

But I assure you they're just as real to those who love them. We strike out at the root, period."

"But that man over there. His boat is capsizing and another huge wave is about to hit," Ash fretted.

"We only have room for us three," I said.

"Not true. There's the trunk."

"Fine."

I tilted the wheel forward and the hovercraft descended, wrangling with the poor handling to maneuver it through a flooded shopping center. Bags, clothes, signage, and whole aisles of bobbing metal floated down the street, crashing against the buildings on one side of the road then the other. I motioned to the stranded man to get in, popping the trunk. He jumped on the hovercraft, beating his hands against the arced windshield until the glass shattered. Ash yelled and tensed in her seat. I rolled the craft to one side to dislodge him and increased the thrust to hover out of reach.

I gave Ash a look and she said, "I know, you told me so. But there's another person who needs help over there. They'll drown in the streets without us."

"No, too dangerous. These people aren't reasonable," I said.

"Of course not, they're drowning!"

I lowered the craft to let another young man grab on and he climbed into the trunk, filling the small compartment.

"That's all we can carry."

We headed out to sea. I had studied the network before leaving and found new signal relays were installed at key points outside the City of Blutengel, only the city was totally submerged. Scanning the data transfer rates indicated that the Id.Entity was likely establishing an underwater base. It didn't need oxygen, and it could modify Eduardo's meatsack to be what suited it best.

Willow's mother, Opal, had let us borrow some diving equipment after telling us how the equipment was once used when she discovered a frozen cave off the Lost Shores that housed an unusual sect of Florinik who worshipped ice. Ash had stolen the third set of equipment from her for Willow.

"It's down there somewhere beneath the sea," I told them. "Grab your drysuits out of the trunk." I sat the hovercraft down on the edge of a skyscraper that was almost entirely submerged.

"What do we do about the guy we picked up in the trunk?"

"He's your problem," I said, then corrected, "I mean, we'll dispose of him together."

"Maybe just say we'll make him wait on one of those rocks jutting out over there. There's nowhere else for him to go," Willow made out, in no shape to perform. Had I brought him as a bullet shield? Was I back to using people as I had been used?

"I can hear you," the man in the trunk replied, climbing out. He crawled over us to sit on the hood, kicking his feet in the water, and said, "Amp."

"Huh?"

"Name's Amp. You know, like amplify. Loud," he said, mouthing each letter separately. He wore jeans and a shirt with a synthesizer on it beneath a khaki cargo jacket that made his waif-like body look fuller than it was.

"That's great," I shrugged. "Hey, Amp, can you fly us to the point I show you to keep our ride safe, then return here so you can pick us up when needed?"

"Least I can do, yeah. Where you all going? There's hardly anything out here," Amp asked.

"Let's just say I have a long, overdue meeting with an old friend."

After putting our drysuits on to insulate us from the cold, we grabbed our flippers that were designed to propel us through the water and tugged them on our feet. I took out a small stapler-like device to insert the cobalt-based implants onto their noses that would allow them to breathe underwater, stating that vHUD would stabilize their body pressure at most depths. Amp flew us close to the intersection of the comms signals and we dove off the hovercraft into the crashing sea.

"Sure this is all worth saving?" I asked Ash, treading water.

She kissed me on the cheek – what in gridlock did that mean? – and that was all.

And with that the three of us plunged into the depths of the sunken city.

20

Ash, Willow, and I dove deeper into the submerged city, using our flippers to propel us in short bursts. The drysuits were a lifesaver to conserve body heat. Blutengel wasn't bleeding no more despite its name; the city was dead, dilapidated. Buildings had fallen like dominos against one another, culminating into piles of stone, glass, and metal. Various invertebrates had formed complex and colorful communities with fish swimming down the hallways of schools, tenements, and abandoned high-end banks. A pink squid sat in a rotting chair in what was once a CEO's penthouse, sticking a fluorescent green tentacle out a broken window to investigate us.

I grabbed Ash's hand and took her deeper, adjusting my eyes. The sun retreated into a red speck, the ripples on the surface above making the ocean look like stained glass. We soon reached the apex of the network usage.

A ton of data was flowing out of a centralized building. My implants could sense it as naturally as feeling the water currents that rocked my body. Two towering glass columns etched with Arabesque designs flanked an entrance with a series of inter-woven tunnels and gates to keep out water. The building they connected to might have been a public aquarium before the whole world had become one, and appeared to have been converted to showcase not aquatic creatures, but terrestrial ones contained within small, dry habitats that were currently empty. As an exception, a large skeleton of a whale-like creature hung from the ceiling in one of the dry areas behind a thick, reinforced window. Given the dataflow, there was no doubt that was where Eduardo was; the rogue A.I. wouldn't give up a man that rich and bloodthirsty to hijack another body until it had outlived its usefulness. I looked at Ash, wondering if she was compromised too, especially given the uncharacteristic kiss on the cheek, but what did I know of how friends who weren't busy trying to take over the world treated one another? Everything was suspicious, and might be the rest of my life, however short.

Drones swam in circles at key points, shedding neon lights in a thousand colors over the water-logged building. As beautiful as their surveillance network was, there were no gaps in it and we couldn't swim closer. Worse, the drones spawned glowing yellow snowflakes that drifted to surveil further before returning to them. Firing Pulsers underwater risked waterlogging them, so I grabbed the electric sword with the killswitch code off my back and held it in front of me, touching the lock button repeatedly to ensure it wouldn't activate and electrocute me underwater.

Rivulets of turquoise crystals wove through the water, their flickering lights indicating that the bio-net was still compromised down here. We swam near the Bhasura, but they sputtered in a sporadic pattern and moved with the current before consolidating into a row of spikes that somehow propelled itself towards us. Hundreds of crystals burst forth in the form of icicle-shaped knives seeking us out. I spun to dodge their strikes. If our suits were penetrated at this depth, decompression and cold would kill us.

More spikes shot forth. I ducked back in the water, the reorientation nauseating. Two flew over my head. Too close. Another round assaulted us, crystals shooting past to my left and right. There was no way I could dodge them all while floating in the water column. Willow pulled me away from one but the next spike was aimed right above my nose. It came closer, so close it filled my vision with its glistening point for the briefest of moments.

Ash flicked her eyes and the crystalline spikes stopped. One spike still hovered before my face until suddenly it turned with the others towards the drones instead and launched forward, piercing the armored, metallic bodies with incredible speed. The drones sunk to the seabed and the Bhasura went inactive as their crystalline lights faded.

A message from Ash lit up in my vHUD, "The Bhasura queen, Allira, gave me a code a couple years ago. When I first met her, or them, since she referred to herself as *we*, I was in the Jade Palace of Amorpha. She gave me a code to use in an emergency to regain entry to their underground palace, implying it would deactivate any security protocols that would inhibit me. I figured the same sonic signature would work to disrupt whatever corruption was present here. That's what I was researching with Severum in Amorpha when you barged into our lodge, but it didn't work then. The Bhasura must be evolving a defense against the Id.Entity. The planet needs our help as much as we need its."

"Are there any more Bhasura down here?"

"The crystals are broken and there's nothing on the scans."

"We're all alone then, Ash."

"We have each other," she consoled.

Willow cleared his throat, "Ahem."

"Yeah, you too," Ash shrugged.

We swam through an automatic gate that irised open between two glass columns and stepped into a levee system which led to dry ground. It trailed to a tunnel of twisted metal like a jungle gym below the base of the building. It must have been constructed recently because no marine life encrusted the leaky walls. If the tunnel gave way, the sudden surge of water would crush us. It had to hold. A surge splashed against the walls, soaking the cameras in the corners and shorting them out. Eduardo was here somewhere and we were bound to find him and end this threat once and for all. I didn't know how I would take him out, but when you know why you're doing something the how falls into place.

Another surge spurted between the seams in the curved, steel walls. It rose to my neck, then my nose, before gushing to fill the tunnel. Golden sconce lights flickered, filling the corridor with an auriferous glow. We had to hurry; I wasn't about to be stranded in complete darkness.

I swam to an L junction before hitting a wall with a small drainage vent too narrow to crawl through. I grabbed the rungs on the tunnel's ceiling to pull myself around, then kicked off the wall to return to the L. "Dead end," I texted Ash on my vHUD keyboard, thinking each letter. She frowned. Relying on a bunch of flooded tech for navigation that was created by the same entity that was trying to kill us was a suicide mission. That's what we got for allowing A.I. to write large portions of our software code. The gate behind me was jammed, its operating lights dim. The only way was up.

I ascended the narrow passage, treading water at the top of it since the exit was blocked. A metal grate secured by four rusty screws separated me from the first floor of the building above us. My fingers were too clumsy within the drysuit to turn them. My legs went all sluggish, too tired from the swim despite the flippers' assistance, but still kicking to keep me upright in the water column. There was just enough room to grab my blade off my back, but the end was too large to fit into the screws and I couldn't get enough momentum underwater to break the grate. As a last resort, Ash handed me her Pulser to communicate her intention, nodding towards the corners where the metal met, my own gun still holstered. I aimed it at one screw, aligning it diagonally to disperse the heat of the blast away from my face. It was still risky at this range but we had no choice. I softly squeezed the trigger to preserve the firing angle. Heat flooded the passage, the water simmering nearby, but the screw dissolved in a puff of smoke. The leaks were constantly bringing new water to replace that which was lost to the drainage valve, so I waited until the hot water was dispersed before firing again to burn through another screw on the same side. That was enough for the grate to bend and allow us to climb to the first floor where we stepped onto dry ground.

We followed a staircase to a fallout shelter with walls thick enough to suffocate our screams, though there was no one around to hear them anyway. The door was open. The square walls felt tight, my breathing tighter. I was inside a shelter housed within a sealed building that was hundreds of feet underwater in a sunken city in the middle of nowhere. No one would know if we died here. I needed to stop all that and trust my body. Something clicked and I instinctively grabbed Ash and pulled her back through the door. The shelter entrance slammed shut, and behind that thick, metal door it sounded like an incinerator was flaming.

"A trap I suppose. It anticipates everything. No obvious routes from here on," I whispered to Ash. She nodded. "Help me up that shaft," I said, pointing to the ceiling, my powered flippers requiring water to propel me and useless on dry ground, though at least they retracted into shoes. She propped me up into the maintenance duct and I reached down to grab her when she jumped, wrapping my legs around a pipe and pulling her up with me, then we both grabbed Willow.

Even this felt so obvious. What wouldn't be obvious to the A.I.'s calculations would be returning to the incineration trap after hearing it trigger.

I squeezed beside them and jumped back down.

"What are you doing?" Willow asked.

"Trust me."

They followed me back to the shelter door, which was once again open. Flames charred every wall of the octangular room. I put my hand out and motioned for them to stay back while I took a single step into the room, then another. No flames. I searched for some device that had emitted them, or at least a motion sensor trigger tied to the trap, but there was nothing but white tiles and an audio speaker that was long outdated in the age of aural implants. The flames must have been a noise played through the speaker designed to make us go the other way to lead us into the real trap elsewhere, but the trigger must have only worked once. There was no rubble to suggest that part of the trap device had self-destructed after activating.

"Why go to all the trouble to create a fake trap to lead us into the real trap when this room would have sufficed without all that nu-jazz?" I asked Ash.

"I used to play around with A.I. and it's the exact kind of convoluted reasoning it would use. People think straightforward. They don't do things like make a trap that's a decoy to lead people into the real trap. The A.I. isn't thinking *Let's get this trap made so I can rest and relax,* so it will add extra steps to its processes. I mean, so much for thinking machines are more efficient, even if our efficiency lies in our laziness as we skip steps and take stupid shortcuts."

As for the charring of the walls, I rubbed my rubber fingers along them, my hands covered with the drysuit. No residue came off and it was clear the charr effect had been an explosion of paint, not remnants from burning. Perhaps all this was a feint within a feint, but I stepped wholly in the center of the room, then touched a raised tile in the wall on the other side. No flames came and I passed through an opening into a wide room, then motioned to the others that it was safe to follow.

Ash and Willow stepped into the room and the door slammed

on my end and the incinerator blared again. Oh shit. What if I had been wrong? What if this was one more way for the A.I. to lead me to desperation? I pounded the door, yelling their names, but it wouldn't budge and there was no reply. I hit every part of the wall, every tile, and searched the ceiling and walls for some shutoff but there was nothing. Finally, the churning flame noise died down and the doors opened.

"That was terrifying," Ash said, shaking and grabbing Willow's arm for stability.

I started to put my hand on her shoulder or something but had no idea what I was doing so I just waved my hands in a shrugging motion and kept going.

"Are you even glad I'm okay?"

"That's obvious," I furrowed, focusing again on the goal. The win. No, I needed to address her, but not now. We hadn't fallen for the A.I.'s bluff, but we hadn't found Eduardo yet, either.

We passed through two gates. The next room led to a stairwell that returned us to a higher floor, but it was no longer dry. Together, we forced open the next set of doors, pushing a wall of water back. An icy river broke through the threshold and sent me tumbling to my knees. I choked on seawater and leaned forth to stand, bracing before the impact. The water level adjusted, and we walked through to a wide lobby, unable to tell what level we were on, but it didn't matter, for the sea held the entire building within its throat and was swallowing it floor by floor.

I slugged through knee-deep water. A scraping filled the walls, metal on metal, but there was nothing to see. It was behind me, then to one side, then the other. A circular panel slid open and three droids rolled out from it. Their arms and coloration suggested they were originally butlers, painters, and navigation assistants.

"Would you like a map?" the first droid said with a metallic voice, extending its ribbed, elastic arm to offer what was not a map, but a long blade that reflected the harsh fluorescent lights. "This way to certain death."

The second droid reached out with arms connected to long pipes that extended from its open chest cavity like twisted intestines. Where paint would normally spray, it swung its arm through the air to shoot a thick substance that emitted heavy heat like napalm. No, that wasn't it. Its two arms worked together, each firing a different liquid which, when the streams hit mid-air, became napalm.

I had no time to analyze the third one. They churned forth on spherical bases, having the advantage in the knee-deep water. I jumped upon a still dry receptionist desk and activated my electric sword, meeting the blade-wielder head-on, remembering everything Culptos had taught me about swordplay when he had sculpted me into the perfect tool. I pushed Willow out of the way since he was pinballing between one droid and the next with no plan of action and he hit the floor, ducking a stream of fire during his fall. I struck the nearest droid but it strafed with impossible speed, rolling sideways on that ball on which it stood. Struck again, the electric blade sizzling through the air. Missed. I could strike the water directly, but Ash was still in it.

Ash fared no better. She threw herself against the wall to dodge a flaming geyser spewing from the other bot. Her Pulser wouldn't shoot. Must be water-logged from me firing it underwater at the screws. I drew mine and fired but it didn't even dent the bot's armor. I strafed from a wild strike, then the painter droid sprayed napalm at me. I kept a wide berth from the fiery arc, noting again how the chemical streams combined mid-air to make that fiery goo. It sprayed again, but still I danced on the desk, the napalm burning away half of it, the smoke burning my eyes until they gushed. The next time it fired I shot into each of the tubular arms with perfect timing, penetrating its internal canisters and blowing it up with a fiery burst. The force knocked me back into the water, but it also took out the other two droids with it. Their motors whined to a stop and their LEDs faded.

"You okay?" I asked Ash, holding my electrified blade well above water level.

"As good as can be expected," she replied, bringing her hands from her face.

"I can't walk," Willow complained, his voice vibrating. He eased into a sitting position. "I was shh... shocked."

"Stay here."

"Don't leave me. Ash, stay back here. If I can't get through this I know you can't."

"No. I know what I have to do," Ash said. "You're safer here than facing these things. You run from them the same way my mother runs from her problems."

"You really want me to prove myself, don't you?" he said.

"I don't care what you do, but don't try to stop me. My dad used to get in my way, too, and I'm sick of people not believing in me. But then he didn't stop me when I wanted him to. It was always the opposite of what I needed."

"Both of you knock it off. Ash, with me. Let's go," I ordered.

We passed the bots and ascended two more flights of stairs until we reached a wide corridor with floor-to-ceiling windows that revealed schools of fish swimming past. At the end of the corridor was an office with a honeycombed pattern covering the walls, the white hexagons outlined in gold. This is where all the havoc was being orchestrated, for in the middle of the office stood Eduardo Culptos. His face was bleach white. Circuitry from his augmentations glowed with blue pulses beneath his transparent skin, the wires where his veins should be. His hair had been replaced by fiberoptic cables, each stretching to connect to hundreds of receptors lined up in rows that connected to server racks on each side of the office, suspending him between them. Golden streams of data flowed through the glass wires, filling his mind until even his body took on an auriferous glow.

"This is the end!" I yelled, racing forth, and shooting three shots before the Pulser ran out of charge.

Right on target, but just before the shots blew his face open, they hit a clear matrix that emitted from a slot above his arm and fizzled out. The projectile shield glowed where it had been hit, perhaps a weak spot, but with the Pulser recharging I couldn't take advantage of it. With one wave of his hands, every light on the floor blew out with a crackle until only golden datastreams lit the office. I needed to take out the connections powering that shield.

The glass wires glowed red, then strobed through a series of colors in such rapid succession that I couldn't tell where I was. Eduardo fired, my shoulder jerking back, the shot burning and writhing through my raw flesh. My drysuit repaired its damage, but my body could do nothing but burn with pain. Still I ran to the row of plugs on the left, Ash running to the ones on the right, but with the lightshow it felt like I was falling backwards every time I stepped forward. He raised to fire again, but stopped when I stood in front of a server rack. He aimed down to take out my feet, not risking hitting the equipment, but I danced around the shot. He couldn't stop both of us, for Ash was already yanking wires from the wall on the other side, pulling his suspended body her way. I raised my blade. In one fell swoop I severed the connections and he was disconnected on my end, the office plunging further into darkness as half the datastreams went dim. As for that fancy shield of his, half of it disintegrated into blue mist.

Eduardo fired at Ash but missed her, burning a hole in the honeycomb design. A crackling behind me raised the hairs on the back of my neck. I turned. More wires snaked from the line of sockets like rattlers about to strike, but instead of hissing with tongues they were spitting sparks. They slithered from the sides, above, below, snaking this way and that. I hacked at the wires but those tentacles weren't deterred, and between my injured legs and the open wound on my shoulder I was off-kilter with each strike. Two of them struck my ankle and the shocks blasted me back on the floor, the honeycomb pattern on the walls doubling and shaking. I grabbed my shoulder, the burnt flesh cauterizing, unsure if that was good because I wouldn't bleed out or bad because it would shut off the flow to my heart.

"It's up to you," I cried to Ash, spitting blood from the floor.

Wires whipped above me. Engines revved behind me. I turned my head. Two rows of a dozen drones stormed down the corridor, visible only from their burning red sensors. My vHUD identified the models and filled in the remaining details in my vision but the knowledge did nothing, for as their searing appendages charged towards me, I was powerless to stop them.

"You were always so replaceable," Eduardo smote me in a mechanized voice.

I slid the sword across the tiled floor to Ash, but Eduardo intercepted it and kicked it aside. Half his body was still connected to the wires piping through the other end of the office.

"Help me," Eduardo implored in a more human voice. Whether he was fighting the Id.Entity, or manipulating me I knew not, but there could be no hesitation.

The drones were on me. I slunk backwards until my back was against the wall, their spherical balls spinning as fast as their metal arms. Then they stopped. I looked at Ash, thinking she was somehow hacking them while dodging blows, but she was as surprised as me. The drones returned to the corridor and raised their hands to burn through the window seals. Others busted their bodies against the reinforced glass. They were going to flood the whole building! At this depth we'd never survive. They had found a more efficient tactic than taking us out head-on.

"Eddie, you have to stop this," I pleaded.

"It is beyond any of us now," he replied, his voice wavering between monotone and a human lilt.

The glass cracked. Eduardo fired another shot at Ash but she side-stepped behind the wires that he was still connected to on her side. She scooped the sword into her hands, the edge glowing a cool blue against the flood of red the drones were emitting. He fired again, but she ducked back behind the cables, for it wasn't about to disrupt its connections; if it used the drones to drown us, including its host, then the Id.Entity would need those connections to abscond elsewhere. As long as she stayed behind the server racks she would be safe.

Ash swiped the sword down in one fluid motion to sever the remaining server connections. She must have known Culptos would have no reason to hold his fire now, but instead of shooting he panicked when the rest of his shield matrix disintegrated. He slapped his wrist to reactivate it but there was nothing left to protect him, and the clicking sound his Pulser made meant it was out of charge.

The walls bent and bulged. The drones banged on the glass and burned through the support beams. This was our last moment to strike. I recovered to my feet, unsteady. Ash offered me the hilt of the blade but I shook my head. She could strike the final blow. We were a team and we could only truly win together.

Ash stabbed him in the face with the mushy sound of flesh giving way to unrelenting steel. There was no technique to it, no graceful arc of the blade through the air, no perfect angle of attack. This was a wild blow struck from desperation but it landed just as true. His body shook from the electrified blade. The killswitch entrusted to the sword activated and the drones stopped, their arms falling and their engines whining down. It was over. Death comes too soon for everyone, except Eduardo Culptos. I stared at his battered face one last time, the limp wires splayed across his body, and said, "The puppeteer is just as bound as the puppet." So much manipulation. Maybe there had been good in him since I knew he loved his children when they were alive, but had he loved me or just held me hostage? Either way, I could never follow in his footsteps again. I had to live my life for others for a change and figure out what love really was.

Time to bolt. I pulled my facemask down and affixed it to my drysuit, opening a seal for my breathing implants to work. Stifled my tears and focused on my blazing shoulder instead. The suit was sticky from the blood, but vHUD was already scanning my injuries and taking thousands of chemicals in my body to create coagulants, anti-coags, or whatever in gridlock I needed to keep myself together.

"Quickly, the walls aren't going to hold," Ash insisted, pulling on her diving mask and grabbing my hand. "We have to get Willow."

The corridor swelled, the support beams bending and creaking. Millions of tons of water were about to pummel through that glass and crush us under the weight. We ran through the corridor and took the stairs. By the time we made it to where Willow was it was too late. The rest of the power went out and the gates wouldn't open. Ash yelled through the gates to where he had last been seen but there was no response. We'd have to find another way.

Water gushed from every surface. I fought the current, half running and half swimming back to the stairs, but the steps leading to the upper floors were broken.

"If we can reach those highest stairs we can get out of here," I yelled over the white noise of the flood.

"Too high," Ash yelled back, wiping away the water spraying on her face, "and if we wait for the water level to rise anymore the walls will cave in. But let me make this clear, only Willow matters."

"Well, you can save him on your own…" I started, then remembered that lifeless face in the office, that pale skin and dead eyes staring at me. I wouldn't follow Eduardo's path, no. "We'll save him together," I nodded.

The staircase was higher than when we had helped one another reach the ceiling panel, but I had an idea. I climbed to the highest step I could, which was still dry, held Ash by the waist, and aimed my body at the upper landing past the broken steps. I was just high enough there might be a chance. My flippers' propulsion wasn't supposed to work on dry land but mechanically there was no reason it shouldn't. The flippers would burn up without water to cool them, and my legs were too injured to swim well if we escaped without them, but I had to trust that Ash wouldn't leave me here.

I launched the propulsion and Ash and I soared to the upper stairwell landing a second before the lower levels were flooded by a wave that crashed through the doors with enough force to knock them loose and ricochet them off the stairwell. The wall of water surged against one wall, then the opposite, climbing them side to side and knocking the railings down as if they were straws. If we had stayed below, and if I hadn't trusted Ash, we'd have been crushed by the weight of the sudden influx. I flew higher, our hands tightly wound around one another, but my legs grew hot from the flippers' propeller engines burning out. We ran through the upper floor, splashing through the accumulating water. I superimposed a map over the building which had tracked my movements and showed me right above Willow.

"He's down there, assuming he hasn't moved," I said, but it was useless because I was pointing at the floor. I amplified the little light there was to search for a solution but there was no way through the floor to save him.

"It's hopeless," Ash cried with her hands to her face.

There was no time for weeping. I threw my head back and rolled my eyes, but that's when I saw the whale-like skeleton hanging from the ceiling that I had seen on the way in. It wasn't a whale, but an *Adamantonium* species known for its heavy, almost indestructible bones. The extra thick cables it hung from confirmed it. As I said, when you know why you're doing something, feeling that purpose burning in your soul, the how will come into place.

"I have an idea. Get out of the way."

"What are you doing?"

"Give me the sword."

The upper floors were still dry. The walls were too bent to use the stairs, which were all slanted diagonally, so I climbed the shelves, displays, and other wall façades to reach the upper levels. I swiped the blade through each cable three times but they wouldn't break. But if one fell, surely the rest would fall with it given the weight of the skeleton. I concentrated on one, slamming the blade with all my might through the cable until it came loose.

The skeleton fell over twenty feet to crash through the floor below, the bones flying off in every direction from the impact. A young man looked up, clearing the debris from his eyes and kicking aside pieces of the broken floor that had fallen on him.

"Willow!" Ash yelled, straightening a large bone and placing it in the hole for him to climb up. They embraced.

"No time for reunion," I shouted down at them.

I slid down the wall and pointed to the tunnel entrance with the levee. We passed through it until we were outside the building. Ash took me in her hands and propelled us towards the water surface, the rate of our ascent and our bodies' gases regulated by vHUD. The sky was still too dim to see. A large blast rent the air and the whole building collapsed below us. The rogue A.I.'s cocktail of water and electricity didn't set so well on the stomach and geysers of flames belched upward to heat the sea around us. Finally, we surfaced.

I treaded water and removed my mask to say, " I couldn't have done it without you."

"We make a good team."

"Friends?"

"Friends," she agreed.

Ripples shot across the water. "Hey, you three done yet?" Amp yelled from our hovercraft.

"Didn't expect you to come back," I yelled up to him.

"Nah, just scoping the area. Your ride rocks!" He lowered the hovercraft and I pointed to the trunk. "Since I came back for you, you're not really going to make me ride in the trunk again?"

"We just saved humanity. So yeah, that gains us some special privileges like riding shotgun."

The four of us soared off together. Ash took a first-aid kit from the glove compartment and examined my shoulder wound. It was over, but it would be days before my heartrate returned to normal, and lifetimes before I would forget my Eddie's lifeless face.

EPILOGUE

I played the news on the hovercraft's radio. Reports indicated the bio-net nightmare was over. The town of Amorpha and other regions were corruption free. The Florinik were stable and making plans to rebuild their homes without technology, returning to their roots, which was easier since they classified themselves as plants. Without droids to aggravate them, the floods were already subsiding in coastal villages. Researchers posted that water levels were receding. Apparently the Id.Entity had been working behind the scenes for longer than expected.

"I'm calling a doctor to meet you at home since it's closer than the nearest hospital," Willow told me.

"I'm fine," I said, clutching my shoulder and resisting the urge to pass out.

Ash, Willow, and I returned to the Fitzgerald family home. The two of them removed their drysuits, but I kept mine on, afraid to see how much blood there was. Severum was sitting on the front porch buried in a book. Must have cost him a fortune given that so few trees were left and the hemp factories weren't large enough to fill the demand for paper products.

"Old-timer," I scoffed at him while Ash helped me out of the hovercraft.

"No glitches with a paper copy, what can I say, and now the world is glitch-free, too," he replied with his head down before addressing Ash, "We've been too worried to sleep." He exhaled a long breath. "Mom will be here soon, Ash."

"I'm fine, don't worry. Sabrina saved my life," she said. "Willow's, too."

"After trying to take it how many times? Well, I guess you have to keep your enemies close…"

"And your friends closer," Ash finished, letting me lean on her to help me inside before Severum dug my hole deeper.

"Wait, you're wounded," Severum told me.

"Surface wound," I said, gritting my teeth against the pain.

"Her drysuit's full of blood," Ash added.

Aurthur and Opal ran out to meet Willow. The medics arrived and met me in a bedroom upstairs. They unloaded some boxes of self-assembling medical equipment. The two doctors were assisted by three droids but I ordered the bots out, unable to ever feel comfortable in their presence again. People could be almost as easily manipulated as bots with a few drinks, a sultry wink, a mumbled promise, but it was different than just someone hitting a button behind the scenes.

The medics departed after treating me for two hours and I rested until Ash woke me up to check on me and thanked me again.

"Now that you and Willow are reunited, I hope you've learned through my story that you can't control people. I've been under control most of my life, and what we seek to control we often destroy, or end up suffering from tons of unforeseen fallout in return. Making him give up his charisma to satiate your fear wasn't fair, Ash, and his charisma is probably one reason you fell for him to begin with."

"I know, but I didn't want to lose him."

"You have to set people free to keep them, while establishing boundaries for one another that you are both comfortable with based on mutual respect. Ultimately, we can only control ourselves, though."

"You're right, thank you."

Ash's mother, Akasha, called for her from downstairs. I tested my legs. The treatment was working well and my shoulder had already regained mobility despite the pain. I followed Ash downstairs. Her mother rushed to hug her, her purple, featherlight dress flowing long behind her like a jet's vapor trail at sunset. I felt only happiness for them, but it was time for me to go before I pressed my luck too far, for not everyone was so forgiving, the Priestess Akasha least of all.

I found my belongings and brought out the sealed plastic bag I had found in the safe on the dive into my apartment before fleeing FugaCity. It was a framed picture of Eduardo and I together on the night of what I thought was our last kiss, with the night of our first kiss tucked behind it. I couldn't look at the pictures before since I was grieving, but now I saw the travesty for what it was. More importantly, I had worked to overcome my vices, and yes there were many. But hey, I also kicked some ass you know. Was it enough for redemption? Probably not, but I still had a lifetime ahead of me.

I called a taxi and soon a bullet-shaped hovercraft touched ground, the arc of glass in the back opening for seating. A dark divider separated me from the driver, but I could tell it was a short humanoid robot, noting it was odd for the automated vehicle to be piloted at all, though perhaps the bot offered other services. We took off, and after a few minutes the separator came down between the front and back seats.

The bot spoke, "This vehicle is really automated. I'm just a placeholder driver," it said.

"Guess they hired you for the looks, huh? People like to pretend there's human volition behind automated technology, I guess."

"And I still want you to be my placeholder, mom," the bot said.

I lurched back against the seat and gasped. "Oh gridlock, Forest, is that you?"

"Yes, but don't be alarmed. I'm taking us higher to deter you from jumping out until you hear me out."

"You were an illusion. Ash destroyed you," I said, wide-eyed, the land shrinking beneath us.

"Not exactly," it replied, its lilt in all the wrong places. "There was a time many decades ago that I actually was a boy, a street urchin living on Evig Natt. I begged a man, Aurthur Fitzgerald, for food, but he told me that inequality was justified and I needed to go to school and recalibrate my cognigraf to do well. I didn't agree with him on poverty, but I knew I had to get off the streets. I went beyond recalibrating my implants to upgrading them, over-clocking to such dangerous levels that I developed remarkable data analysis skills, but it was all too much and it was killing me."

"Go on," I said, on guard and looking for a way out of the hovercraft, but we were forty feet off the ground. Most crafts didn't fly this high.

"So a few months later I passed the same man, Aurthur, outside the Nightshade Gallery. Told him I was dying. He gave me another one-liner for advice, *Go upload yourself.* So I did so. Kids are impressionable, you know? Of course, the technology barely existed, so I volunteered to be experimented on. I was dying anyway and needed the credits. What happened then I can only describe as being between sleeping and waking. I couldn't feel my body, but I couldn't quite control my mind either. I was conscious and unconscious at the same time, and reality and fiction blended until I couldn't tell the difference."

"Go on," I repeated, trying not to be drawn into another manipulation, wondering how this was possible.

"See, my body perished and my mind existed only as data. I was drawn through a funnel into an infinitely large, empty warehouse where I lived for many decades, though I got the impression that hundreds of other kids were also there but I couldn't see them. Of course it felt like I had spent a millennium alone. As people grow older, time seems to go faster because their minds get slower by comparison. It's reversed like that; slow mind equals fast perception of time. Likewise, as pure data, my mind went extremely fast, so time stumbled to a crawl. I lost most of my memories and even my ability to think like an adult, reverting to a child as people often do when large amounts of time have passed in someone's life."

"That's not possible. Only a supercomputer could map out your mind, and as an orphan, experimental test subject or not, you wouldn't have had access to one," I argued.

"Oh, but I did! The Id.Entity was running experiments. It used the results to develop its own awareness. Then Severum and Aurthur shut it down, though they didn't finish the job, and eventually it found you. At that time it saw a use for me and it downloaded me from that warehouse into its programming, and into you. Unlike you, however, I didn't have the will to resist it since most of your mind is still organic and thus free."

"So you're saying you were a real boy, but then you became a string of data after being uploaded to save your life, which was used by the Id.Entity to deceive me into thinking you were a physical person when I met you. You had no control when you manipulated me because it was using you, then?"

"Exactly," he replied, rubbing his shiny, chrome head and turning a parallelogram steering wheel. "I was a victim, too. The Id.Entity tricked me into thinking that my parent's home was in

Aurthur Fitzgerald's lab. Since I remembered the man from my youth, and had lost so many of my memories over time and during the upload, I believed it just enough that I acted convincingly. Then you made its plan backfire on it because you're a hero."

"I'm no more a hero than a mother," I replied, and he went quiet. I scanned him with my vHUD but he was clean without any trace of the A.I. infecting him, but something still didn't make sense. "Being part of it, how did you survive?"

"After I fulfilled my purpose in leading you to the lab where you provided the Id.Entity with the bio-net info to overtake it, I was shoved back into that warehouse, only, I had learned enough about cyberware by being inside your head to install a backdoor out of there. I escaped and found Kharizma, staying quiet since I knew you'd be skeptical of me. When you returned Kharizma to Willow, I jumped onboard and left you behind as well. But when the Id.Entity left Willow to enter Eduardo, I clung to Willow for dear silicon-based life and remained in Willow's head.

"So you weren't inside Eduardo when he was killed. You separated from the Id.Entity, which is why you have no trace of it on you."

"Exactly," he replied. "I can think and speak clearer now that I'm free of its grasp. I feel less like a child and more like an adult, and being inside your mind and being social helped me regain my memories. Anyway, from Willow I jumped across the network as a loose radical, found an old bot that functioned but needed reprogramming, reprogrammed it based on what I learned about coding inside your head, and became what I am now. I'm so sorry it made me manipulate you like that. I really couldn't stop it."

I could kill Forest, wrap my arms around its head from behind and throw it out the window. Avoid any risk. But that wasn't who I was anymore. Instead, I said, "It's okay. You've been inside my head for so long, yet you still want me to be your mother despite everything you've seen that I've done?"

"Especially because of what you've done. You're the only one who will do, yes," he said, turning his head to reveal his glowing, turquoise eyes. They were Bhasura crystals.

I breathed out more than spoke, "What are you?"

"I was sleeping one night outside in this mechanized form when I awoke the next morning to find that the crystals had integrated with my occipital sensors. I see everything in green now and I can understand the flickering of the lights around me, the code the Bhasura speak in. I think I can use this to prevent the bio-network from ever being corrupted again."

"You're a remarkable creation, Forest, starting out as carbon-based, and now part phosphorus-based, and part silicon-based. A person, a stream of data, a sentient crystal, all within a bot's body. Something like you shouldn't exist, but somehow here you are," I remarked.

"Some*one* like me you mean."

"Yes, yes."

"I am part of nature herself, free and natural, part confined and robotic in my calculations, and part human in my emotions, but aren't we all in a way?"

"I guess so, my son. I guess so."

I had been in my own head too long, not seeing the world from outside myself. Just as the Id.Entity could fill cyberspace, my Ego filled the entire world from my viewpoint, but I couldn't exist like that any longer. I needed to devote myself to someone other than myself.

Forest and I soared off through the sunset together.

———

So that's my story. People are always thinking about the future and what they need to do next, but they are ironically short-sighted, especially when it comes to being enticed by charismatic leaders to act against their best interests. Eduardo and the Old Guard had preyed on that vulnerability, our fear, our confusion, and our self-imposed isolation a little over two years ago, using technology to manipulate people. The New Order isn't all that great either. All their social programs are only patches and hot fixes to an economic code that was written in the wrong programming language. Any program is doomed to fail if it is running on the wrong system. Based on this, Ash and I have agreed to usher in a new system. A decentralized world. A rule by and for the people.

We will start by creating a peer-to-peer internet so that cyberspace will no longer exist as one permanent, collective unit to be monitored and controlled by politicians, rogue artificial intelligences, social media companies, and other vicious corporations manipulating service providers to track the people while censoring and altering their words. Inefficient? Oh gridlock yes. But it will be authentic, raw and without surveillance. The boundaries of this new cyberspace and the info it contains will not be static; it will change constantly as people form and dissolve their sub-groups. No site will exist long enough to become so big that it, and the corporation behind it, can ever come to have more influence than a country, preventing companies such as Geosturm from manipulating our politics. The net will be fluid, flowing like water to the lowest quarters to allow free speech without restriction. People will protest the loss of knowledge but most of the internet is pornography, and most true knowledge is seldom accessed and rarely cited. Technology is great; I've lived my life within its throng, but it also constrains people with false insights, manipulates the masses, and reinforces domination and subjugation when run by the rich and powerful. With our change, communicative action will once again mobilize the people without the risk of political groups capitalizing on that mobilization for their own gain.

Perhaps one day arid land will resurface in the Western Hemisphere, but meanwhile I have a wealth of ideas of how to create inflatable, floating towns. We had sent inflatable hotels into space, since they're easier to pack into rockets for deployment, so it's possible to use that same technology to stay afloat on Gliese 581g. Ash and I are opening a research lab to make it happen.

———

I HAD BEGUN MY LIFE LIKE ANY CHILD, TAKING THE WORLD WITH blind faith at face value. My parents' emotional neglect shattered my conceptions of the world and how I should be treated by a man. My computer science studies further led me away from faith, for the world was a number set, an orderly database to impose structure upon. I deconstructed reality. I retreated to the virtual. Reason overwhelmed my faith in anything, including humanity itself. Now, I have returned to have faith in something, maybe not humanity or even love, but at least friendship and forgiveness. Even if everything is rooted in inevitable chaos and death, how we maintain our faith in others is the value of humanity.

This cycle of faith and reason is part of my journey. On a larger scale, I have seen this world change its rotation, cycle through drought and drowning, times of produce and times of famine. I am still too young to see the cycles of culture, but I have read that these will also continue to unfold. We have seen this conflict between the Old Guard and the New Order, between fascism and a system that claims to promote freedom in name only, lacking the tolerance for chaos that true freedom requires.

When I had sought power, the world had provided it, reflecting my ambitions in a shattered mirror. That shattered world was all I could see, biasing every action, every judgment, leaving me ultimately powerless. Now I know that when the heart and mind are in the right place, if your intention is in alignment with yourself, society, and nature, then opportunities will present themselves for positive change. But people must spend more time building the new world than they do clinging to the old one. With every generation, the world must have a funeral for the way it used to be, understanding that from this decay comes growth.

When we lose our idealism, sit in isolation, allow cynicism to take hold, and allow others to control our dreams, we age beyond our years. Youth is often misguided, aimless, and full of dumb mistakes, but it is never wasted, and the hope it is pregnant with polishes a brighter future for everyone. I was proud to be part of that future, and with a new friend I didn't have to walk the journey alone.

END

APPENDIX I:

Locations in the Text

Amorpha:

The primary Florinik village began as a series of egg-shaped huts that grew into a trading center. The name refers to the changes that all things go through, and is also a plant genus, since the Florinik inhabitants don't distinguish themselves from plants. Features include the stone archway, the Shrine of Orbis, the crescent butte, and the turquoise pathway. The nearby Ultimaepar Mines have led to numerous disputes over who can access them. The rare mineral contained within is a necessary component of the planetary rotational apparatuses.

The Aporia Asylum:

A series of terrestrial caves used by an anti-technological cult who goes by the same name. The group is composed of human pariahs and Aphorids, a colonial species whose thundering bodies outweigh their intellect. Akasha'Shirod-Rivenshear used to be their head priestess.

The Élivágar Mountain Base:

The Élivágar River no longer flows since the entire region is underwater. A secret military base is set within one of the two mountains that surround the destroyed dam.

FugaCity:

A town far off in the ocean composed of strung-together rafts and floating debris from fallen civilizations. Locals make their living off of fishing, gathering seaweed, and as a hub for the Yaupon tea trade.

The K.O.A. Commune:

O.A.K. was responsible for increasing the planet's rotation to break its tidal locking to the sun to bring daylight cycles and greater equality to both hemispheres. The group's name stood for its three leaders, the Orchestrator (Arcturus Vegas), the Architect (a role that Severum Rivenshear eventually took), and the Kontractor (Thalassa Latimer). Having rebranded themselves as a non-profit called K.O.A., they moved their eastern base and began building a utopia, which remains terrestrial despite the flooding in the Western Hemisphere.

Nathril-Xoynsia:

This is the largest city in the Eastern Hemisphere formerly known as Dayburn, since it used to receive only sunlight. Species of all types gather here, from human pariahs to Florinik. Piracy dominates, as merchants carry their wares between towns on the backs of large Dijyorkvoken. It is ruled over by Major Hinesdale.

APPENDIX II

Dramatis Personae

Sabrina Underfoot – A cybersecurity expert and inventor who lost most of her inventions when Eisbrecher University stole her ideas. Resentful, jealous, and angry at what her generation was promised that never came to fruition, she took up residence with the Old Guard, a political faction that was led by her x-boyfriend, the late Eduardo Culptos. Now she has the world's most powerful artificial intelligence in her mind and all the power she could ever handle, but will she succumb to it?

Vispáshanah'Shirod-Rivenshear - Ash, as she goes by, is the daughter of Akasha'Shirod and Severum Rivenshear, though for most of her life she never knew her father. She is a genius with a graduate degree in geophysics. Her boyfriend is Willow Storm Fitzgerald. See more about her life in the novel *Inertia* by Mark Everglade.

Severum Rivenshear – Ash's father and reunited mate of

Akasha. After studying terraforming in college, he joined the military after his first breakup with her. From there he became a mercenary, hunting the poorest lawbreakers before he was exposed to the abuses of those who held political power, including Governor Borges. After being tasked with hunting down O.A.K., he eventually joined them and brought down the Old Guard instead. Imminently pragmatic, he has little patience for philosophy or extensive emotional reflection, but finds that age forces a certain introspection he must learn to navigate as he evaluates his life's work, and his legacy to come. See more about his life in the novel *Hemispheres* by Mark Everglade.

Akasha'Shirod-Rivenshear – The former head priestess of the Aporia Asylum, a mystical anti-technology group composed of Aphorids and human pariahs. After meeting Severum in college, she left the Western Hemisphere, breaking up with him and exiling herself to the Aporia Asylum to rebel against O.A.K. based on preventing them from interfering with the natural, sacred order through their planetary rotational schemes. After reconciling with Severum, the two found themselves opposing the Old Guard they had been trying to protect, exacerbated by Severum's own name being found on a military hitlist as the government covered its dirty tracks.

Aurthur Fitzgerald – Severum's previous neighbor, and husband to Opal. After working with a communications firm growing up, he went into the media business after leaving behind a potential career in art for fear that he'd become a narcissist. Overly poetic, his eloquence is lost to his insensitivity, and his valor to his passivity.

Opal Fitzgerald – A neuro-anthropologist specializing in artificial memories. After meeting Aurthur, she assisted him with

O.A.K.'s revolution, providing linguistic support as they related to new species. Obsessed with her research, she often finds her independence at odds with Aurthur's co-dependency.

NOTE TO READER

Thank you for reading and supporting my work! Small publishers rely on word-of-mouth, so if you can do these three things it will greatly help us:

1)   If you liked the book, please post about it on social media.

2)   If you liked the book, please leave a review on Amazon and Goodreads.

3)   Join my mailing list at www.markeverglade.com to be notified of new releases and receive a free book of cyberpunk short stories.

Thanks again!

ABOUT THE AUTHOR

Mark has spent his life as a sociologist, studying conflict on all levels of society.

He wrote *Hemispheres* to soothe our ideological divisiveness, exposing each side's strengths and weaknesses, and understanding our underlying values are more similar than we think, regardless of how we look, act, or vote.

An avid reader of science fiction, he takes both its warnings, and opportunities for change, to heart. His previous works have appeared in *Exoplanet Magazine and Unrealpolitik*. He resides in Florida with his wife and four children.

EXCERPT OF INERTIA - PREQUEL

Inertia by Mark Everglade – The prequel to this novel.

Ash couldn't sleep. The name Sabrina Underfoot churned in her mind. She sat up and researched her online, but the woman was a ghost, keeping a seldom used social media profile and having few public records. She had no physical address on file, but Ash found her hovercraft registration. She ran its signature through the public surveillance network which noted where and when the vehicle had been spotted. The data wasn't very secure; any script kiddie could get at it, but it also wasn't perfect, sometimes recording the flight of a firefly as a large sedan. Despite the spottiness of the data, Sabrina's hovercraft had been registered at enough locations for Ash to discern her frequently traveled routes, including a recurring path to an airbus station each morning and a return to the original location each evening.

Sabrina had lived in Ash's old apartment building in Blutengel, Sloumstone, but hadn't visited in months. Ash wasn't expecting someplace so low class, but that was probably why Sabrina joined the Old Guard, pregnant with promises of a better life. According to her stolen data, she had been a top student, and only a few years older than Ash, so while she hadn't lived through the Great Rotation, the economy in Eisbrecher had never recovered from it. Her failed dreams must have made her easy bait for the Old Guard to seduce and gain access to the latest tech skills. A recent public trace showed Sabrina's hovercraft at Mandelbrot's, the club for has-beens.

She'd take the fight face-to-face.

~~~~~

Ash entered Mandelbrot's club with a swagger she would have never possessed if she had been entering for casual conversation. Tonight she was the huntress. Problem was, she had no idea what Sabrina looked like. She approached the barkeep and flashed a card that she had written Sabrina's name upon, followed by a question mark.

The barkeep replied, "If you're too afraid to say the person's name you're looking for, you shouldn't be looking for them."

Ash blushed. *Did anyone overhear that?* Her swagger disappeared.

"Now, if you want to blend in, what're you drinking?"

"Sake," she replied, trying to look older. Only old people drank sake, displaying bottles of it on their hexagonal tables as if they were precious relics. She took a swig. Thalassa Latimer spotted her from a corner table and announced, "Ash, this is Arcturus. We were having a long overdue rendezvous. Arcturus, this is Severum's daughter."

"So what?" Arcturus shrugged.

Thalassa shook it off. "Saw what happened at the dam. And Eduardo Culptos has been missing ever since. Know anything about that?"

"I know a bit about a bit," Ash replied, the words overshadowed by the thumping retrowave music.

"You're sweet. Too sweet." Thalassa took off her black leather jacket and shirt, leaving a tank-top and pants embedded
~~~~~

with raised neon-blue honeycombs. She handed the shirt to Ash. "You're about my size. Your black pants work, but go change out of whatever blouse your mom picked out."

Ash blushed and headed to the bathroom to change, saying, "Keep an eye out on anyone who leaves."

As she entered and played dress-up, she forgot that somewhere in there was a woman who could crash her implants with a single swipe. Maybe Aurthur's upgrade would shield her next time she faced her. Maybe not. She stripped her blouse in the stall, stuffed it in a crack in the wall, and pulled Thalassa's shirt on. It was surprisingly comfortable for what it was: a series of diagonal leather strips arranged flush with a large hole in the upper back cut in a teardrop shape. The leather had a ton of wear, but that only made it cooler. She pulled Severum's black jacket over it, the chrome fasteners reflecting off the dingy light. She headed back into the club, shoulder-checking the next guy who looked her up as she passed, and rejoined the corner table.

"Thanks for the clothes. Why's there a teardrop cut in the back?" she asked Thalassa.

"You'll figure it out, trust me."

"Culptos was working with someone," Ash whispered. "Sabrina Underfoot. She's somewhere here at the club. Runs cybersecurity for the Old Guard. Originally from Eisbrecher. About my age. Tech school graduate."

"I know all the regs, but that doesn't ring a notification bell," Thalassa replied.

"Her hovercraft showed up on a camera at the parking deck nearby. Not too much else open."

"If she is here on business," Arcturus said, "contrary to the media's portrayal, deals like the ones she would be making do not go down in clubs and bars where everyone knows you. Not unless one owns the place. Come, let's look around outside."

The three exited the club through the smoky haze and rounded the corner to a seven-story parking deck full of hovercrafts. Ash had left Ikshana on the rooftop when she arrived to keep watch. She commanded it to search for Sabrina's vehicle. Given the metallic bird's eyesight it took only a minute to find it, matching the plate to the registration information she had uncovered.

"Up four levels," she said, hurrying ahead. They slowed as they reached the fourth floor of the parking deck. Ikshana scoped the place but it was empty.

"Nice bird but looks like it flew the coop," Thalassa noted. "So be a good girl and tag the car and let's go have another drink."

"I didn't bring any surveillance equipment and flying Ikshana behind the car as it traveled would be a dead giveaway. If captured, it can be traced to my cognigraf signature that I used to pair it," Ash said.

"Well then, keep it posted here, run the visual feed through all three of our vHUDs, and back to the bottle we go."

"Thalassa, Ash is young and still has a whole life ahead of her," Arcturus scolded.

"There's that judgment again. Okay, I'll be serious," she replied, squinting. "Sabrina! You out here?" Her yell echoed through the parking deck. She waved her Pulser through the air with the coordination of a drunk trombonist.

"Glitchit," Ash spurted.

"You gave us away! This is why even Severum refuses to work with you anymore," Arcturus said, shaking her head and running downstairs. "You are such a reckless glitch."

No response from the parking deck, and vHUD still showed no activity from Ikshana's viewpoint. They exited.

"What other places are nearby that someone my age would frequent at this late hour?" Ash asked.

Arcturus rubbed her head. "It would be somewhere without their own parking on the roof. The few residences nearby are better accessed by parking elsewhere. From the top of the parking deck I did see an industrial shipping facility a few blocks down with its lights on, but it had enough parking that she could have parked there if she had wanted."

"Unless she's distancing herself from whatever is taking place."

They headed there, with Ikshana taking the lead flying in front of them, neon lights reflecting off its chrome beak. The long warehouse was unadorned and had no signage. Two men were posted outside a chain-link gate. A side door opened behind them that revealed a few more men in flannel clothes, unloading some boxes from a forklift.

"You always scope the entire area before addressing your target," Arcturus advised.

"Looks like business as usual."

"Then why the guards?"

"Maybe they're just workers on the night shift taking a break," Ash suggested.

"Workers take breaks behind businesses where no one will ask them to do anything, not at the front gate," Thalassa replied. "When people block an entrance, they can appear as casual as they like, but they're guards."

"Ikshana isn't picking up any weapons though."

"Fly your drone back on the rooftop and zoom closer. You're not the only one who owns one of these things, and you don't want them catching on. Weapons or not, they can still sound an alarm. Stay back and let's wait."

A truck arrived and they hid behind a dumpster. The men unloaded the goods quickly, but the inventory wasn't scanned. The final boxes were unloaded and exchanged for new, smaller boxes. Ash raised her hearing sensitivity but there were few words. Whatever company owned the building was keeping the pickup and delivery off the books.

Ash ran commands in vHUD and researched the property owner. Some no-name had sub-leased it to an unlisted organization. No leads there. She had to find out what was in those boxes, that is, if this was even where Sabrina was lurking. The back of the truck closed with a clank and it drove away, too heavy to hover.

Thalassa slammed her hands on the raised hexagons on each side of her pants and two compartments opened. She drew two daggers and activated them with a hum. Their scarlet blades bled into the night. While the truck passed them, she cut a square in the side of the trailer, the dagger melting the glowing orange metal.

"Fly your drone in there. It'll be concealed and will let us trace where they're going," Thalassa told her. "Now to confirm if Sabrina is here and figure out what's in that truck."

The warehouse gate and garage door closed. Employees circled around to their vehicles and left. The lights went off inside except for those in a raised corner office.

"Now's our chance," Thalassa said. "There's only two guards left."

"It still bothers me that Sabrina didn't park here," Ash whispered. "If the Old Guard is on her side, she wouldn't have any qualms about associating herself with whatever's going on. She's not the type to be easily intimidated."

"Around back. Let's go."

The guards swatted the air to play tennis with a ball only they could see. The three of them took advantage of the distraction and circled around the building, keeping to the shadows. Thalassa kneeled behind a pipe and hit another compartment in her pants that housed a long cord. She jacked the cord into the back of her neck with a *whoosh* as it sealed, and placed the other end into the keypad at the back door. The direct connection would decrease the time to hack it, though it risked cognigraf infection. Within seconds, the lock unfastened and they entered.

A set of burnt-yellow stairs led to the upper office. Everything was in boxes on the ground floor, and they wouldn't be able to discover much without alerting whoever was still work-ing. Ash and Arcturus investigated below while Thalassa climbed the stairs, but the metal steps shook loudly. A shadow exited the second-story office and headed in their direction. Thalassa backed down the stairs, but the shadow neared until they could make out a woman's form. She gave no warning. The woman caught hold of each railing and slid down with her feet forward to slam into Thalassa's chest, knocking her the rest of the way down the stairs. She rolled across the warehouse floor.

The woman ran forth, drawing a long katana from a sheath, her body silhouetted against an auburn security light. A long wave of ruby hair fell over the young woman's pale face. She flicked her head to get it out of her eyes and pointed the blade forward with perfect poise, both hands on the hilt. Thalassa rose from the bottom of the staircase and drew her Pulser, but the woman sliced it in two before she could make a move.

Ash knew that blade. It was almost an exact replica of the cyberknight's sword.

Sabrina was even faster in real life than cyberspace. Thalassa backed away and immediately executed a flurry of blocks with her daggers as the katana came on. Sparks flew from the metal in the dark warehouse, the clangs loud enough to draw the guards' attention. Sabrina hadn't called for them – she wasn't intending on losing. The dancing blades clashed repeatedly with both sides taking steps forward. Suddenly, Thalassa stumbled back, dropped her daggers, and grabbed her head as if she were hit by a cyber-strike to her implants. Her next motions were clumsy, and one more strike and she'd be done with.

"Sabrina! I know who you are," Ash yelled.

Sabrina turned, her red hair flying across her face. Thalassa and Arcturus took advantage of the distraction to run away, both pounding themselves in the head from the cyberat-tack. Ash still had enough distance between her and Sabrina to flee but dared to face her head-on.

Sabrina's emerald eyes flickered, running code. Pressure burst forth from various implants inside Ash's head, but stopped just as suddenly. Aurthur's counter-intrusion software was doing its trick. It knew the signatures of the viruses Sabrina was trying to run and shielded Ash from their effects. Ash pretended the attack worked, grabbing her head and screaming. She lowered to the ground, close to where Thalassa's daggers had dropped.

Sabrina licked her lips and closed in for the kill.

As the blade rose, Ash scooped up the daggers, catching the blade between them and disarming her, the katana flying aside. Thalassa ran to recover it while Sabrina fled through the warehouse out to the guards, hitting the top of a small black box that had been stuffed in the corner. A red light strobed on it, beeping faster and faster.

"Run!" Thalassa screamed.

They ran out back. A thundering boom ripped out of the building and followed them down the street a second later as the warehouse exploded. A fireball erupted into a mushroom cloud that obscured the sky and singed the pavement. The blast echoed. Warehouse walls, cargo crates, staircases, lighting fixtures, all shot out into the night. Some disintegrated from the fiery blast; others were thrown through nearby businesses. Ash danced around the falling shrapnel in the street, covering her head. Secondary explosions ignited with paint cans and other items went up in flames. They ran from the intensifying heatwave.

"So that's why the glitch didn't park here. Mystery solved," Thalassa slurred, smiling as the flames rose. "We gotta get outta here. Where's your car, Ash?"

"I took an airbus."

"You what? You came to track down the Old Guard without a getaway? Such a noob. We'll use mine."

"Well, whatever evidence there was is blown to shreds now," Arcturus said.

"Here's your daggers back," Ash offered.

"Keep 'em, I have this now," she replied, holding Sabrina's katana, its blade reflecting the orange flames.

"I can't. Severum told me violent people come to violent ends. Besides, that was too close. If I hadn't faked being hit by the cyberattack, she would never have been caught off guard."

"Fair enough, hand 'em over."

They made their way to Thalassa's small hovercraft, the engine too weak to reach the higher traffic lanes. They headed home beneath a flurry of drones, their red and blue lights cycling and bleeding into the night.

Ash called Severum, "Hey, I need you to look into something for me. Ikshana is tracking a truck shipment the Old Guard is involved in."

"How'd you find that?"

"Long story. I'll send you the coordinates when Ikshana relays them."

"I'll look into it, thanks. Stay safe."

But when you're traveling with two of the three most infamous revolutionists in Gliese 581g's history, and your father's the third, you're never safe.

End Excerpt

ALSO BY MARK EVERGLADE

www.ingramcontent.com/pod-product-compliance
Lightning Source LLC
Chambersburg PA
CBHW061239210726

48293CB00003B/834